Shadow Lover

by

Anne Stuart

Bell Bridge Books

This is a work of fiction. Names, characters, places and incidents are either the products of the author's imagination or are used fictitiously. Any resemblance to actual persons (living or dead), events or locations is entirely coincidental.

Bell Bridge Books
PO BOX 300921
Memphis, TN 38130
Print ISBN: 978-1-61194-377-1

Bell Bridge Books is an Imprint of BelleBooks, Inc.

Mass market paperback was originally published in 1999 by Onyx, an imprint of New American Library, a division of Penguin Putnam, Inc., in the United States and Canada

We at BelleBooks enjoy hearing from readers.
Visit our websites – www.BelleBooks.com and www.BellBridgeBooks.com.

10 9 8 7 6 5 4 3 2 1

Cover design: Debra Dixon
Interior design: Hank Smith
Photo/Art credits:
Scene (manipulated) © Ievgenii Tryfonov | Dreamstime.com

:Llsa:01:

Dedication

For Jennifer Todd Taylor, who consistently saves my butt from egregious errors.

And thanks for letting me burn down the Edgartown house as a surrogate for the Big House.

I enjoyed it immensely.

Chapter One

THE BLINDING WHITE light of a late-spring snowstorm woke her. Carolyn rolled onto her back with a muffled groan, but the glare speared through a narrow crack in her heavy drapes and forced its way beneath her eyelids. There was no way she could ignore it.

She let out a deep, long-suffering sigh. She slept alone, always had, probably always would, and she could sigh to her heart's content. "I hate Vermont," she muttered, her voice low and bitter.

Snow in April was obscene. So was snow in September, and she'd had to suffer through that as well. Eight months ago she hadn't minded. Some naive part of her had reveled in the flurries melting against the brightly colored leaves. Eight months ago she hadn't known just how long and deadly a Vermont winter could really be.

The house was very quiet. Which was only to be expected—the MacDowell family compound was maintained by the best-trained servants money could buy, and nothing, not a speck of dust, not an untoward noise, ever disturbed the surface tranquility.

There were times, even now, when Carolyn wanted to race down the oak-floored hallways barefoot, singing at the top of her lungs. There were times when she wanted to laugh out loud, to scream in anger, to weep in loneliness. Those times came less often nowadays. She was a sensible woman, one who accepted the good and the bad in life. She muttered the serenity prayer under her breath at all hours, and most of the time she felt as calm and accepting as she appeared. Good, sweet Carolyn. Loyal, faithful Carolyn, always there when she was needed.

Heavy snow was one of those things she couldn't change. She climbed out of bed and pulled the curtain, letting in the blinding glare. It was still and cold out there—the night had dropped more than a foot of snow on southern Vermont, but the maintenance people were already clearing it away with their usual silent efficiency. Carolyn leaned her forehead against the frosted glass, breathing deeply. Maybe she'd feel better if she got outside in the fresh, cold air. Even if she desperately needed the sun to warm her bones, not ice them.

She could always climb back into bed, pulling the duvet up around her ears, but for some reason that had never been an option, not since she'd moved into Alex's old room last fall when she'd come back home to be with Sally. Sally had removed all of his belongings and put them in storage more than a decade ago, and Carolyn had bought new furniture, new curtains and rugs, and a big, old-fashioned bed in a vain effort to make it seem like home. It didn't work.

Alex had been gone a long time—if she were a fool she'd think they'd forgotten about him. But no one forgot about lost children, not even the powerful, unsentimental MacDowells.

She sighed. Maybe she should just reclaim her small, utilitarian bedroom in the east wing where she'd usually slept during her visits. At least there she'd felt a sense of belonging, not the odd feeling that she was an imposter, that she'd usurped the best room in the place.

She was being ridiculous and she knew it. But she felt oddly unsettled; she'd felt that way for weeks. As if something monumental was about to happen.

She started to push away from the window, and then froze. Someone had parked at the head of the circular driveway, smack in front of the deceptively simple entrance to the main house. An ancient, rusty black Jeep stood up to its hubcaps in snow, and the inches on its roof told her it had to have been there for hours. It wasn't there when she went to bed last night, sometime around eleven. She'd slept later than usual, but even so, it was still only a little past eight. Who in God's name could have showed up in the middle of the night? Had something happened to Aunt Sally while Carolyn had been lying in bed bitching about the weather?

She had a closetful of silk nightgowns, presents from the various unimaginative members of the MacDowell family. Carolyn slept in oversized t-shirts, and she ran into the hallway, barefoot, not bothering with a bathrobe.

The main house in the MacDowell compound consisted of a huge center building and two wings off either side. Carolyn's room was on the second floor; Aunt Sally's sprawling apartment took up the first floor of the west wing. The house was silent as she raced down the stairs, arriving at the open door of Sally's rooms breathless, panicky.

The old woman lay in the hospital bed in the inner room, still, silent, her eyes closed. The curtains were drawn, and only a dim light penetrated the artificial gloom. For more than a year Aunt Sally had been bedridden, hovering closer and closer to death, but there should have been more warning.

"Aunt Sally!" Carolyn's voice was a broken whisper as she started forward into the shadows, ready to fling herself on the bed and weep.

An arm shot out, catching her before she could hurl herself across the room, and she was too startled to do more than strike out in sudden panic.

Aunt Sally's faded eyes opened, and she peered through the darkness. "Is that you, Carolyn?" she said in a sleepy, surprisingly strong voice.

Whoever held her seemed to have no intention of letting her go, but Carolyn's attention was centered on the woman who'd been a mother to her. "You're all right!" she said, not bothering to disguise the relief in her voice. "I thought something might have happened."

Aunt Sally's lined face looked oddly luminous. "Something's happened, all right, Carolyn. The best thing in the world."

Belatedly Carolyn realized that someone was still keeping her from Aunt Sally. She turned, and he dropped his arm, stepping back. She stared up at him in astonished silence, letting her distrusting eyes travel the length of him.

"He's back," Aunt Sally said, her soft voice unmistakably joyful. "He came back to me." She sounded as if her lost lover had returned.

The man had to be somewhere in his mid-thirties, ruling out that possibility, however. He was tall, though not as huge as some of her relatives, lean, and dressed in faded jeans and a thick cotton sweater that had seen better days. His streaked blond hair needed to be cut; his handsome face needed a shave. There was nothing to be done about his astonishing eyes, except to wish that they weren't surveying her with quite such a cynical expression.

She'd never seen him before in her life; she was utterly certain of that fact.

"Who?" she said, staring up at him. "Who's come back?"

His smile wasn't particularly unpleasant. Just faintly mocking, as if he'd expected that reaction from her. "You don't remember me, Carolyn?" he murmured. His voice was low-pitched, faintly husky, the voice of a smoker. "I'm wounded."

"I don't know you." She didn't want to know him. There was an aura of danger to him that was both illogical and unmistakable.

"It's Alex, Carolyn," Aunt Sally said joyfully. "My son has come home to me."

Carolyn froze in disbelief. She should have been shocked, but deep inside, some part of her had guessed who he was. Who he was pretending to be.

Alexander MacDowell, Sally MacDowell's only child, heir to half the MacDowell fortune, had arrived back in the nick of time, almost twenty years after he'd disappeared. And she didn't believe it for one moment.

"Aren't you going to welcome me home, Carolyn?" he asked after a long, strained silence. "The prodigal son, returned to the bosom of his loving family?"

She could feel Sally's anxious gaze, and it was stronger than the sheen of mockery in the man's blue eyes. She wanted to scream at him, but her love for Sally stopped her. Sally had accepted him; Sally was fooled. Carolyn would have to be very careful indeed.

"Welcome back," she said, forcing the words.

Sally leaned back and smiled, closing her eyes. But the man calling himself Alexander MacDowell wasn't fooled for a moment. "I think my mother needs to sleep," he said softly. "I'm afraid I woke her up when I arrived last night, and she was too excited to do more than drift off."

"She's been very sick," Carolyn said, trying to keep the anger from her voice.

"She's dying," he said flatly. He glanced down at her. "Why don't you come have some coffee with me and tell me how she's been doing? I'm sure Constanza will find us something to eat."

"How did you know Constanza was still here?"

"I saw her last night. She and Ruben wept all over me," he said. "You don't seem very happy to see me, Carolyn. Have I ruined something by my unexpected reappearance?"

"Hardly."

He smiled then, a cool smile that was still surprisingly sexy. "Why don't we talk about it? Don't feel you have to get dressed on my account. You've grown up very nicely indeed."

He probably meant to fluster her, but even if Carolyn wasn't a MacDowell by blood, she'd spent her entire life surrounded by them. She lifted her head regally, ignoring the fact that she was wearing only a bright red t-shirt with Tigger emblazoned on the front, and it came halfway down her long, bare legs. "It'll take me five minutes to get dressed," she said coolly. "I'll meet you in the breakfast room." She waited for his response.

"I haven't been here in almost twenty years, Carolyn. There wasn't a breakfast room back then."

"Ask Constanza," she said, turning her back on him, resisting the impulse to pull the t-shirt down closer to her knees.

She waited until she was back in her room before she let reaction set in. Closing the door behind her, she leaned against it, letting a shiver wash down over her body at the memory of the stranger's eyes, watching her, mocking her.

Because he *was* a stranger—she was absolutely sure of that. She had spent most of her early childhood in the proximity of Alexander MacDowell, and she still bore the scares to prove it, both psychic and physical. And that man in Aunt Sally's bedroom was nothing more than an imposter, and given the huge sums of money involved, that made him a criminal as well.

She pulled on her clothes hurriedly, slamming drawers and barely pausing to pull a brush through her hair before she left the room again. She didn't trust him alone in this house. She didn't trust him at all.

She'd been almost fourteen years old when she'd last seen Sally MacDowell's only real child. Alex had been a monster from infancy, or so she'd been told, and adolescence hadn't served him well. He was wild, dangerous, far too pretty for his own good, and absolutely no one could control him—not his stuffy Uncle Warren, who tended to view him and all children as distasteful aliens; not his strict mother, who ruled her world but melted when faced with her beloved son. He stole, he lied, he raised hell, and Ruben and Constanza kept finding both cigarettes and marijuana in his room.

Ruben kept covering for him, but Carolyn had heard the grown-ups talk. And she had prayed, every night, that they'd send him away, to military school, to reform school, to someplace where they'd beat the crap out of him and make sure he never came back to torment the young girl who wasn't really his sister, and who would never truly belong with the grand MacDowells. The young girl who had a ridiculous, debilitating crush on him that nothing would destroy, no matter how horrible he was.

In the end, they didn't send him away. He simply took off, with every spare piece of cash in the house, including the kitchen money, Constanza's savings, Carolyn's piggy bank full of quarters that at last count had equaled eighty-three dollars, and sixty-seven hundred dollars in cash. He hadn't been able to get his hands on his mother's impressive jewelry collectic 1, but thirteen-year-old Carolyn had already been given inappropriately valuable gold jewelry on birthdays and Christmas. He'd made off with that as well.

The best private investigators, the most determined police forces had been unable to find any trace of him over the ensuing years. Warren had sniffed and informed his sister she was well rid of him, and the fight that had erupted had kept Warren and Sally apart for almost a decade.

And now the black sheep had returned. Or someone pretending to be Alexander MacDowell was back. And Carolyn wasn't sure which would be more dangerous—the real Alex or a phony one.

She found him in the breakfast room, his long legs stretched out over an adjoining chair, a cup of coffee in one hand. The delicate Limoges cup that Aunt Sally loved looked ridiculous in his large, strong hand. It was tanned, and he wore no rings, she noticed. The Alex she had known would have worn rings. He was staring out at the wintry landscape, squinting against the bright white glare, and she stood in the doorway, allowing herself the dubious benefit of watching him.

There should have been no reason why he couldn't be Alexander MacDowell. The teenaged Alex had had pale blond hair, but it could have darkened into the brown-streaked, shaggy mass on the stranger. His pretty, boyish features, his petulant mouth and hypnotic, slightly tilted eyes could have matured into the man who lounged there, entirely at ease. There were a million reasons why he could be Alex MacDowell, and only one reason why he couldn't.

"Are you going to hover there like a vulture?" he said lazily, not bothering to turn and look at her. Her reflection was clear in the bank of windows—he must have seen her the moment she appeared.

"That sounds more like you than me," she said calmly enough, moving into the room and pouring herself a cup of coffee. The Limoges cup fit perfectly in her hands. Her hands were delicate, long fingered, graceful. Aristocratic hands, in stark contrast to the stranger's hands.

He swiveled around to look at her. "You think I'm a vulture?"

"Don't they hover at the side of the dying, waiting to scavenge?" He was sitting in her usual chair. The table was large enough for eight, and yet he'd somehow managed to hone in on the one thing she claimed for herself.

He smiled up at her, a slow, wicked smile. "You never did like me much, did you, Carolyn?"

He meant to be ingratiating, but Carolyn was immune. She sat across from him, taking a strengthening sip of her black coffee. "I never liked Alex much," she said carefully, though the real Alex would have known better. "I'm not sure what I think of you."

"Ah. You don't think I'm Alexander MacDowell? What am I doing here, then?" He didn't seem the slightest bit perturbed by her doubt.

"Sally MacDowell is dying. When she does she'll leave a substantial amount of money to her heirs. Alexander MacDowell has been missing for more than eighteen years, long enough to be declared dead. Warren's been itching to do just that for at least ten years now. If someone hadn't shown up, claiming to be Alex, then there'd be that much more money to go around."

"Greedy, are you?" he said, spooning sugar into his coffee with reckless abandon.

"Not particularly. I'm not one of the heirs. Whether Alex is alive or dead makes no difference to me. At least financially." She was proud of her cool, unemotional voice. She'd worked hard on perfecting it, on being the perfect MacDowell—she who never was a true MacDowell at all.

"You mean my mother isn't leaving you anything? I find that hard to believe—you've been a part of this family almost since you were born."

"Not legally," she said. "I was never adopted."

"Not even after I left?"

"Why would you think that?" she countered sharply. "You didn't have anything to do with my being kept as a foster child, did you?"

"You overestimate my influence," he said. "Besides, I liked having you as a little sister. I wouldn't have minded if they'd made it legal. You didn't answer my question, though. Are you trying to tell me that my mother hasn't left you anything in her will?"

"Why are you so interested in her will? How do you know you're even still in it?"

"You've as good as told me so, Carolyn," he said gently. "Besides, my mother was so happy to see me last night she told me all about it herself, and how grateful she was that she had never given in to pressure and changed it. So how much did she leave you?"

She stared at him in profound distaste. "Whatever Alex's other flaws," she said, "he was never crass."

He laughed, a light, mocking sound that grated on her nerves. "You've been around Sally too long. You've got that arctic edge down perfectly. Did you have to practice or did you just absorb it by osmosis?" He obviously didn't expect her to answer. He swung his feet down onto the floor and reached for the coffeepot, filling his delicate flowered cup and ladling in an indecent amount of sugar. The real Alex had always had a weakness for sweets. "I've lived a crass life for the last eighteen years. You'll have to forgive me if my social skills are a bit rusty."

"I'm sure you have," she said stonily. "But you aren't Alexander MacDowell."

"It must be nice to be so sure of yourself." He poured cream in as well, turning the coffee a pale beige. He glanced up at her, and she expected to see a flare of anger in his eyes. Instead, he smiled at her. "Are you going to be the hardest one to convince? My mother, Constanza, and Ruben welcomed me with open arms. Of course, they wanted me back."

"Unlike me."

He glanced at her. "Why don't you want me back?"

"I don't want an imposter worming his way into the family and defrauding them of money."

"And if I'm the real Alex?"

"I don't want Sally's heart broken. She doesn't have much time left, and I want it to be peaceful. She'd learned to live without her son. She mourned him, and then got on with her life."

"Peace is a highly overrated commodity," he murmured. "I think Sally would prefer a few weeks of joy to a few months of fading away."

"It's not your place to decide," she said fiercely.

"It isn't yours, either."

Stalemate. She looked across the table at him, making no effort to disguise her dislike. "I assume you have proof," she said.

"Assume anything you want," he said airily.

"Warren and Patsy aren't going to accept you at face value. They're going to want answers, physical proof. There are fingerprints, dental records—"

"Alex MacDowell never had his fingerprints taken, even when he was caught with a bag of pot when he was fourteen. His family was too powerful. And there may be dental records, for all I know, but since I never had a filling before I was twenty-three, I don't think they'll tell you much."

"You've researched this very carefully," she said, not bothering to keep the bitterness from her voice.

"Look at it this way—at the absolute worst I'm making an old woman very happy, and there's more than enough money in this damned family to go around. They won't miss my share."

"Are you admitting you aren't Alex MacDowell?"

He rose, graceful, as the young Alex would have been, and moved around the table. She didn't flinch, didn't back away from him. She merely wrapped her hands tightly around the delicate cup and sat there, looking at him.

He put his hands on the linen tablecloth in front of her, leaning over her. Too close. She found she was holding her breath, unwilling to breathe in the same air he did.

"Why are you afraid of me, Carolyn?"

He was too close. She could see the streaks of gold in his brown hair, the streaks of green in his blue eyes. He was so close she could smell the coffee on his breath, the melted snow, the faint scent of shampoo. She looked at him, and for a moment she thought of Alex, long, long ago.

"I'm not," she said.

"Are you afraid I'll take your place again? That Sally will love me more than you? That you'll be on the outside again, looking in?"

She let go of the cup, knowing that in another moment she would have crushed the fragile bone china in her delicate hands. She sat back, away from him, and she made her mouth curve in the cool, unemotional smile she'd perfected long ago.

"I'm not worried about a thing," she said, "except for Sally's well-being."

"You weren't so saintly when you were a little girl," he said. "I remember you were always whining, always trying to follow me. When did you get in the running to become the next Mother Teresa?"

"Back off." She couldn't help it; the words came out, tight and angry.

It was what he wanted. His smile widened, and she wanted to hit him. She put her hands in her lap, keeping her back straight, as he moved away from her. "They've trained you well, Carolyn," he murmured. "They did what they could never do with me."

"And what's that?"

"They made you one of them. They sucked the life and soul from you." He shook his head. "Too bad I didn't take you with me when I ran."

"You've forgotten some of the details you should have memorized. I was thirteen years old at the time."

"So you were," he said softly. "That didn't mean you didn't know how to kiss."

She could feel the color drain from her face. There was no way he could know. No way anyone could know. "What . . . what are you talking about?"

He headed for the arched doorway. "I think I'll check on my mother. I hadn't realized how much I missed her."

"You didn't answer my question." She rose, standing at the table, holding on to the surface so he wouldn't see she was trembling.

"No, I didn't." He smiled sweetly. "Better call Warren and Patsy and have them get up here. Maybe they'll do a better job of unmasking the imposter."

He was gone before she could say another word.

Chapter Two

"WHAT THE HELL is going on here?" Warren MacDowell stormed into the small, perfectly decorated library and proceeded to loom over Carolyn.

She closed the leather-covered checkbook with deceptive calm. Warren's stuffy, bombastic temperament always had the ability to shake her composure, but she'd learned to disguise it years ago. Warren was the kind of man who thrived on other people's weaknesses, and Carolyn had enough sense not to exhibit hers any more than necessary.

"I tried to call you," she said, looking up at him. "But you'd already left."

"Sally called me in the middle of the goddamned night," he snapped, even more bad-tempered than usual, "with some ridiculous story about Alexander returning from the dead. Where is he?"

"I haven't seen him since this morning. I've been working in here."

"He would have to pick a blizzard to come home. It took me forever to drive up here. So what do you think?"

Warren was not a man who usually asked for anyone's opinion, particularly hers. "What do I think about what?"

"Don't be obtuse! What do you think about the prodigal son? Is it really him?"

"Who else could it be?" she said carefully.

"A con man. We all assumed Alex was dead, had been for years. There's a lot of money involved—it would be worth someone's while to try and pull this off. Have you asked him any questions? Asked for proof?"

"I didn't think it was my place. Aunt Sally believes him, and she's happier than she's been in years. I'm not about to tell her that he's a phony."

"But you think he is," Warren said shrewdly. Carolyn looked up at him. Warren was a good-looking man in his late sixties, but then, all the MacDowells had been blessed with abundant physical charm as well as money. A perennial bachelor, he cared more about his appearance and his possessions than anything else, and his gray suit was undoubtedly Armani. He was a little too old for it, but he still looked elegant and untouchable.

He had never been one to encourage intimacy, and she was in no mood to confide her doubts. "I don't know," she said. Lying.

Warren shook his head. "I'll have to see the boy. Ask him a few pointed questions—"

"He's not a boy anymore."

Warren shrugged his dapper, narrow shoulders. "Who is? Where will I find the black sheep?"

"Probably by Sally's bedside. That's where he was headed after breakfast."

"How cozy. Sally's a smart woman. She'll see through an imposter easily enough. It shouldn't take much to uncover the truth."

"No," Carolyn said, "it shouldn't." But for some reason she didn't think it was going to be that simple.

"Well?" Warren said, growing impatient. "Aren't you coming with me?"

The day was getting stranger and stranger. Warren usually treated her as a cross between a poor relation and an upper servant, which, in fact, described her position in the MacDowell family fairly well. He'd never sought her opinion or her company in the past, he'd simply accepted her presence.

She rose. "If you want me to."

"You knew Alex as well as anyone. You grew up with him, in a manner of speaking. I want to see if you can put a dent in his story."

It wasn't an enticing thought. The man with Aunt Sally was a liar and a fraud, but Carolyn was in no particular mood to be the bearer of bad tidings. It was up to someone else to unmask him, not her. The most important thing was to protect Aunt Sally now that her failing health made her unable to protect herself. The truth, and the money, were only secondary issues.

But Warren was standing by the door, practically fuming with impatience, and now wasn't the time to finally stand up to him. That time was coming, with Aunt Sally's impending death. But it wasn't here yet.

Sally's room was bathed in gentle shadows. This time Carolyn didn't jump to any macabre conclusions as she saw her dozing peacefully in the hospital bed that had been moved in several months ago. This time she didn't miss the figure stretched out on the green velvet Victorian fainting couch, reading peacefully.

Warren cleared his throat with awesome majesty, and Aunt Sally jerked into wakefulness. The man pretending to be Alex didn't move, simply raised his head to look at them with sublime indifference.

"Warren." If Aunt Sally sounded more resigned than enthusiastic, it was only to be expected. She had tolerant affection for her younger brother, but not much more. "Your nephew has returned."

"So it seems," Warren said in a deliberately lukewarm voice. But then, he was never a man to show enthusiasm. "Welcome back, Alex."

"Uncle Warren." Was there a trace of malicious humor in his eyes as he looked at the older man? Of course, the real Alex had always viewed his stuffy uncle with amused disdain.

"Why don't we go into the living room so we don't disturb Sally? As you can imagine, there are a great many questions I want answered—" Warren said smoothly.

"No!" Aunt Sally's voice was surprisingly strong.

"Don't be ridiculous, Sally," Warren protested. "I just want to ask the boy a few questions. Arrange for a few medical tests. Just a formality, of course, but it's only reasonable to be cautious. After all, it's been eighteen years, and while I will admit there's a surface resemblance, we should have some form of proof. Papers, answers—"

"No," Sally said again, more calmly. "I won't have you cross-examining him. Do you think I don't know my own son? It could have been fifty years, and I'd still recognize him, with my heart if not with my eyes."

"Your eyes aren't any good," Warren interrupted tactlessly. "And I doubt your lawyers are going to find this acceptable without some form of proof."

"Fuck the lawyers," Alex said in a calm voice.

After a shocked moment, Sally laughed. "Yes, Warren," she said, a little short of breath. "You heard what my son said. Fuck the lawyers."

"Sally!" Warren protested, clearly shocked, but Sally ignored him.

"Come over here, Carolyn," she commanded with her usual high-handed charm. "I haven't seen much of you today."

"I thought you might want some time alone with Alex." She didn't even hesitate—she was proud of herself—that she could swallow the lie so easily.

Her reward was Aunt Sally's bright smile. "We'll have dinner tonight, the four of us. I'm feeling quite wonderfully strong right now, ready to take on the world. Why don't you take Alex to his room and make sure he gets settled? He hasn't had more than a moment to himself since he arrived last night."

She'd already anticipated it, but she stalled. "What room shall I put him in?"

"Don't be silly, Carolyn. His old room. It's been waiting for him all these years." She turned her head to the imposter. "I had it redecorated when the house was enlarged, but I think you'll still like it. If you want anything changed, just let Carolyn know and she'll see to it."

She could feel his eyes on her, an unpleasant sensation. "What does Carolyn do nowadays? Besides see to any changes?" His mother wouldn't hear the faint mockery in his voice. Carolyn couldn't miss it. And couldn't stop from bristling.

"She takes good care of me," Sally said. "She's been wonderful, Alex. She insisted on quitting her job to take care of me when the cancer came back this time. I couldn't have asked for a better daughter."

His eyelids drooped over his mesmerizing eyes. "I can imagine," he said. She knew what he was thinking, even without him saying anything. He thought she'd come back for the money. Left her apartment in Boston, her career as a school social worker and come back to nurse a dying old lady during her final days. A very rich dying old lady.

After all, that was why he'd appeared, wasn't it? And it was a waste of time to insist she had nothing to gain but some sort of peace of mind.

"You're very noble," he said. And for some reason Carolyn suddenly remembered the real Alex, his voice laden with sexual innuendo.

There was nothing sexual going on here, she reminded herself belatedly. Just a con man, out to bilk an old lady out of her fortune, and the only thing that stood between them was her loving family. But the MacDowells had never seemed particularly loving, though even now Warren was surveying the interloper with surprising acceptance.

"Go along, then, and get settled," Warren said expansively. "We'll talk later. I'm sure Carolyn will take most excellent care of you." He hesitated. "Good to see you back, my boy."

Sally reached up her gnarled hand and patted Warren's approvingly.

"It's good to be back," Alexander MacDowell said. And Carolyn didn't miss the faint undertone of mockery in his low, husky voice.

She could feel his eyes on her back as she led the way up the wide center staircase. Thank God she'd already managed to strip her borrowed room of all her clothes and belongings. If the imposter knew she'd been sleeping there it would be one more weapon he could use.

She went in ahead of him, giving it a last-minute check to make sure no trace of her temporary occupation had remained. Alex paused inside the door, surveying it critically. "She wasn't expecting me back," he said.

Carolyn paused in the center of the room, watching him. "Alex disappeared more than eighteen years ago, and in all that time there's never been any word, any hint that he was even still alive. Aunt Sally is a realistic woman—she accepted the obvious years ago."

That faint, unfamiliar smile twisted his mouth. "And aren't you happy for her?" he asked softly.

She kept her mouth shut, ignoring the unmistakable taunt. "The bed's new, and everything's very comfortable—"

"Who used the room while I was gone?"

"No one important," she said, glad she was able to be completely honest. "Just an occasional guest."

"Why is it filled with chintz and flowers? It doesn't look like Aunt Patsy's style. Too much bare wood. Patsy likes things plush and padded."

She tried not to show how startled she was. He'd done his homework, that much was certain—he had the pampered Patsy MacDowell down to a tee. "If it's too feminine I can go out and buy some hunting prints," she said in a slightly caustic voice. "Dead animals ought to macho it up a bit."

"Was this your room?"

This time she couldn't hide her reaction. Of course he was well versed—a con man would have to be. He'd need to be observant as well, and she'd probably given it away with the unavoidable tightening of her mouth.

"I was living in Boston until Sally got sicker," she said, offering no real answer.

She owed the real Alexander MacDowell absolutely nothing—she owed his impersonator even less. Constanza had helped wipe out any trace of her presence, and she was back in the small room on the first floor where she'd spent most of her life. "There's a new bathroom off to the left that you should find more than adequate," she said briskly. "I'll have Ruben bring up your suitcases—"

"I can handle it."

He was standing between her and the door, and she had no choice but to look at him dead on.

He could have been Alex. He had the same clear, almost luminous blue eyes, faintly slanted so they had almost a Slavic look, and his sulky, pretty teenaged face could have matured into the starkly elegant bone structure, the high cheekbones and lush, sensual mouth. He could have been Alex, except for one thing.

Alex was dead.

He moved, and she breathed an imperceptible sigh of relief. She didn't want to pass too close to him as she made her exit.

But he didn't move out of the way. He moved closer, coming right up to her. She stood her ground, because she'd learned long ago never to show fear, but this time it was an effort. He was tall. Tall enough to make her feel just slightly threatened. Alex hadn't been that tall, and Alex had been seventeen when he disappeared. He would have reached his full height by then, wouldn't he?

"So I stole your room," he said in his soft, husky voice. "And I stole your place as Aunt Sally's caretaker. It's no wonder you're not welcoming me with open arms."

"I'm not much for open arms in the best of circumstances," she said.

"I bet not," he murmured. "Though I have to admit it's a shame. Are you going to help Uncle Warren prove I'm an imposter?"

"If you are."

"And what do you think, Carolyn?" He was too close. He reminded her eerily of the real Alexander, and it disturbed her, confused her. Made her doubt the truth she'd never been quite sure of in the first place.

It was no wonder he had a powerful effect on her. Only someone who could successfully impersonate the real Alex would have attempted such a masquerade, and the imposter knew all the tricks. All the slight, sensual little habits Alex had had, to make her feel vulnerable, make her feel a strange, despicable kind of longing.

She stared at him stonily, fighting it. "I think that if you hurt Aunt Sally I'll make you wish you'd never tried this."

"Tried what?" His voice was soft, taunting. "What are you going to do to me?"

But Carolyn wasn't going to fall for it, no matter how much he goaded her. She wasn't ready to declare her outright enmity, even if he already recognized it.

"I think you'll be very comfortable here," she said, taking a small step back and moving around him with what she hoped was a politely casual air.

"Oh, I'm sure I will," he said softly. He was deliberately letting her escape, and she knew it. She didn't care—getting away from him was suddenly very important. "If you ever start missing your old room, feel free to visit," he added.

"I'll be fine," she said.

"It's a big bed. I don't mind sharing."

She jerked around, stung beyond endurance. "It'll be a cold day in hell."

He glanced out at the wintery landscape. "It already is, Carolyn."

THE MAN CALLING himself Alexander MacDowell allowed himself a small, wicked grin as the door slammed shut behind the departing Carolyn. He'd been trying to get an honest reaction out of her since she'd first raced into Sally's bedroom, but she'd been impressively, annoyingly controlled, unwilling to let her raging disbelief and disapproval surface no matter how he pushed her.

He wondered why. Affection for the woman who'd provided her with a home and a family might have something to do with it. For all that Carolyn Smith seemed to be a calm, slightly repressed young woman, she clearly had strong affection and loyalty for Sally MacDowell. Perhaps her one weakness.

He knew more about her than she could ever guess. He knew where she'd worked, he knew her friends, he'd even seen her apartment near Beacon Hill. He knew the names of every man she'd ever slept with. Since that list came to a grand total of three, it wasn't a difficult feat, assuming his sources were reliable. So far they had been, but he was prepared for anything.

She looked at with cool dislike in her clear blue eyes, and it both annoyed and aroused him. He was going to need an ally in this rambling old house. He was going to need someone he could count on, someone he could use. Carolyn Smith was the obvious, perfect choice.

She wouldn't be easy. But then, few things worth having came easily. If he could make cool, protective Carolyn believe in him, then no one would dare doubt him.

She hadn't responded all that well to his attempts to be wryly charming. She had some unresolved business with the teenaged Alex MacDowell, and it probably had something to do with adolescent desires. Alex MacDowell had been the quintessential bad boy, raising hell with a mastery impressive for one of his youth. And very few women, particularly impressionable adolescent ones, could resist a wickedly charming black sheep. She'd had a crush on young Alex, and everyone in the MacDowell family had known about it.

The man who'd arrived back at the MacDowell compound in southern Vermont could raise a certain amount of hell himself. And he had every intention of doing so. He could be wickedly charming, and he intended to have Carolyn find him completely irresistible. Too much depended on getting her to believe in him. If he had Carolyn on his side, no one would dare question him.

The old lady wasn't long for this world—he recognized that fact with calm assurance. He'd seen enough people die to know when someone was living on borrowed time. Sally MacDowell would be dead by summer—all her hundreds of millions of dollars couldn't do a damned thing to stop the inexorable hunger of cancer.

He could make it through that time with no difficulty whatsoever. He was used to manipulating people, to having them do what he wanted. He had a talent for it. Sally would die peacefully, her long-lost son by her side. Carolyn would get her teenaged romantic fantasies fulfilled in the bed she'd unwillingly abandoned. And when he left, all his questions would be answered. He could go back to being plain Sam Kinkaid, alone in this world and liking it just fine.

Probably the safest thing might have been to keep his distance from Carolyn Smith. She was a smart woman—he knew that more from looking into her clear blue eyes than from the reams of information passed to him. It didn't matter that she'd graduated from Bennington with honors. All she had to do was look at him with that guarded, withering expression and he had the sense not to underestimate her.

He'd been carefully primed for all the people he'd find in the Vermont house, but his informant had failed when it came to describing Carolyn. Beneath the conservative clothes, the neatly coiled hair, the quiet, seemingly demure manners, lurked something unexpected.

Something fierce and passionate, carefully repressed.

She'd been brought into the MacDowell family when she was a two-year-old, and twenty-eight years later she was back at Sally's side when everyone else had left. What had brought her back to Sally MacDowell? Money? Loyalty? Greed?

He had a healthy respect for greed. It was a powerful motivator, one that could be used to his advantage.

He knew why Sally loved her, why the MacDowells approved of her. She was essentially an unpaid companion, loyal, unquestioning, willing to go to any lengths for her unofficial family.

And she had the one thing all the MacDowells considered of primary importance.

She was beautiful.

Odd, how physical beauty was of such value to the extended MacDowell family. To start out with, they'd been blessed with extraordinary genes and generous health. And they'd bred wisely. There were no dogs in the MacDowell family—even on her deathbed, Sally was a gorgeous creature, with papery-fine, pale skin and dark, beautiful eyes.

Carolyn had been a fitting complement to the glorious MacDowells. The photo albums had traced her development from a solemn, delicate toddler through a coltish adolescence. Now she seemed muted, like a fine painting seen through bad lighting, the colors dim and faded. Her clothes were classic, uninspired, hanging on her body with tailored severity that nevertheless seemed to hide her.

He moved over to the window, staring out over the snow-covered landscape. He hadn't been in Vermont in years—he'd forgotten what a late-spring snow could be like. He couldn't have timed his reappearance better—the turmoil of the weather paralleled the unsettling effect of the prodigal son's return.

He was a man who was more alert than most—he heard the footsteps in the hall outside his door and knew immediately who they belonged to. Ruben's tread was soft soled and discreet; Constanza's footstep was sturdy. And there was no way Carolyn was going to come back to this room without an exceptionally good reason.

Alex stretched out on the bed, staring up at the beamed ceiling. It was a comfortable bed, big enough to fit his frame and room to spare. He didn't move when the knock sounded on the door.

"Come in, Warren," he said lazily, contemplating the cracks in the ancient beams.

Chapter Three

"SORRY TO INTRUDE, young man," Warren said pompously, moving into the room and eyeing him with disapproval. "But I thought you and I might take this chance to get a few things clear."

Alexander glanced over at the tightly shut door. "Cut the crap, Warren," he said lazily. "This isn't 'Mission: Impossible.' The room isn't bugged; no one is listening to us talk."

Warren's elegant face creased in dislike. "One can never be too careful," he said, and Alex half expected him to sniff in disdain.

"The only one doubting me is Carolyn, and I've seen to it she'll keep her distance, at least for the time being."

"I warned you she'd be the hardest one to convince," Warren said. "She's quiet, but she's sharp. And she was closer to the real Alexander MacDowell than I was."

The man on the bed smiled lazily. "I'm not worried about it. I think she was half in love with Sally's son when he left. It shouldn't take much to rekindle that feeling."

"Don't be absurd!" Warren protested. "She was thirteen years old. She may have had a crush on him, but it was hardly serious. She was far too young to be interested in boys."

"From what you've told me, Alex MacDowell wasn't just any boy. And don't underestimate the hormonal urges of puberty. She was probably lusting after him."

"Disgusting," Warren said, and this time he did sniff.

"You think I can't do it?" Alex said calmly.

"Oh, I have every confidence in your abilities," Warren murmured. "I expect you'll end up convincing everyone you're Alexander MacDowell. I just think you'll have an easier time tricking Carolyn than seducing her. I don't think she's a woman who has much use for the opposite sex."

There was a faint, unexpected undertone of pride in Warren's voice, and Alex thought he could understand why. Sexual indifference was a matter of power to a man like Warren MacDowell. A power Alex had no intention of cultivating, at least not in this lifetime.

"We'll see," he said. "If I can get her to trust me enough to sleep with me, then we should have no problem whatsoever. Unless Patsy decides to be difficult."

"Leave my younger sister to me," Warren said. "I know how to handle her. She doesn't waste much time thinking about anything other than her own interests. The family business holds little charm for her. She's more concerned about her own greedy pursuits."

"But won't my sudden reappearance put a dent in the funds she uses for those pursuits?"

"I can handle her," Warren said again. "She's married well—three times—and she trusts me. We're actually quite close. If I accept you, she will."

"And her children?"

"They might not be so easy," Warren conceded. "But then, I never would have gotten involved in this charade if I didn't think you were the man capable of pulling it off. Once you manage to convince Carolyn, the others should be a relatively simple matter if you watch your step."

Alexander surveyed him out of half-closed eyes. He had no illusions about his coconspirator. Of all the celebrated MacDowells, Warren had the strongest sense of self-interest, coupled with a useful lack of morality. When he'd first come up with the crazy idea of passing himself off as the missing heir, Warren had been the obvious choice for a partner in crime.

He'd considered other possibilities before approaching Warren, discarding them quickly. Constanza and Ruben were too loyal, Patsy too caught up in her endless quest for pleasure to make an effort to ensure she could continue to pay for it.

And Carolyn Smith. She would have been his first choice. After years on her own she was living with Sally MacDowell, taking care of her during her final illness. She knew more about the MacDowell family than anyone else—with her help no one would dare stand up to him.

But some sixth sense had sent him in Warren's direction instead, and now he basked in his customary good luck. Carolyn would never have tolerated such deceit—she was obviously cursed with a strong sense of morality.

"You think Sally has any doubts?" Warren asked after a moment.

"Not a one. She needs to believe in me. She's dying, and she doesn't want to leave this life without finding her son again."

"Just make sure she doesn't start agreeing to things like DNA tests and the like. There's a limit to what we can do, who I can bribe."

"Don't worry, she won't," Alex said with calm assurance.

Warren stared at him for a long moment, then nodded, satisfied. "I won't deny it's gone extremely well so far. The next few days will be the test."

"The next few days will be simple," Alex murmured. "If you do your part."

"I'm the one with the most to lose," Warren said huffily.

"I doubt it. If I get unmasked you'll just insist you were taken in like everyone else. I'm willing to bet there isn't a shred of proof tying us together. Is there?"

"You think I don't trust you?"

"I think you don't trust anyone. Neither do I." Alex sat up, turning to look at him. "Don't worry about it, Warren. I'm not going to get caught. If I am, cover your ass and don't worry about me. I'm very good at getting out of tight places."

"I'm supposed to believe you won't betray me?"

"If you don't believe that, why did you get involved in this?" Alex countered smoothly.

"Because you look eerily like him," Warren said after a moment.

"And because I showed up on your doorstep and offered you a chance to get your hands on all that lovely money," Alex said bluntly. "Don't forget that."

"My sister's dying," Warren said. "She'll die happy if she thinks her son is back—"

"You don't give a shit whether your sister dies happy or not. You only care that she dies with her estate settled, not tied up for years proving that the real Alexander MacDowell is dead."

"What if he's not?" Warren said suddenly. "What if the real one does suddenly appear?"

"He's dead, Warren," Alex said in a low, cool voice. "Trust me, he's not coming back."

CAROLYN HAD probably had to suffer through worse dinner parties in her life, but at the moment she was too miserable to remember them. A table had been set up in front of the bay window in Sally's room, and Sally even managed to sit in her wheelchair, the bright color of happiness in her pale cheeks. Alex sat beside her, attentive, charming, and Warren was surprisingly expansive. Carolyn sat across from the interloper, quiet, saying little, eating even less, listening to the liar as he spun his web.

Not that he reminded her of a spider, she thought objectively. He was too golden and glorious for that, with his slanted blue-green eyes, his sun-streaked hair, his tanned skin stretched taut over his high cheekbones. He had the same slightly Slavic look that the real Alexander had had, which was probably what made the deception work.

His mouth was what fascinated her. It was the mouth of a satyr, cynical, voluptuous, utterly and completely sexual. He smiled, he laughed, showing perfect white teeth; he talked with lazy charm, holding the rest of them spellbound. Holding Carolyn spellbound, even as she fought it.

He was good. He was beyond good—he was masterful, enchanting Aunt Sally, charming Uncle Warren, telling old tales of a childhood he hadn't lived. Someone must be helping him, Carolyn thought, plastering an expression of polite interest on her face as her brain worked feverishly. Some of the little bits he was coming up with would only be known to members of the family. Someone must have told him about the time Alex had gone skinny-dipping at South Beach on Martha's Vineyard and the police had caught him. Someone must have told him that Alex was dangerously allergic to shrimp.

He glanced at her across the dish of scampi, a faint, knowing gleam in his eyes. "Did you suggest the menu, Carolyn?" he murmured, making no attempt to serve himself.

"I have a weakness for shrimp," she said lightly.

"So do I," Alex said. "A fatal weakness."

"Oh, my heavens!" Sally said in a shocked voice. "I'd forgotten, darling! You're allergic to the stuff. Carolyn, how could you have done such a thing?"

"It's been eighteen years." Her calm voice didn't betray her unexpected flash of guilt. Not for endangering the imposter. But for troubling Sally. "I'd forgotten as well."

"So you weren't trying to kill me?" he asked gently.

She toyed with her wineglass, then gave him a cool smile. "It wouldn't have been a very effective way to do it, now would it? After all, the shrimp is quite recognizable. If you were someone who knew he was allergic to shrimp you simply wouldn't touch it."

Her barbed statement went over Sally's head.

"Don't talk to Carolyn of murder," Sally said brightly. "She's an expert on the subject."

"Oh, really?" His eyes were deceptively languid. "How many people have you murdered?"

"No one," she said. She smiled at him. "Yet."

"She loves reading trash," Warren explained broadly. "Murder mysteries, all that sort of garbage. She fancies herself an expert on modern crime because she's read a few whodunits."

"Hardly." Carolyn managed to keep the irritation from her voice.

"You'd better think twice before committing a crime, boy," Warren went on. "Carolyn's the type to catch you red-handed. She's a regular Miss Marple."

"Don't be ridiculous, Warren," Sally said with surprising vigor. "I read spy thrillers and I'm not about to join the CIA or the KGB. What do you read, darling?" She turned to Alex with an almost flirtatious smile.

"I don't have time to read," Warren announced loudly.

"I wasn't asking you," Sally said. "And anyone with any sense finds the time to read, or their brain atrophies and their soul shrivels."

"Even when they read trash?" Warren snapped.

Carolyn drained her wineglass. She had a splitting headache, but there was no way she was leaving Sally alone without her protection. Warren had a tendency to upset her, and the unexpected stimulant of her prodigal son would no doubt take its toll as well. She'd been going downhill steadily since last fall—Carolyn dreaded the thought that something might accelerate the inevitable process.

"Depends on what you define as trash, Uncle," Alex said smoothly. "I like reading horror novels, myself."

"You would," Carolyn muttered. Indeed, the teenage Alex had been reading Stephen King when he disappeared. Once more, the stranger had done his homework.

"Tell me, Alex, do you have any plans now that you've finally returned to the bosom of your family?" Warren demanded.

"Warren!" Sally's voice held a distinct warning note.

"I'm not quizzing him about his past," her brother said impatiently. "Though I admit I'm curious. There's no reason not to ask him what he plans to do now, is there?"

"He doesn't have to answer anything he doesn't want to. It's wonderful just to have him back."

Alex met Carolyn's eyes across the table, between the bickering siblings. The light was a soft glow of candlelight, and for a moment she let herself be drawn in by the sheer intensity of his eyes, the rich, disturbing promise of his mouth. "Are they always like this?" he asked with just the right note of amusement.

Carolyn was not amused. "Don't you remember?"

He rose, towering over the table and stretching with lazy, unconscious grace. No true MacDowell would ever stretch, Carolyn thought, surreptitiously moving her cramped muscles. They were all too well-bred, too carefully instilled with polite behavior.

"They used to argue about me," he said.

"They still do."

Sally looked up mid-tirade, her faded eyes troubled. "I'm sorry, darling. You shouldn't have to listen to us two old buzzards fighting on your first night back."

"Don't call me old," Warren snapped. "You're ten years older than I am."

"And dying to boot," Sally snapped back. "You're old, I'm antique." She wheeled her chair away from the table. "You go along now, the pair of you. And Carolyn, send Mrs. Hathaway in to help me, would you? I'm quite tired."

"You don't need the nurse tonight," Carolyn protested. "I can help you—"

"I wouldn't think of it, dearest," Sally said fondly. "What's the use of having a private nurse on call if I don't use her? Besides, I'm having a bit of . . . discomfort. She can give me a shot."

Sally never admitted to pain. A MacDowell never did. She probably referred to her long, hard labor to bring forth the two-week-overdue Alexander MacDowell as a slight twinge. According to family legend, she'd spent two weeks in a private hospital, refusing all visitors until she emerged with her infant son.

"If that's what you want," Carolyn said reluctantly, knowing when she was beaten. She wouldn't stay with Sally until she slept, but no force on this earth could make her spend the rest of the evening in Alex's company. "I'm tired as well. If you don't mind, I'll just head for bed."

"Carolyn, you can't leave Alex alone on his first night back!" Sally protested.

"Warren's here." It sounded rude, almost a refusal, and Carolyn had never refused Sally any of the small requests she'd made of her over the years.

"You and I both know that Warren is a pest who'll start cross-examining Alex the moment he gets a chance. Now, don't glare at me, Warren, I know you can hear me, and I have no qualms saying it to your face. Carolyn will keep you both company and make sure you leave Alex alone."

"You want her to spy on me, is that it?" Warren demanded huffily.

"I want you to behave yourself," Sally said, her voice fading. "I just wish I felt well enough to throw a party—"

Carolyn felt sick horror fill her at the very thought. "Don't worry about parties, Aunt Sally," she said swiftly. "Just concentrate on getting better."

"Don't be absurd, child. I'm not going to get any better and we both know it."

"I don't know any such thing—"

"Keep your fantasies if it makes you feel better," Sally said with a weak wave of her hand. "At least Alex can face the truth."

It shouldn't have hurt, Carolyn thought, allowing no expression to cross her face. She'd worked that all out years ago. She stood quite still as the imposter moved past her to take Sally's hand in his strong, tanned one. Sally loved her, she knew that. There was no reason to feel bereft, abandoned.

"Get some rest, Mother," the liar said softly, leaning down to kiss her cheek. "I'll be here in the morning."

Sally sighed happily. "You don't know how long I've wanted to hear someone call me Mother again. Good night, dearest." She reached up and touched his face with a gentle caress.

And Carolyn slipped quietly out the door.

IT WAS A STILL, cold night, with the quarter moon hanging low in the sky. In a few days the unnatural cold would lift, the heavy wet snowfall would melt away into nothingness, and spring could once more begin its slow assault on the bleak, frozen fields of Vermont.

But for now all was an icy silence, spreading out over the snow-shrouded landscape. The tree limbs were black against the whiteness, and in the distance the mountains hovered over them, an ancient, protective presence.

Carolyn moved behind the house, her down coat bundled tightly around her as she walked along the neatly shoveled paths. Her booted feet made soft, crunching noises on the cold snow, and somewhere in the distance she could hear an owl cry. There were creatures out there in the darkness, wild ones who lived their lives with stunning simplicity and freedom. Someday that freedom would be hers.

She'd never been fool enough to think she'd been free during her Boston years. Sally was the only mother she'd ever known, a calm, dispassionate figure who had always been there. If there hadn't been much outward affection or involvement, at least Carolyn had felt Sally's caring and stability.

And she'd felt that caring over the years and the miles.

She owed Sally. Not on a physical level—that debt had been paid. She owed her emotionally, for giving her someone to belong to. No one else among the mighty MacDowells had even noticed the quiet girl child growing up in tempestuous Alexander's wake, but Sally had noticed, and watched over her, and loved her in her own way.

And Carolyn owed her everything in return. For a few months she could put her life on hold. For a few months she could stay.

Until Sally died.

All the denial in the world wouldn't change what would happen—Carolyn had learned that lesson long ago. She would mourn her deeply, but finally her life would be her own.

She would even have money. Nothing like the huge sums that the real MacDowells would inherit. Nothing like the kind of money the imposter would be trying to con out of a dying old lady.

It didn't matter. It would help reclaim her tentative independence. Despite her affection for the extended MacDowell family, even including stuffy Uncle Warren, Aunt Patsy, and her diverse offspring, once Sally died her ties would be severed. Her debt of loyalty and love would be paid, and she would be completely, gloriously free.

She supposed she should feel guilty about that, about the longing for freedom, but she couldn't. If she could change things, give years off her life to keep Sally happy and healthy she would gladly do so. But God didn't make those kinds of bargains, and Sally was dying. And Carolyn would be gone.

She could see her breath in the night air, soft puffs of vapor spilling out, as she made her way down the path to the frozen pond. She used to skate there, years ago, when the MacDowells had come to Vermont each Christmas. Before she had brought Sally here to die. She hadn't skated in years, but Ruben saw to it that the surface was always cleared of snow. It was smooth and clean now, this last dumping already pushed to one side if anyone was silly enough to want to skate.

Carolyn stood on the edge of the ice, staring out across the glassy surface, a sudden absurd urge rushing through her. She didn't even own a pair of skates, though a pair would be produced almost immediately if she expressed an interest.

She stepped out onto the ice gingerly, the tread on her flat boots keeping her from slipping. The ice was almost a foot thick, and she tried to push along against it, but her boots gave her too much traction.

She moved to the center of the pond, gathering the stillness about her. It had been years since she'd tried to skate. It was so long ago she couldn't even remember when she'd last worn skates.

Yes, she could. Christmas, twenty-two years ago, when she'd been nine years old. She'd gotten new skates, and a surprisingly patient Alex had brought her out to try them. She should have known better than to trust him. She'd ended the day with a fractured wrist, courtesy of Alex's attempts to teach her the niceties of ice hockey, and she'd never picked up her skates again.

Even now, she could remember the cool, taunting expression on Alex's face as Sally had blistered him, then forgiven him, as she always had. But somehow, in her memory, Alex's face looked exactly like his imposter.

"Done much skating lately, Carolyn?"

His voice came across the ice on a whisper of smoke. She barely moved. She knew he would come, she realized belatedly. She knew he would follow her.

She lifted her head to look at him across the expanse of ice and snow. He was standing at the edge of the woods, silhouetted in the moonlight, and he was dressed lightly, in a thin jacket and no gloves. He didn't look cold.

She huddled deeper in her down coat. "Not for twenty years," she said.

"You should try it again," he said. "Maybe I'll give you another lesson."

He'd been told about that, had he? She shouldn't be surprised. "I don't think I need any lessons from you about anything."

"Sure you do," he said gently. "You need lessons in not giving a damn about anybody but yourself. You need lessons in telling people you don't like to fuck off. You need lessons in fighting back instead of being used."

"Fuck off."

She could see his alarmingly sensuous mouth curve in a wry smile. "So maybe you don't need lessons in that. How about learning how to stop caring? They'll hurt you, Carolyn. Even an outsider can see that."

"You admit you're an outsider?"

"I haven't been here in eighteen years. That hardly makes me intimate with the workings of this household. I can tell you one thing, though. You haven't changed."

"Haven't I?" she said, not moving from her spot in the center of the ice.

He was coming toward her. His running shoes were covered with snow, and he skidded a bit on the slick ice. He seemed to enjoy it. "You're still the little girl with her nose pressed up against the storefront window," he said, his voice cool and unfeeling like the hard ice beneath her feet. "You still want what you can't have."

He was coming too close to her, but she stood her ground, refusing to back away. "And what is it I can't have?"

"A real family."

She took a sharp intake of breath. "Is the ability to hurt people part of being a con man?" she said. "Or is it just an added gift? I'm afraid you've been misinformed—I have a real family. Sally."

"I don't want to hurt you, Carolyn," he said. "I never have. Are you afraid to face the truth? You never were before."

"I'd say your acquaintance with the truth is superficial indeed."

"You wound me," he protested with mock solemnity.

"I would sell my soul," she said meditatively, "for the ice to crack beneath you."

His smile was wintry bright. "Not a good way to kill someone, I'm afraid. Someone might hear my calls for help. And chances are, you'd fall in as well."

"It might be worth it," she said.

"You want me dead?" There seemed more than casual interest in his question.

"I want you gone where you can't cause any more harm," she said.

"And you're willing to kill me to ensure that?"

She sighed. "Don't flatter yourself. I need a better motive for murder."

She started past him, suddenly claustrophobic. He moved, blocking her way, as somehow she knew he would. "Maybe I could convince you I am who I say I am."

"And maybe pigs will fly, but I don't expect either thing to happen in the near future. May I go?"

"Am I stopping you?" He was standing uncomfortably close, but his arms were crossed over his chest, and he made no move to touch her.

The night was bitter, and she could hardly keep from shivering inside the protecting folds of the down coat. He stood there, barely dressed, seemingly comfortable.

"Aren't you cold?" she asked suddenly.

"Don't worry about me," he said. "I learned how to take care of myself more than eighteen years ago."

And on that point, at least, she believed him.

Chapter Four

THE DREAM CAME again that night, when it hadn't come to her for years. She'd thought, hoped, it had gone forever, but she should have realized that the return of Alexander MacDowell would trigger her recurring nightmares and the ever-shifting memory of the night he died.

She'd lost the ability to separate truth from her dreams. There had been a time in her early twenties, when she'd been in her final year at Bennington and the nightmares had grown to unmanageable levels, that she'd finally sought help. The therapist had suggested she write down her dreams, and then write down everything she remembered from that night, and compare the two. The effort had proven a dismal failure. She had gotten to the point where she doubted everything that she ought to remember—where reality, memory, and nightmares all blended into one psychedelic swirl. Finally she'd just learned to let go of it, refusing to think about it all. There was no way she could make sense of it, no way she could ever learn the truth of what happened that night. She wasn't even sure she wanted to know. She just wanted to be free of the dreams.

And she had been. Until a man claiming to be Alex MacDowell had appeared out of a freak storm and set her life on end.

The dream started as it always had. They were in the old house in Edgartown, on Martha's Vineyard. It was late at night, after midnight, and she was asleep in her small bedroom at the back of the house, over the kitchen—part of what used to be the servants' rooms. But in the summer Constanza and Ruben stayed in an apartment over the garage, and the rooms had been made over into cheery little bedrooms. Carolyn slept in one of them.

She was almost fourteen at the time. She'd heard them arguing, the sound muffled through the walls and ceiling, but they hadn't bothered to lower their voices. Alex must have done something wicked again, she'd thought sleepily, putting the pillow over her head.

He was the bane of her existence, a spoiled, selfish creature who was utterly wild. He drove Aunt Sally to distracted tears, he tormented his cousins, and he taunted Carolyn with a lethal combination of casual bullying and seductive charm that was far too potent for a young girl to handle. And she wasn't sure which she hated more—the charm or the bullying.

She heard him in the room. He was silhouetted against the moonlight flooding in her uncurtained window, and he looked taller, almost like an adult in that shadowy light. He was standing at her dresser, rummaging through her things.

"What are you doing?"

He turned at the sound of her voice, but she hadn't managed to startle him. "I'm getting the hell out of here, Carolyn," he'd said in a strange voice. "I need money."

"I don't have any."

"You have this." He held a handful of gold jewelry in one fist, and she sat up, a cry of protest strangled in her throat.

"You can't," she said. "Those were presents from Aunt Sally. Listen, I'll see if I can get you some money—"

He shook his head. "I don't have the time. She'll buy you more. My mother has no problem buying love with her checkbook." His voice was cool and bitter.

"At least leave me the charm bracelet." She shouldn't have admitted that weakness. Each year Sally had added a new charm, something whimsical, charming. It had marked her years with the MacDowell family, and it was the most precious thing she owned.

"Can't do it. Sorry, kid. If you have any sense you'll get the hell away from here as soon as you're old enough. They'll destroy you." He sounded odd to her, distant, as if he'd already left.

"They're my family," she'd protested. And immediately regretted the words.

He came up to the bed, looming over her in the moonlight. "No, they're not," he said. "And be glad of it. They eat their family alive."

He reached out his hand and touched her face in the moonlight. "Too bad I can't take you with me, Carolyn," he said. "But you're too young, and I'm not into jailbait. Take care of yourself." And he kissed her.

He'd never kissed her, apart from brief, dutiful pecks on her cheek when ordered to do so. This was on her mouth, but it was no Prince Charming awakening the sleeping beauty. It was rough, hurried, and completely sexual, his mouth open on hers, his arms pulling her young body against his. It was a hungry, lost kiss, and she didn't even hesitate, putting her arms around his neck and kissing him back with all her inexpert passion.

It seemed to go on for a breathless lifetime; it was over in a heartbeat. And he was gone, disappearing into the darkness, out of her life forever. Taking a fistful of her gold jewelry, including the only thing she'd ever cared about.

She stood there in shock, trembling all over, and then she moved, throwing on clothes with abandon. He'd taunted and teased and tormented her all her life. He wasn't going to get away with robbing her as well, making up for it with a good-bye kiss that was everything she'd ever fantasized and more. By the time she reached the front sidewalk she thought she could see him heading toward Lighthouse Beach, and she started after him, silent, determined.

Running away from an island six miles off the coast of the mainland was not the easiest thing to do. Alex had tried it before, when he was fifteen, stealing a friend's catamaran and disappearing for over a week. The police had found him in Boston and brought him home, unrepentant and hostile and enticingly experienced.

Whose boat was he planning to steal this time? Or was he going high-tech and planning on taking one of the small private planes parked at the island airport? Sally had paid for flying lessons for his sixteenth birthday, and she'd regretted it ever since.

But he was heading toward the beach, not the airport, and if she could only see where she was going she could catch up with him. Threaten to scream at the top of her lungs if he didn't give her back the charm bracelet.

He could have the rest, with her blessing. She was willing to pay almost anything to get him out of her life, and he was right. The MacDowells were more than generous with their checkbooks, if not with their emotions. If he were gone she could have Sally to herself, with no wicked, beautiful bad boy to distract either of them.

The light from the quarter moon was fitful, and there were dark clouds scudding across the sky, obscuring it. She slipped on the loose stones that led to the beach, going down on one knee, and she could feel the bite of the broken shells through her jeans. She didn't care. She scrambled back to her feet, keeping his tall, straight back firmly in sight.

She wasn't afraid of him, she told herself, over and over again, for all that he'd taunted and tormented her during the years he'd been an almost-brother to her. She wasn't worried that he could try to silence her by force.

If she started screaming for someone to stop him from leaving, he'd probably just shrug his shoulders and grin.

And disappear.

The tide was high that night; the sea was rough from the remnants of a late-summer storm. He came to a stop at the edge of the beach, staring out across the narrow channel of water to Chappaquiddick, then turned and looked back toward Water Street and the old house.

Without thinking Carolyn ducked down, out of sight behind an overturned dinghy. She hid there, trying to catch her breath. Silly to be so panicked, she told herself furiously. She started to rise, to go after him, when she heard the voices.

He wasn't alone out there at the edge of the water. She should have known that—he wouldn't be planning to swim off the island. He must have arranged to meet someone.

They were arguing, she could tell that much and nothing more. Cautiously she raised her head, peering over the boat. The clouds had covered the moon now, and the two figures were in shadows. Much of the same size and the same build, she couldn't even tell which one was Alex. Whether the person he was arguing with was male or female, young or old, stranger or almost-relative.

"Fuck you!" Alex's furious voice carried on the night air, and he shoved the other person, turning away and starting down the beach.

It happened so quickly Carolyn thought she'd imagined it, staring in frozen horror as ghastly images danced in her mind. The moonlight glinting off a gun. The sudden, swift move of the dark, anonymous figure, the explosion of sound in the night, a sound that could have been a car backfiring but wasn't.

And Alex's recoil and his crumpled body lying on the sand. Even from a distance she could see the dark circle of blood pooling around him from the hole in his back, and she tried to scream, but the only sound she could make was a faint moaning noise.

She sank back down, shivering, unable to catch her breath as wave after wave of horror washed over her. She had to move, had to go for help, but her body was frozen, rigid. Her breath caught in her chest, strangling her, and she had to struggle to stay conscious, to fight the merciful blankness that wanted to overtake her.

She had no idea how long she sat there, fighting for breath, fighting for calm. By the time her gasping sobs had shuddered to a stop, by the time she managed to scramble to her knees and peer over the side of the dingy, it was too late.

The beach was deserted. The clouds had passed, and the sliver of moonlight lit the empty sand.

There was no sign of footprints. The tide had risen up to the rocks, and whoever had walked on the sand had left no trace behind.

The tide had washed the blood clean. It must have carried Alex's body out to sea. With the fierce storm currents, he might not be found for days or weeks. Maybe never.

She had to get help. It might not be too late—she'd lost all sense of time, but it could have been only a matter of minutes since Alex had been shot. Maybe he wasn't really dead, maybe the bullet had missed his heart. She started to rise, then sank down again in panic.

Someone was standing at the edge of the path, waiting. Watching. The streetlight was far enough away that she could only see the silhouette, but she knew without question that it wasn't Alex. It was the man or woman who'd shot him. And he was waiting to make sure there weren't any witnesses.

It was cold and damp. The t-shirt she wore was soaked with dew, and the wind off the ocean was bitterly cold against her skin. She curled up in a ball, wrapping her arms around her body in a vain effort to keep warm. She hadn't been seen, she was sure of that. Whoever had killed Alex was just being careful.

She didn't even know that Alex was dead, not for certain. He'd been shot, and she'd seen him fall, seen the blood on the sand. But she hadn't actually seen him die.

She closed her eyes, burying her head against her bony knees, breathing hard, seeking warmth in her damp breath. She just had to wait. As soon as the coast was clear she'd run back to the house on Water Street and wake Aunt Sally, and tell her . . .

Tell her what? Her only child was dead? Murdered by someone, and she couldn't even tell if it was a man or a woman? And that Carolyn had done nothing to save him? She lifted her head to stare out at the sea. The waves were rough, surging in toward land. There was no way even a strong swimmer could survive for long in that rough surf, and certainly not someone who'd just been shot. It was too late to go for help.

The figure was still standing there, facing the horizon, waiting with seemingly endless patience, and there was nothing Carolyn could do but wait as well, shivering in the cold.

The sound of the children woke her. Squeals of delight, as a nanny brought her charges down to Lighthouse Beach to feed the seagulls.

Carolyn tried to move, but she felt encased in ice, her bones and muscles frozen.

It was a sunny day, even in the early morning. Overhead the seagulls wheeled and screeched in pleasure, and the tide was already going out again, taking with it all trace of the boy who was once Alexander MacDowell.

It took all her strength to pull herself to her feet. She felt battered, beaten, and she moved back up the pathway like an old woman. The children looked at her strangely, and their German nanny herded them quickly out of harm's way.

The house on Water Street was still and silent. No police cars parked outside, no lights on. She could see movement in the apartment over the garage, but even Ruben and Constanza had yet to begin their day. She crept in the back door, into the silent and deserted kitchen, shaking with the cold. She climbed up the back stairs, back to her bedroom, and collapsed on the narrow bed, pulling the covers tight around her. She should strip off her wet clothes, but she didn't have the energy. She needed to get warm. She huddled deeper beneath the pile of blankets, shivering so hard she could hear the creak of the old bedsprings beneath the new mattress. She listened, remote, removed, and then closed her eyes.

She'd almost died. When the rest of the house had stirred and discovered that Alexander had taken off with every piece of loose cash or jewelry he could lay his hands on, full panic had set in. Someone must have checked to make sure Carolyn was asleep in her bed, bundled beneath a surprising amount of heavy blankets, but then she'd been forgotten in the hubbub, the police, the FBI, the panic and anger and recriminations. By the time Constanza realized she hadn't been seen all day, Carolyn's fever was one hundred and five and her body was shaken with convulsions.

They didn't tell her Alexander had disappeared until she was released from the hospital some five days later. Sally had stayed with her the entire time, sleeping in a chair by her hospital bed, her once-beautiful face ravaged by grief and worry. It wasn't until later that Carolyn knew that she'd remained by her side rather than go in search of her spoiled, errant son. Sally really did love her after all, and she never spoke Alex's name out loud. Her son had failed her, and in her hurt and anger she simply ignored his existence, turning instead to Carolyn.

It wasn't until years later that Carolyn remembered anything at all, when she woke up screaming with a nightmare, and the horrifying night came back to her full force.

Alexander MacDowell was dead, she remembered that much. Someone had shot and killed him. Beyond that, dreams mixed with memories that sent her into a mindless panic. She'd learned not to think about it. Not to question.

The dreams had eventually stopped, and she'd pushed them all away, into the forgotten past. Sally had never asked if she knew anything about that night, and as the years passed and she began to long for her missing son, she never thought to question Carolyn, and Carolyn had never wanted to take away her hope. It was easier to forget that summer night so long ago, pretend it hadn't happened.

She didn't have that luxury anymore. Not with a stranger, a liar, a criminal trying to worm his way into Sally's good graces and into her fortune. Not with the dreams coming back to rip her from her sleep.

She should have told the truth years ago, even though it would have shattered Sally. But she hadn't. She was unwilling to dredge up her own imperfect memories, unwilling to bring that much pain to the person she loved most in the world.

She could hardly come up with the truth some eighteen years later. She could only keep her mouth shut and her eyes open, and wait for him to betray himself.

And hope the dreams wouldn't keep coming back.

PATSY MACDOWELL looked younger than her son George, and only marginally prettier. Which was only to be expected, given that her fifty-eight-year-old face and body were a work in progress, an ongoing testament to the wonders of cosmetic surgery, compulsive exercise, and every fad diet known to womankind. She was a perfect shade of golden bisque, a combination of seventy-five-dollar-an-ounce makeup and state-of-the-art tanning machines. The MacDowell brown eyes stared up at Carolyn with their usual vague disinterest, and she lit a cigarette with practiced grace.

"How are you, Carolyn?" she said with her patented greeting. She had absolutely no interest in Carolyn's response, but that didn't keep Carolyn from telling her the truth.

"Disturbed," she said flatly.

Patsy's response was less a smile than a grimace. "Aren't we all? Where is the mysterious missing heir? I didn't disrupt my schedule and drag myself all the way up here to sit around and waste time."

She was stretched out on the sofa in the living room, her perfect legs crossed decorously. It was no accident that she reclined on a rose-colored sofa that accented her pale beige suit. Patsy knew how to choose her accessories, even when it came to which furnishings she graced.

"I haven't seen Alex this morning," Carolyn said, omitting the fact that she had done her best to avoid him since his appearance in Vermont some three days ago. "When did you get here?"

"It seems like hours ago, darling," Patsy said with a delicate yawn. "Dear George drove me up—he's always been the best son. But even so, the whole thing is too exhausting, don't you know? Find Alex for me, will you, and tell him his devoted Aunt Patsy is positively dying to see him again. Not to mention his cousin George. The two of them were the same age, and dearest friends when they were children."

"They're still the same age, and they could never stand each other," Carolyn pointed out. Patsy ignored her, always ready to revise family history to suit herself.

Things had gone from bad to worse. Patsy and Warren were bad enough—George Clarendon, better known through youth as George the Pig, was the final straw. An elegant, beautiful, sneering young man, he always seemed to be watching everyone, making a mental list of their failings.

"I think Alex is off with Warren again. The two of them seem to have hit it off," she said coolly.

Patsy stared at her. "How astonishing!" she murmured. "I wouldn't have thought Alex and Warren were the type to cozy up. Of course, eighteen years have passed. People change."

"Yes."

"Still," Patsy continued, "I find that very interesting indeed. If Warren accepts him completely then I don't suppose I have any reason to doubt that it's the real Alex. After all, Warren is far more observant and distrusting than I am—he's always telling me so. I suppose I should take his word for it that he's the real thing." Carolyn said absolutely nothing, a fact that wasn't wasted on Patsy. "Sally believes it's him, doesn't she?"

"Absolutely," Carolyn said.

"And what about you, dear Caro?"

Carolyn hated being called Caro, and she suspected Patsy knew it. She managed a cool smile. "I have a suspicious nature."

Patsy shrugged. "I suppose I'll have to make up my own mind." She glanced out the window. It was a gray, chilly day, and the recent snowfall still lingered on the flat brown landscape. "Not the best time of year for a family reunion. Tessa and Grace are arriving today as well, but at least I talked Grace out of bringing her obnoxious offspring. Children give me hives."

Carolyn hadn't realized things could still get dramatically worse than they already were, but the imminent arrival of the rest of Patsy's grown children was the final blow. "I'll talk to Constanza," she said, whirling around, desperate to escape and go kick something.

"No need, dear," Patsy said with a languid wave of her hand. "I've already warned her. Though I gather you've been sleeping in the room Tessa usually uses. You don't mind vacating, do you? She is so particular about her surroundings, and if she has to share, she'd much rather share with Grace. You can understand that, can't you?" She smiled sweetly.

"I don't mind," Carolyn said numbly.

"It's a good thing Sally had this place renovated a few years back, or you'd be stuck in the servants' quarters with Ruben and Constanza. Not that there's anything wrong with that—Sally spoils them dreadfully. But then, she's always been a soft touch." She gave Carolyn a gracious smile.

It took Carolyn a moment to realize that her fingers were tingling. Her hands were clenched so tightly she'd cut off all feeling in them. She forced herself to relax, to meet Patsy's pampered smile with one of her own. She'd known Patsy all her life, and she knew just what was pure malice and what was simply the by-product of determined self-interest.

"I'll go move my things," she said. "When do Tessa and Grace arrive?"

"Oh, at some point," Patsy said airily. "Find Alex, will you?"

"Of course," she said, lying through her teeth. The last person in the world she was ready to face was the phony Alex MacDowell. Though running up against George the Pig was a close second.

Naturally Alex was waiting in the hallway, just outside her room.

"You look ready to kill someone," he said lazily. He was leaning against the wall, watching her, his eyes hooded, his expression unreadable. He was wearing faded jeans that fit his lanky frame, a thick cotton sweater, and running shoes.

She paused, looking at him with a critical eye. "You don't dress like a MacDowell," she said abruptly.

"That doesn't even wound me, much less kill me," he said. "And just how does a MacDowell dress?"

"Didn't your research tell you that?"

He made a clucking noise with his tongue. "Harsh, Carolyn. Why do you refuse to trust me?"

"You figure it out." She pushed past him, into her room, slamming the door behind her. He caught it, moving inside and closing it very quietly behind him. Closing them both in.

She ignored him, yanking open a drawer and pulling out her neatly folded clothes. He stood there watching her. "Is this what a MacDowell wears?" he asked curiously, leaning forward to pick up her neatly ironed khaki slacks. "Looks pretty boring to me."

"If you want to know how to dress you can watch your cousin George."

"He's coming?" Alex made a disgusted noise. "Is he still a little pig?"

"No," she said. "He's here already, looking for a touching reunion with his favorite cousin. If you'll excuse me, I have to vacate this room for his sisters and I don't have time for small talk."

"They're kicking you out, too? You can always come back and sleep with me."

It was the final straw in a series of long, horrible days. Without thinking she reached out and slapped him, the sound loud and shocking in the stillness of the room.

He didn't flinch. Didn't move. His blue-green eyes hardened for a moment, and then his wickedly sensual mouth curved in a smile. "A mistake, dear Carolyn," he murmured.

"On your part or mine?" She was horrified at herself. She'd never hit another human being in her life, and yet there he stood, the imprint of her hand red against his golden skin.

"Let's call it a draw. I'll keep my lascivious thoughts to myself, and you'll keep your hands to yourself." He looked charmingly repentant, and so much like the real Alex when he was trying to worm his way back into someone's good graces that a fist closed around her heart.

He held out a hand. He had strong, beautiful hands, worker's hands, with long, elegant fingers. She couldn't remember Alex's hands at all. "Truce?" he said, charming. Lying.

She looked at his hand pointedly. "Over my dead body."

She expected rage from him. Contempt and fury. Instead his smile widened, into one of knowing smugness that was still infuriatingly attractive. "Ah, Carolyn," he murmured. "You're going to be such fun to convince." And then he was gone, closing the door softly behind him.

Chapter Five

THE THIRD OF THE elder MacDowell siblings, Patsy, was a piece of cake, Alex thought smugly, surveying her across the dinner table. She didn't care whether he was the real Alex or not, as long as he didn't tax her concentration. She was on something—he'd kicked around the world for too long not to recognize even the subtle symptoms, but Patsy was in a pleasant enough fog, aided by a suitably impressive Cabernet.

Her three children were another matter. George the Pig was looking at him as if he were a wild-eyed terrorist out to bomb everyone into oblivion. Tessa was tossing her auburn mane of hair every chance she got, glaring at him out of her magnificent, smoldering eyes, and doing everything she could to remind him that she was a) a highly paid and much sought-after fashion model and b) she didn't believe him for a moment.

She was getting a little long in the tooth for high fashion, Alex thought cynically. She had to be near thirty, though she looked a decade younger, fighting the encroachments of age with the dedication of her mother. The little sneer that pursed her collagen-enhanced lips was going to leave nasty little wrinkles if she didn't watch it.

Grace, the youngest of the cousins, would have been six when Alex left, and there was no way he would have remembered her. She seemed a cut above her self-absorbed siblings. He might even go so far as to say she was pleasant, except that she barely spoke to him, though when she did she was civil enough. She spent the entire time talking in a corner with Carolyn, while the other cousins concentrated on Alex and ignored Carolyn completely.

As did Sally. She hadn't felt up to sitting at the table, but she held court in her bedroom, and Ruben had wheeled her hospital bed to the French doors that opened onto the formal dining room so that she could be a part of it all. He could feel her eyes watching him, and he wondered what she was thinking. Whether deep in her heart she really believed he was Alexander MacDowell.

It didn't matter—she wasn't about to protest. Or call for proof, or

DNA testing, or any of the like, of that much he was absolutely certain. She'd made up her mind that he was her son, and nothing would make her change it.

"Carolyn?" Her soft voice, weak from pain, nevertheless carried down to the end of the table, where Carolyn sat with Grace.

There was immediate, dutiful silence in the room. Carolyn rose, and as usual he had to admire her grace, even in the boring gray cocktail dress she'd worn down to dinner. Without effort she made Tessa seem overblown and obvious, and anyone with taste wouldn't look twice at the famous beauty.

But Carolyn wasn't interested in clothes, adornment, or his opinion, he thought wryly, watching her out of hooded eyes. As he'd watched her all night long, now that she was no longer capable of avoiding him so assiduously.

"Are you tired, Aunt Sally?" she asked solicitously. "I'll have Ruben bring you back to bed—"

"Don't fuss over me, child!" Sally's faint smile took most of the sting out of the reprimand. "I'm just fine. I'm perfectly capable of knowing when I'm tired or not. I have a favor to ask you, darling. If it's not too much of an imposition."

Alex kept his expression bland. He suspected Carolyn would have slashed her wrists for Sally, but they obviously preferred to keep up the polite fiction. He couldn't figure out what Sally had ever done to deserve such devotion, but Carolyn was obviously loyal to a fault.

"Anything," Carolyn said rashly.

"Alex and I were talking," Sally said, and Carolyn's eyes narrowed, though she kept herself from glancing toward him. "He wondered where that childhood portrait is? You remember, the one I had done when he was twelve?"

"You got rid of it," she said flatly.

"Don't be absurd, Carolyn," Warren protested. "That was a Wicklander portrait—they're worth their weight in gold. She wouldn't have thrown it out."

"I didn't mean that. I meant that she was so upset she couldn't bear to look at it anymore," Carolyn said, and this time she did toss an angry glare in Alex's direction.

"Where is it, Carolyn? Is it in storage?" George demanded, sounding, if possible, even more pompous than his elderly uncle. George had been born with an old soul, sour and disapproving, a fact that was at odds with his strikingly handsome appearance. As a child he'd been a sneak and a tattletale, as an adult he simply passed judgment on all around him.

"It's in the Edgartown house," she said reluctantly.

"That's what I thought. I want it back," Sally said.

"I'll make arrangements to have it shipped—"

"No! I don't want to wait, and besides, as Warren pointed out, it's a Wicklander. It's too valuable to be entrusted to any commercial company. I don't want strangers rummaging around my house. The Vineyard house is a family treasure—we don't want to endanger it."

Did she know what was coming? Alex thought lazily. She looked wary, but trusting.

"What do you want me to do about it, Aunt Sally?" Carolyn said.

Sally gave her the smile that had charmed men, women, and children for all of her seventy-eight years. "I knew I could count on you, darling. I want you to drive down there and get it."

"Of course I will," she said warmly.

"Alex prefers to use his own car, even though I told him the Rover would be better—"

"Alex?" Her voice was a strangled shriek of horror. He gave in to temptation and gave her a beatific smile.

"I told Mother I wanted to see the Edgartown house again, and that I'd be happy to drive you. That way you won't have to drive all that way alone."

"I like driving alone," she said sharply.

"And the portrait's fairly big. You'll need help with it."

"I don't need help with anything." The harshness of her words momentarily silenced the room, and Sally looked at her out of wide, hurt eyes.

"Carolyn!" Sally protested in shock. "You'll make Alex feel unwelcome."

"Of course he's welcome," Carolyn said through her teeth, and he was reminded of the phrase, 'spitting nails.' "I just think you'd be a lot happier with him keeping you company. After all, you have all those years to catch up on—"

"You won't be gone that long, Carolyn," Sally said with a long-suffering patience calculated to infuse Carolyn with guilt. "Just one night, or two at the absolute most. I'm not about to drop dead in the next few days, you know. It would mean a great deal to me." She didn't bother to wheedle. She knew she had Carolyn in the palm of her hand.

Carolyn caved, as he'd expected her to. Obviously, she was saving her fighting strength for him. "Of course I'll go," she said with deceptive calm. "And if Alex wants to drive, then I'm sure that will make things easier. I don't think we need to be gone for the night, though. If we leave early enough we can be at the Woods Hole ferry by midmorning, and be back here late the same night."

"I wouldn't want you to push. You've given up so much to take care of me—you've been at my beck and call for the last eight months. Enjoy yourself with a handsome young man." Alex kept his face gravely composed, but she glared at him anyway. Before she could say anything, Tessa broke in.

"Carolyn's never been particularly interested in handsome young men, Aunt Sally," she said airily. "She likes them stuffy and intellectual. If you want I'll be happy to drive down to the Vineyard with Cousin Alex. It would give us a chance to catch up on old times."

Not what he wanted at all. Tessa was only a bit player in this particular drama. He couldn't care less whether she believed he was the real Alex MacDowell or not. Carolyn was a different matter, and he wasn't interested in wasting time. Looking at Sally's pale, pain-wracked face, he knew there wasn't time to spare.

"That's a wonderful idea!" Carolyn sounded positively exuberant at the thought of her reprieve. "I can stay here and make sure everything runs smoothly and Tessa—"

"No," Sally said, and there was no disputing the finality of her voice. "I may be dying, but I'm still in charge of this household. You aren't needed to run things, Carolyn. Constanza is entirely capable of seeing to matters, and besides, my sister and brother will be here. You've been cooped up with me all winter, and I want you to get out in the real world for a change."

"But I don't want to." She sounded like a stubborn child. "I'd much rather stay here with you."

Sally closed her eyes, suddenly looking very tired. "Don't fight me on this, Carolyn," she said wearily. "I really don't have the strength for it."

Game, set and match, Alex thought, as Carolyn's face flushed with guilt.

"When do you want us to go?" she asked.

Sally's smile was dazzlingly bright, but the wily old lady didn't overplay her hand. "That's my girl," she murmured weakly.

And Carolyn managed a weak smile in return.

CAROLYN'S HANDS were shaking so hard she dropped the bottle of tranquilizers onto the deserted kitchen floor. The small yellow pills spilled out over the wide oak plank, rolling under the huge refrigerator, and she watched them go with a blank expression. Sally's doctor had prescribed them, insisting she might need them during Sally's long, slow journey toward death.

She hadn't touched them until Alexander MacDowell had showed up. If things didn't take a sharp turn for the better, she was going to need every one of those little yellow pills and more besides.

She knelt down, scooping them up, when she heard someone push open the kitchen door. There was never any question who it was, she thought bitterly. Of the nine people in the house, it could only be the one person she most wanted to avoid.

"What are you scrabbling around on the floor for?" George's faintly supercilious baritone startled her into dropping the pills she had.

She ignored them, rising gracefully, too distracted by the unavoidable knowledge that she was disappointed it wasn't Alex, when she'd been so certain it would be. "Can I help you, George?"

George, like his sister, had fashion-model looks and the personality to match. "I'm hungry. You want to rustle me up a sandwich?"

"No." She'd learned long ago how to deal with George. He was a user, adept at getting people to do what he wanted, and she had no intention of joining his mother and sisters in catering to his whims.

George shrugged, obviously expecting her answer, and slouched on into the kitchen. His tan was deep and perfect, the product of his top-of-the-line health club. It kept his body in excellent shape as well, and he had a tendency to close in on people, press that trim, well-muscled flesh against them. Carolyn kept the kitchen island between them.

"So what do you think of him, Caro?" he asked casually. "Do you think he's the real McCoy?"

"What do you think?"

"I haven't the faintest idea. It's no skin off my nose—I wasn't in line for any of Sally's money anyway, except indirectly, and I have more than enough for my needs."

"I find that hard to believe."

George's smile revealed small, perfect teeth. "Well, I will admit that the more money, the better. But I'm a patient man—and good things come to those who wait. You, on the other hand, have a very great deal to lose if this man is actually who he says he is."

She stared at him stonily. "Don't be ridiculous."

"Oh, I'm not talking about money," he said softly. "After all, we both know you aren't legally family. I'm sure Sally's left you a generous stipend, but you're a clever girl. You wouldn't be expecting more. No, you stand to lose something more important than money."

"I didn't think you realized there was anything more important than money, George."

But George was undeterred. "You'll lose Sally's single-minded devotion. For the last few months she's been totally dependent on you, and you've had her all to yourself. She won't need you anymore, Caro. She'll have Sonny Boy for love and affection. You'll be relegated to the position of unpaid companion." George was not the brightest of men, but he had a certain animal instinct shared by the rest of his family, and he had an uncanny ability to draw blood. Fortunately, Carolyn was expecting it.

"I'm not worried about it, George. My apartment's still waiting for me back in Boston, and I shouldn't have any trouble finding another job. Though it's very nice of you to be so concerned about me."

He blinked, and then his smile widened as he recognized the irony. "If he's an imposter, Carolyn, it's up to you to expose him."

"Why me?"

"Because you're here, for Christ's sake. You knew him better than any of us, and you'll be around him day and night. This little visit to Edgartown will give you the perfect time to get to know him better. See if you can trip him up in some of his lies."

"Lies?" she echoed. "You don't believe he's the real Alexander?"

"I didn't say that. I'm a careful man. I watch, and I listen. As I said, it's not my money, but since it belongs to my beloved aunt, I don't want to see her handing it over to some criminal."

"Noble of you," Carolyn said lightly.

He moved closer. "Listen, Caro, why don't you come down to New York after you get back from the Vineyard? I know you must miss the city, living up here in the boonies. We could go out, have a good time. I know a marvelous Moroccan restaurant that you'd adore."

She stared at him in disbelief. "Why would I do that?"

"You can tell me what you've found out about Alex. And you know I've always liked you. You're a very attractive woman, Carolyn." He dropped his voice to a husky note that was obviously supposed to sound seductive.

The swinging door opened, and Tessa strode in, breaking up the awkward moment. "I've been looking for you, Carolyn. You're needed. Warren, Mother, and Grace want to play bridge, and I'd rather slash my wrists."

"No." It was the second time she'd told a MacDowell no, and the experience was heady. "Sorry, I have too much to do. They'll have to play three handed."

"Don't be absurd. I'm sure whatever you have to do can wait," Tessa said grandly.

"No." Number three. Carolyn was so pleased with herself she even managed a gracious smile. "They'll have to entertain themselves."

Without another word she scooted around the kitchen island, leaving the pills scattered over the wooden floor, making a graceful escape.

DESPITE THE extensive remodeling, the MacDowell family compound wasn't large enough to comfortably encompass the entire extended family. With the newcomer in Alex MacDowell's remodeled bedroom, and Tessa and Grace sharing her old one, Carolyn was officially dispossessed. Patsy, Warren, and George had claimed the three self-contained suites, and there was no moving them, short of using dynamite.

Which left Carolyn with a foldout sofa in the library.

Normally she didn't mind. But these weren't normal times. George was getting odd ideas. Warren was far too chummy, and worst of all, there was a lying stranger in the house.

On top of that, the library was the room equipped with a large-screen TV and a bar, and two of the younger MacDowells had taken up residence there.

At least Alex had made himself scarce. Probably sucking up to Aunt Sally, Carolyn thought bitterly. She didn't know how she was going to survive the next few days, the next few weeks. The very thought of being trapped in a car with him for untold hours filled her with dread. He disturbed her, in ways she didn't even want to think about. He was a liar and a cheat and possibly far worse, and there was nothing she could do or say to stop him from using the MacDowells for his own nefarious purposes.

It was a huge, rambling house, but she had nowhere to hide. The older generation was in the living room, the younger in the library. She didn't dare go back to the kitchen, even to retrieve her scattered pills, and it was a bitterly cold night. She wasn't in the mood for another moonlight stroll, especially considering who she'd run into last time.

It was after one in the morning when Tessa and George finally decided to vacate the library. Carolyn waited until the house was still and quiet, secure in the knowledge that everyone was asleep, before she crept back to the kitchen to find her tranquilizers.

They were gone. Some helpful soul had cleaned up, and there was no sign of the scattered pills or the empty bottle. She could only hope Constanza had returned to the kitchen to make certain everything was cleared away after midnight raids and the like, but she doubted she'd be so lucky.

Constanza had moved most of her clothes to the bedroom Tessa and Grace now occupied, but at least she'd managed to grab an armful and stash them in the little-used storage room. She threw on an enveloping flannel nightgown and headed for the dubious comfort of the foldout sofa, travel alarm firmly in hand. Most of the MacDowells would be sleeping late, but she wasn't about to be caught in bed by any of them.

There were no shades or curtains on the library windows, and the moon was bright and clear, reflecting off the melting snow, shining in Carolyn's eyes no matter how much she shifted.

It was after four when she finally fell asleep, the deep chime of the grandfather clock still echoing in her head.

It was after six when she awoke in the dark, murky stillness of the room. Dazed with sleep, disoriented, she couldn't remember where she was, and she blinked groggily, wanting nothing more than to settle back beneath the soft down comforter and forget all the things that lay ahead of her.

"Rise and shine, beautiful," a low, seductive voice whispered in her ear. "It's time to hit the road."

She struck out, in sudden, inexplicable panic, connecting with solid bone and flesh. Alexander MacDowell was leaning over her, and he caught her arm as she tried to hit him.

"Calm down, angel," he said. "I wasn't about to climb in bed with you. I just thought you'd want to make an early start, since you're hoping to do this in one day."

She yanked her arm away from him, shivering in the early-morning stillness as she tried to regain her shattered equilibrium. "Today?" she said in a voice of horrified disbelief.

"Why put it off? You'll just dread it all the more," he said.

She didn't deny it. "Go away," she said sharply.

He didn't move. "How long will it take you to get ready?"

She wanted to tell him till hell froze over, but she was neatly trapped. She'd promised Sally, and she never went back on her word. Sally asked very little of her—she should welcome the sacrifice.

"An hour," she said.

"Well, don't waste time primping on my account," he said.

"Trust me, I won't."

He rose, and she almost wished he hadn't. It was a disturbing sensation, lying in the soft, warm mattress with him leaning over her, staring down at her out of his enigmatic blue eyes.

His smile didn't help matters. Cool and calculated, it played around his impossibly sensuous mouth and seemed to say that he saw right through her. "I brought you some coffee," he said, nodding toward the table.

"I don't drink coffee in the morning."

"Constanza says you like it with milk and no sugar," he continued, ignoring her blatant lie. "Seems to me you could do with a little added sweetener."

"If you don't leave now it'll take that much longer," she said coldly.

He let his eyes run over her body. There was nothing to see—most of her was beneath a fluffy duvet and the rest was covered by the flannel nightgown she usually reserved for the coldest parts of January. She could feel a slow heat envelope her skin beneath the layers anyway.

"I'll wait for you in the kitchen. At least Constanza is glad to see me back." He started toward the door, stopped, and then turned back. "Oh, I forgot something." He tossed a small object onto the bed, and she knew by the rattle that it had to be her pill bottle. "You left your drugs scattered all over the kitchen. You have to watch that stuff—Aunt Patsy's a druggie. She would have scarfed them down if she'd seen them."

She didn't bother denying it—her name was on the prescription bottle. "It's for my headaches."

"They're tranquilizers, Carolyn," he corrected her. "Mild ones, but tranquilizers nonetheless. And I intend to make sure you need them."

With a wicked smile he was gone.

Chapter Six

HE WAS SO BUSY charming Constanza that he barely looked up when Carolyn entered the kitchen, setting her empty mug down on the granite countertop.

"It's good to have Mr. Alex back," Constanza said cheerfully.

"Hmmph." She poured herself another cup of coffee, then deliberately took a tranquilizer from her pill bottle and tossed it down. Alex failed to look suitably impressed.

"I'm not sure Carolyn agrees with you, 'Stanza," he said lazily.

Someone must have told him about Alex's nickname for the woman who'd been half cook, half nanny to him growing up. It had been years since she'd heard it.

"She's not happy you're back?" Constanza said in shocked tones.

"She's not certain it's me."

Constanza laughed. "Don't be silly, Mr. Alex. How could she not know it's you? How could she have any doubt? Mrs. MacDowell knows you—how could a mother not know her own son? Besides, you're just the same."

"God, I hope not," he said devoutly. "I'm older and wiser."

"Maybe," Carolyn muttered.

Constanza shook her head. "You two were always bickering. I shouldn't be surprised that you're still at it. Now sit down and I'll make you some eggs."

"I'm not hungry, Constanza. I'd rather get on the road."

"You're never hungry," Constanza scolded. "It's an insult to my cooking, and I won't have it. Sit down and eat, or I'll tell Mrs. MacDowell on you, and you know how she worries."

It was an empty threat, and both of them knew it. Neither of them would add to Sally's cares, but Carolyn sat anyway, resisting the impulse to stick her tongue out at Alex. "Just some toast," she muttered, sipping at her coffee.

"You'll starve to death," Constanza said. "What are you in such a hurry for, anyway?"

"I want to get back as quickly as I can."

Constanza came and stood over Carolyn, her hands at her hips. "What nonsense is this? You need to get away from here—you've barely left the house in the last eight months. Mrs. MacDowell isn't going to die in the next few days, and there are plenty of people to keep her busy. You take a few days and enjoy yourself. The sea air will do you good."

Alex was watching this with great interest, and it took all Carolyn's willpower to ignore him. "Maybe later," she said.

"You mean after my mother's dead?" Alex murmured. "How morbid of you."

She'd had too little sleep and too much coffee. "I've been dealing with the fact of Sally's upcoming death for more than a year now. Sorry if it's a little rough for you, but you haven't been around to get used to the idea."

"Make up your mind, Carolyn. Either I'm a wicked imposter who shouldn't be around in the first place, or I'm a rotten, ungrateful son who's returned too late to do much good."

"I've made up my mind."

"So you have. And I don't need to ask what the judgment is, do I?"

"Either way, you're despicable."

"Don't you mean 'dethpicable'?"

She dropped her coffee cup, staring at him in sudden shock. She had shared only one thing with the wild young terror that had been Alexander MacDowell—an unexpected love for Bugs Bunny and friends. "Dethpicable" had been their password, along with "no more buwwwetts." But Alex was dead. And Daffy Duck was making a comeback—anyone Alex's age would have seen those old cartoons a thousand times. It was coincidence. It was logical.

It was nerve-wracking.

He rose before she could respond, and she made herself look at him. He was dressed in the same loose, casual clothes he'd worn before—faded jeans, cotton sweater—and he hadn't bothered to shave that morning. Maybe he thought the faint stubble was attractive. Maybe he was right.

"Come on, princess. You're the one who's in such an all-fired hurry. If you're hungry we'll stop at McDonald's on the way."

She managed a graceful shudder. "MacDowells don't eat at McDonald's," she said.

"But you're not a MacDowell."

There was no malice in the simple statement. It took all her enormous self-control not to let her reaction show on her face, not to reply with the obvious "neither are you." She ignored him, rising as well.

"I'll just go and say good-bye to Sally." She started toward the door, but he caught her arm, bringing her up short, and she had the sense not to pull away from him.

"She's sleeping. She had a bad night. I already said good-bye for both of us."

For a moment she didn't move. There was nothing she could say, no way she could fight back. She simply nodded. "All right. I'll just go and get my bag."

"What do you need a bag for? I thought you were determined we wouldn't be gone overnight?"

"Miss Carolyn is a very careful woman," Constanza announced with a proud air. "She always likes to be prepared for everything."

"Ah, but you can't be," he said softly. "Fate has a habit of playing dirty tricks."

She looked at him for a measured moment, making certain he knew she considered him one of fate's dirtiest tricks. "I'll meet you at the car."

CAROLYN SMITH amused him. He knew it was crass and coldhearted of him to find her pride and anger entertaining, but he had no illusions about his better nature. He'd lived a hard life, though he blamed no one but himself for it. It left him less than sympathetic toward foolish, worthless emotions. You took what you could get and made do with it.

Carolyn Smith would never get what she wanted. She'd never be a MacDowell, never belong to this family of smug hypocrites, and she ought to be glad of it. But she wasn't. And all he had to do was wave that lack under her nose, and she responded like a laboratory rat.

Not that she was particularly ratlike. He'd stood over the makeshift bed in the library, looking down on her, and she ought to thank God he'd resisted his worst impulse and hadn't gotten in bed with her.

God knows he'd wanted to. It would have been simple enough—he could have covered her body with his, and before she had time to scream he would have stopped her mouth.

She would have hit him. She would have kicked and struggled for approximately thirty seconds. And then she would have kissed him back.

It wasn't any particular vanity on his part. Some women were attracted to him, some women despised him. Carolyn Smith just happened to fit in both of those categories.

He ought to leave her alone. She'd managed to carve a peaceful life for herself, and his appearance was already disruptive enough. Seducing her would only make things worse.

Then again, he didn't particularly approve of her safe, peaceful life, and he was lazily egocentric enough to pass judgment. She was too young to immure herself away in a living tomb. Too young to devote herself to a family of dinosaurs that had no use for her, and obviously never had. What she desperately needed was some shaking up. And he was the man to do it.

She was standing outside the front door, waiting for him by his battered old Jeep. With her pale blond hair tucked in a tight little knot at the back of her neck, and the enveloping black raincoat pulled around her slender body, she was doing her best to look like a no-nonsense schoolteacher. She was failing miserably.

He considered holding the door for her, then decided against it. The Alex that she once knew wouldn't have bothered to open the car door for his almost-cousin. The Alex he had become was far more interested in bank vaults and bedroom doors.

Constanza was right—she was a careful little soul. She unearthed the seatbelt and buckled herself in, keeping her leather purse held tightly in her lap as some sort of protection. He could have told her that nothing would keep her safe.

They drove in silence for the first twenty minutes—a hostile silence on her part, an amused one on his. It wasn't until he came to the golden arches and put on his turn signal that she roused herself to speak.

"I don't want anything," she said. "It's too early in the morning for grease."

"It's never too early for grease." He pulled up to the drive-thru window. "Look at it this way—you'll need energy to keep battling me. You can't put up a good fight on an empty stomach."

"Who says I want to fight with you?"

He looked at her. "Maybe I'm imagining the waves of hostility wafting toward me," he said lightly.

"Go to hell."

"On the other hand, maybe not." He pulled forward, took the food, and dumped a bag in her lap. "Eat it."

"You can't make me."

He laughed softly. "Yes," he said, "I can." She believed him.

He'd never seen anyone take so long to eat one Egg McMuffin and one Hash Brown. She picked at it, crumbling it into tiny pieces.

"You're too skinny," he observed, watching the road.

"If you think you're going to win my heart with that kind of garbage you might as well save your breath," she said tartly.

"What makes you think I'm trying to win your heart?"

"Bad choice of words. You're trying to win me over like you've won over the rest of the MacDowells. You have most of them eating out of your hand, believing every word. And don't tell me again that I'm not a MacDowell—I'm perfectly aware of that fact."

"Then why do you still let it bother you? If I were you, I wouldn't want to be one of them. You'd be much better off without them."

"Were you? Assuming for a wild, crazy moment that you really are Alexander MacDowell, were you better off without them? Trying not to be one?"

He wasn't going to answer her questions. Not when they cut close to the bone. "What do you think?"

She crumpled up the paper and remaining bits of food and shoved it in the bag. "I think you're a cheat and a liar. A con artist, out to bilk a dying old lady out of her fortune."

"If she's dying, then she's not going to need her fortune for much longer."

"You doubt that she's dying?"

"No. I can see she doesn't have much time left. I can also see that having her long-lost son return to her is the best thing that can happen. She's happy, Carolyn. You have a problem with that?"

"I have a problem with false happiness. With believing a lie."

"She's not going to live long enough to find out whether it's a lie or not. She's going to die knowing her beloved son has finally returned to her. She's going to die surrounded by her loving family. What more can anyone ask? Do you want to deprive her of that? Do you want to take her son away, now that she's finally found him again?"

Carolyn was silent for a moment. "I don't want to talk about this anymore," she said finally, and her voice was weary. "I didn't have any choice in coming with you, but that doesn't mean I have to argue for five hours down and five hours back."

"We can talk about something else."

"I don't want to talk at all. I want to forget you even exist," she said ruthlessly. She turned away from him, facing out the window.

"Don't worry, Carolyn. As soon as Sally dies, I'll be gone from your life, and it'll all be over. You'll never have to think about me again."

She didn't respond. Her profile was distant in the gray morning light, and he allowed himself the dubious pleasure of watching her as he watched the road. He had known plain women, beautiful women, kind women, and cruel ones. Carolyn Smith had perfect features—a narrow, straight nose, high cheekbones, a sweetly generous mouth, and wide-set, wonderful blue eyes. Her skin was flawless, her body long and nicely curved, though she could have used a few extra pounds. All in all, she should have been physically irresistible.

But she had a wall around her, a wall of barbed wire and ice, and no matter how lovely the creature behind that barrier, she was still out of reach. The warning signs were all around—*no trespassing*—and yet her cool beauty was perversely tempting. Most sensible men would keep clear of her.

He wasn't a sensible man. He was a man who enjoyed a challenge. He was a man who knew far too much about Carolyn Smith, probably more than she did herself. He was a man who enjoyed danger. Otherwise, he'd be Sam Kinkaid on the other side of the ocean, basking in the Mediterranean sun in his house in Tuscany.

But here he was. And here she was, her arms folded tightly across her body, turned away from him, cold, silent, withdrawn. Here she was, at his mercy for at least the next twelve hours. He was looking forward to it.

THE FRONT SEAT of the Jeep felt as cramped and stuffy as a race car. Carolyn was doing her absolute best to ignore him, pretending to be asleep, staring out the window, answering his occasional comments with a discouraging "mm." But try as she might, she couldn't rid herself of the overwhelming sense of his presence, crowding her, pushing at her, physically overpowering her. He was there, beside her, all around her, intrusive, demanding, even when he didn't say a word.

It was her own damned fault, and she knew it. At the advanced age of thirty-one she'd learned how to let go of distractions, rise above disappointments, inure herself to annoyances. And yet the con artist pretending to be Alexander MacDowell seemed impervious to all her defenses. He managed to get under her skin with his faint, mocking grin, his luminous blue eyes, his sexy, lazy slouch.

She took a deep breath, then let it out slowly, trying to relieve the tension that had built up inside her. It was the fifth or sixth time she'd tried it, and it didn't seem to be working. It only made her feel light-headed.

"Need more tranquilizers?" he drawled, pulling to a stop outside the ferry office. He'd found the Woods Hole dock without any trouble, and she knew a moment's doubt. The way was well marked, and he was a thorough, well-versed man. He'd drive directly to the house on Water Street once they got on the island, too. She shouldn't let his cleverness surprise her, or make her doubt what she knew was true.

"I'm fine," she said in a tight little voice.

"You're wrapped tighter than a watch spring. I'm surprised you're not a little more resilient."

"I'm worried about Sally. I haven't been away from her for the last year, when she started going downhill. I don't like to leave her."

"That's a long time to devote yourself to someone with a full-time nurse and a household staff. She doesn't need you hovering at her bedside every moment."

She turned to look at him. "No, she doesn't. But I need to be there."

She half hoped there wouldn't be room on the ferry for their car. She shouldn't have underestimated him—he'd already reserved a space, and they arrived promptly in time to make the sailing.

It had been so long since she'd been on the ferry, so long since she'd seen Edgartown. At one point the old house had been a battleground for the MacDowell siblings—everyone wanted their piece of it. Of all the MacDowell houses, this was the important one, far more precious than the Park Avenue apartment or the sprawling Vermont compound. But Sally had lost interest in the house not long after Alex's disappearance, and Carolyn had been equally happy to skip coming to a place so full of painful, hidden memories. Warren and Patsy and her children put the house to good use, with George holding regular parties. But Carolyn hadn't returned in more than twelve years.

She could have thought of happier ways to return than with a man pretending to be a dead man. Alex MacDowell, seventeen years old, with wild, angry eyes, haunted her. His ghost wandered this island, roamed Lighthouse Beach, lingered in the shadows in the formal garden behind the old house. The ghost of Alexander MacDowell lived here, and bringing an imposter into his presence seemed like a very grave mistake.

She left the car and the man and went in search of a cup of coffee, sipping as she watched the island loom up out of the afternoon sea. It was later than she expected—it was already midafternoon, and the ferry was taking far longer than she remembered. Probably because she was so eager to get this over with.

He was already waiting for her in the car when she reached it, just as the ferry docked. She had no idea how thorough his briefing had been, but she had no intention of giving him any help in finding the house on Water Street. He didn't need any help.

She'd known that huge old Victorian house since childhood, yet it looked strange, different in the off-season. Like the rest of the houses along Water Street, the shades were drawn, the porch furniture in storage, the no-trespassing signs glaringly in place. Spring was further along down here—tiny leaves had already shot forth, and the front lawn was a dewy green.

She glanced at Alex, but he seemed entirely familiar with the place as he parked the car and climbed out. Of course, it was always possible he'd come here before, as part of his training. He knew too much about the real Alex MacDowell not to have help from someone close to the family. Maybe an actual MacDowell.

He glanced back at her. "You want me to open the door for you?" he drawled.

She'd been sitting there in a trance. She shoved at the door handle, forgetting she still wore her seat belt. She cursed beneath her breath, finally exiting the car with a complete lack of grace. Lighthouse Beach was behind her, and she turned, unable to resist the impulse. It looked bleak, barren, and deserted in the early-spring chill.

She hadn't realized that Alex had come up behind her, following her gaze out to the abandoned lighthouse. "It hasn't changed much, has it?" he murmured.

She glanced up at him. He was too close, but then, even at opposite ends of the country the man would always be too close for her peace of mind. He was looking out at the place where the real Alexander MacDowell had died with no more than casual curiosity. Totally unaware of its history.

"Some things never change," she said quietly.

He met her gaze. "And some things do." His smile was faint, self-deprecating. Sexy. That was the one thing he had in common with the lost Alex.

He was sexy as hell. And just like the vulnerable thirteen-year-old he'd left behind, she was far from immune.

He glanced around him, as if seeing the place for the first time. Which, in truth, he probably was. "There's something depressing about a seaside community in the off-season, isn't there?"

"I prefer it."

He grinned. "Okay. How about something depressed about an unused lighthouse?"

She shook her head. "It's still used. It's just automatic. It's to keep people from dying on this beach." She used the words deliberately, almost as a taunt.

But the man pretending to be Alexander MacDowell was oblivious. He merely shrugged. "I hope it works," he said.

Chapter Seven

THE HOUSE WAS cold, musty, damp, and dark. Spring had come early to the Vineyard, but the warmth of the sun hadn't penetrated the shadowed recesses of the old house, and Carolyn shivered as she stepped into the gloomy front parlor. The furniture looked bulky and ominous in the holland covers, and the shades let in no light at all.

"Let's get the painting and get out of here," she said, unwilling to explore the old house any further. It had been a long time since she'd been here, and yet the painful memories still lingered. If it had been up to her, she never would have come back.

Alex walked past her, into the darkness, and pulled one of the shades, flooding the room with light. "What's the big hurry?"

"I don't want to miss the last ferry."

He turned to look at her. "I thought you realized."

If she'd been cold before, it was nothing compared to the sudden chill that invaded her bones. "Realized what?"

"We've already missed it. Didn't you look at the schedule? I'd assumed you realized once we got on the boat there was no getting back till tomorrow morning."

"Don't be ridiculous! The ferries run till eight o'clock at night, and longer on weekends."

"In the summer, Carolyn. This is off-season. The last boat left the island an hour ago. We passed it on our way out here."

"No! What about the ferry we rode on? That was getting ready to leave—"

"It was heading on to Nantucket. It won't be back here till morning. We're stuck here for the night. We might as well make the best of it."

"There are planes—"

"What about the car?"

"You can stay here and keep it company."

He leaned against the wall. "I hadn't realized you were quite so scared of me."

"I'm not."

"Then why are you so desperate to leave? You'd have to rent a car once you got to the mainland, and then the drive north would take you a good five hours."

"I want to get back to Sally."

"Why? She's not going to die in the next twenty-four hours. Her doctor said she'd stabilized for the time being."

"You talked with her doctor?" She tried to keep the anger out of her voice.

"Why not? I'm her son. Her closest living relative."

You're a cheat and a liar. She didn't say the words, she even schooled her expression into one of deceptive calm. "Of course," she murmured, turning away from him.

"Look," he said. "If you're that desperate I can see if there are any small planes flying off the island tonight. But you're making a fuss over nothing. You don't have to be afraid of me."

"I'm not," she said again.

"Then what is it you're afraid of?"

She looked at him, cool and fierce. "Absolutely nothing."

"Now, that's not true," he said lazily. "You're afraid of spiders, and commitment, and Alexander MacDowell. You're also afraid of losing whatever dubious sense of family the MacDowells have given you. You're like a child in a candy store, looking inside at all the treats you can never have. But you don't realize all those things are tasteless, useless. A mirage."

"Spare me," she drawled. It was easy enough to find out she was terrified of spiders—the entire family knew it and mocked it. If she'd reached the age of thirty without forming any serious romantic attachments, it was only logical that she'd been uninterested in getting involved. As for whether she was actually afraid of Alex, either the real one or the man pretending to be him—well, she wasn't going to think about that, not right now. "What about the hotels? The bed-and-breakfast places?"

"Off-season, remember? Is it this house you're afraid of? Did some monster pop out of a closet and molest you?"

"It holds unpleasant memories," she said in an icy voice.

"Like what?"

"Like the day Alex died." Immediately she knew that she'd said too much. For a moment his face was entirely blank, and then he moved toward her, a slow, almost stalking pace, and it was all she could do to hold her ground, to look up at him with absolute calm and not back away.

"The day Alex died?" he echoed. "What made you think I died? I just ran away. That's what everyone else thought, isn't it?"

His eyes were mesmerizing, a deep blue that sank into her bones. "Yes," she said.

"Yes, what? Yes, you thought I died? Or yes, that's what everyone else thought?"

She didn't want to be having this conversation with a ghost. Even though she knew he was flesh and blood, with no connection to the real Alexander MacDowell beyond an eerie resemblance. "Everyone assumed you simply ran away."

"But you didn't believe that. Why, Carolyn? Why did you think I was dead? What did you see?"

She was hypnotized by the sound of his voice. By the soft insistence that was reaching past all her careful defenses. "Nothing," she said.

"Then why were you certain I was dead?"

"Because the real Alex loved his mother. He wouldn't have just disappeared into thin air and never be heard from again. Sally had the best private investigators looking for him—a seventeen-year-old wouldn't have been able to avoid them."

"You'd be surprised what a clever, determined seventeen-year-old can do. So what did you think really happened to me? Did someone cut me into little pieces and bury my body all over the island?"

She hated the faint mockery in his voice. "I think someone shot Alex in the back and threw him into the ocean. His body was probably carried halfway to France before the fish made good work of it."

"Gruesome, aren't you?" He was watching her with utter stillness, his face giving nothing away. "Was that a morbid fantasy on your part, or do you have any particular reason to believe that was what happened?"

He knew. Whoever and whatever he was, he knew that Alex MacDowell had been murdered that night; she could feel it in her bones. And now he knew she knew too. She realized she'd just put herself in danger, and she could have kicked herself.

"Just wishful thinking," she said lightly.

He smiled then, a faint, humorless smile. "And then I suddenly return and blow your theory out of the water. What a disappointment for you. On many levels."

"Not particularly."

"Did you ever tell Sally you thought I was dead?"

"I never told anyone."

"Why?"

Unbidden, the memory of the dark figure came back to her, the blood on the beach, the icy mist covering her as she crouched behind the rock. "It was just a theory," she said, shrugging. "Obviously a mistaken one. Because here you are, big and strong and healthy."

"Obviously," he said, looking at her, the expression in his suddenly opaque eyes unreadable. And the truth, the possibilities were strung between them like a spider's web, sticky and entrapping. "So where did you put the portrait, Carolyn?"

She didn't say a word, simply walked away from him, into the adjoining back parlor. He followed her, then stopped in front of the portrait, staring up at it with an unreadable expression on his face.

It was a marvelous painting. Edward Wicklander was the premiere portraitist in the seventies, and he'd done a magnificent job with the gorgeous, sulky features of Alexander MacDowell, age thirteen. He could have been a symbol for all disenchanted youth, tasting the first fruits of the forbidden and not certain he liked it. Carolyn stared up into the painted eyes, but this time she didn't marvel at how snide and mocking and lifelike they were. Instead she was riveted by the clever blue gaze that was an absolute twin to the man who stood just behind her.

Somewhere she found her voice. "The resemblance is amazing," she murmured.

He didn't misunderstand her, but he had his own way of playing this game. "Isn't it? He captured me to a tee, didn't he?"

"Do you remember posing for it?" The real Alex had raised holy hell about the hours he was supposed to sit, motionless, while the renowned Wicklander worked his magic. It was only the promise of a racing catamaran that had kept him marginally still for even a few minutes at a time.

"Now, now, Carolyn, you know better than that," he chided gently. "You aren't supposed to cross-examine me about the past."

"How very convenient for you," she murmured. "What will you do, tell Sally on me?"

He moved in close, but she held her ground, determined not to flinch. "No," he said. "George was always the tattletale, remember? I can be much more wicked. I can simply refuse to answer your questions." He reached out and caught a stray lock of her hair, letting it drift through his fingers. She didn't move. "Or even worse, I can answer them." Their eyes locked. It was something she'd been avoiding, and she knew she'd been right to do so. There was something unbearably intimate in his cool blue gaze, as if he could see past all her diversions and defenses, deep into the very heart of her where she let absolutely no one in. The small, soft vulnerable part of her that still throbbed and ached and bled. The part she'd tried so hard to stifle and control.

She stared up at him, unable to break the moment, even as she felt the breath catch and strangle in her throat, and she was transported eighteen years back, to a hot summer night in this very house, when Alexander MacDowell had looked down at her with those same eyes full of wicked longing and she'd been ready to give him anything he wanted.

With the small exception of her gold charm bracelet.

But they weren't the same eyes, no matter how similar they were. And that longing had been the lovesick imagination of early adolescence, and nothing to do with the reality of Sally MacDowell's wayward, thieving, randy son.

She jerked away, not caring if he pulled her hair, but he let her go with a faint smile. "Poor Carolyn," he murmured. "I won't torment you any longer. Why don't we go see if there's a way to get you off this island so you don't have to spend another moment in my company?" It was as if the odd, breathless moment hadn't even existed. "If worse comes to worst, maybe one of the guesthouses will be open."

She couldn't do it. At that moment she couldn't willingly get back in the close confines of his car, breathing the same air he breathed, feeling his body heat envelope her. He had far too powerful an effect on her, and she needed physical distance, a few moments away from him to pull her tattered self-control back around herself. "You go ahead," she said. "I'll wait here."

He looked at her in surprise. "You trust me?"

"Not particularly. I just want a few minutes' peace."

He didn't argue. "I didn't come to disturb your peace, you know."

"Didn't you?"

"A thirty-one-year-old woman who's lived the life you've lived shouldn't be desperate for peace. You need unsettling."

"How do you know? Alexander MacDowell hasn't been around for eighteen years."

"I admit I'm curious. I asked."

"Who?"

"Ah, you want me to name my accomplice in crime," he said lightly. "Sorry, Carolyn, but I asked Sally why you were still dancing attendance on the lordly MacDowells."

"And what did she say?"

"That you loved her. And that you were afraid of leaving, of living life out in the cruel, cold world."

"Sally doesn't know me as well as she thinks she does," Carolyn said with deceptive calm.

"Sally doesn't know anyone that well, including her own mind."

"Including her own son."

"You couldn't resist that, could you?" He was unoffended. "My mother is a woman of narrow vision and indomitable will. She knows just enough about the people who surround her to make them do exactly what she wants them to do. Anything beyond that is extraneous and she doesn't bother with it."

"Your filial devotion is inspiring."

"Maybe there was a reason I've been gone for eighteen years."

She wanted to scream at him, but she bit it back. One more minute in the darkened back parlor and she'd start hyperventilating, and she hadn't had a panic attack since she was twenty years old. She wasn't going to let a con man bring her back to that vulnerable state.

"I thought you were going to see if there's a way for me to get off this island," she reminded him with pointed calm.

"True enough. Let me just dump my bag before I go in search of a telephone. That way you can rummage through it if you get bored."

"I doubt you'd leave anything incriminating within my reach."

"Oh, you never can be too sure. Maybe I like to live life dangerously. Maybe I want you to find out the truth," he taunted her.

"And what is the truth?"

He didn't move any closer to her, didn't say a word. He didn't need to. His presence was powerful, intimidating, even from across the room. He simply smiled.

SHE SEARCHED THE bag he dropped inside the front door. His clothes were good quality but well-worn. He obviously hadn't invested in a new wardrobe as part of his impersonation scheme. He wore silk boxers, he shaved with a disposable razor, and he had a bottle of aspirin. He also had condoms.

She zipped up the bag, shoving it away from her in distaste. The jeans were American, the t-shirts French, the aspirin was actually paracetamol from England. He was as well traveled as he claimed to be. Or at least his possessions were.

She wandered toward the back of the house, through the dining room and butler's pantry to the large, old-fashioned kitchen. Constanza had steadfastly refused to let Sally refurbish it, insisting she liked the old ways. The heavy iron sink still stood separate, the aging refrigerator let out a soft hum. It took Carolyn a moment to realize just what that humming noise signified.

The refrigerator had been turned on and stocked. There was fresh fruit, coffee beans, heavy cream, and orange juice. And a six-pack of Alex's favorite dark beer.

She slammed the door shut and moved to the sink. The water gushed forth obligingly, when it should have been turned off for the winter.

The telephone was dead—at least Alex hadn't lied about that. Though he had a cell phone in his Jeep—he could have found out whether there was a way off the island without disappearing.

She moved back into the front parlor, sinking down in one of the linen-covered chairs. The light was strange, and she realized she'd never been on the island in any time other than high summer. She wasn't used to the way the spring light cast long, eerie shadows across the water.

She closed her eyes, and she could see him. Alex—the real Alex—young and strong and healthy, a lithe, beautiful creature as irresistible and untamed as a unicorn. How could she have resisted, even having felt the sting of his torments and teasing over the years? She'd watched him that summer, bare chested and tanned and smooth skinned, wearing only a ragged pair of cutoffs, and she'd dreamed about him.

Her knowledge of the basics of sexuality had been woefully inadequate back then. Alexander MacDowell had been the center of her first romantic fantasies, and her first full-fledged sexual fantasies. Dream sex had been idealistic and delicate, a worshipful experience consisting of closed-mouth kisses and disembodied pleasure. She shuddered to think how she would have reacted to the reality of it all. But Alex had disappeared, giving her just a taste of what real sexuality was, leaving her more shattered and vulnerable than ever. He'd had more than his share of older, wiser girls—he didn't have to prey on his own family. If he'd stayed, if he'd lived, he probably wouldn't have touched her again.

Though she hadn't been family, she reminded herself. She had belonged to nothing and no one. Not even Alexander MacDowell.

She tried to summon up the remembered golden beauty of the lost boy, but the interloper kept forcing his way into her imagination. Instead of Alex's sexy, youthful pout she could only see the stranger, with his elegant, Cossack eyes and wary beauty.

Maybe he was an actor, hired by a mastermind to bilk Sally of her millions. Or maybe he'd been hired for a kinder motive, to give Sally peace of mind during her final days, weeks, and months. To give her back her beloved, long-lost son so she could die in peace.

Even Carolyn couldn't quibble with a motive like that—she would have done anything to make Sally's passing easier, even if it meant lying, stealing, or putting up with a dangerously seductive con man. But for some reason, she couldn't quite believe that altruism was behind the imposter's arrival.

He had to be working with someone close to the family, someone who would be privy to all the private goings-on, the layout of the houses, the nuances of relationships between the three disparate MacDowell siblings, the family memories, family secrets. Alex was smart enough, subtle enough, and brass-balled enough to try to carry off such a masquerade, but he needed help. It was all well and good in a detective novel or a romance, but in real life posing as someone else should have been just about impossible to carry off.

There was no way he could convince her, even if he'd managed to bamboozle the rest of the MacDowell family. Even the usually paranoid Warren had accepted him with barely a protest. Obviously, the imposter was damned good.

Would she have believed him if she hadn't seen the real Alex die? She liked to think that she wouldn't, that she would have known immediately, instinctively, that this wasn't the bane and delight of her adolescence, come back to haunt her.

Except for the fact that he seemed to arouse most of the same emotions within her. Rage, frustration, and an overpowering, unwilling fascination.

"What are you thinking about?"

She hadn't even realized he'd pulled up outside the house. He was already climbing out, her overnight bag in one hand, a large paper bag in the other.

She roused herself to look down the walkway as he approached. "I was thinking you were going to come up with some kind of excuse to keep me on this island."

"Actually, I think I would've enjoyed having the place to myself for twenty-four hours, without anyone watching me like a hawk, waiting for me to trip up," he said pleasantly. "Unfortunately, no one's flying out tonight, and every hotel, motel, and bed-and-breakfast on the island is closed down or has no vacancies available."

"Every one, eh?" She didn't bother hiding her disbelief.

He reached the top of the steps and set down her suitcase. "Almost every one. There are a few rooms available at the Red Cow Tavern, but I think you'd be happier here. There's so much room in this old place that we don't even need to see each other till we leave tomorrow."

"What about the plumbing? The electricity? The house has been closed for the winter." She waited for him to start stumbling over words and excuses.

He didn't. "Constanza said she'd have someone come in and turn things on for us. Bring in a few supplies in case we need them."

She should have known it wouldn't be that easy. "Then what's in the grocery bag?"

"Dinner, my precious. If you can stand my company long enough to partake of it." She knew what it was—she could smell it. It had been more than twelve years since she'd had fried clams from the Red Cow Tavern, but the aroma was unmistakable.

Alex had been the only one in the family who'd shared that particular weakness. Just two days before he'd disappeared, he'd showed up at her door at midnight, a bag full of greasy fried clams and french fries in his fist, and he'd lured her onto the roof overlooking the inlet to feast in companionable silence.

"How long has it been since you've had fried clams, Carolyn?" he said. "Whole-belly clams, the kind that would make George turn green?" He could have found that out from anybody. There was no way he could know about the midnight feast—no one had known about it but the two of them.

She realized belatedly she was hungry, hungry enough to eat fried clams with him, hungry enough to let the questions go. There'd be other ways, other times to trap him. Besides, hostility wasn't getting her anywhere. Maybe she could be halfway pleasant and trip him up that way.

"There's beer in the refrigerator," she said evenly. "I'll get plates and silverware—"

"Don't bother," he said. "Why don't we eat out on the porch roof, using our fingers? There's no proper MacDowell around to drill us on etiquette."

She could feel her face freeze. He couldn't know, unless he was Alexander MacDowell come back from the dead. Unless someone else had been watching, listening.

She wasn't going to start doubting herself at this point. It didn't matter that the man looked down at her out of Alex MacDowell's eyes, that he smiled with Alex MacDowell's luscious mouth. It didn't matter that he knew things no one else could possibly know.

And most of all, it didn't matter that he left her feeling angry, confused, and irrationally yearning.

Alexander MacDowell was dead. And this man was a charming liar.

"The porch roof sounds just fine," she said after a moment.

Chapter Eight

THE MOON HAD risen across the inlet, sending a path of iridescent silver light over the water. The empty food containers lay scattered over the flat porch roof, and Carolyn pulled her knees up to her chest, hugging them, as she stared out over the night.

It wasn't that late—daylight savings time wouldn't start until next week, and the night poured down around them, carried on a breeze that held only a faint bite. A reminder of the snow that lay melting on the hills of Vermont.

"I think I'm going to be sick," she said with utmost calm. "I'm not used to all that grease."

He was leaning against the house, his long legs stretched out on the shingled roof, a beer in one hand, a faint smile on his moon-shadowed face. "You're not used to indulging your appetites, Carolyn. Greasy seafood is one of the glories of nature. And you've barely touched your beer. Don't you drink, either?"

"Not much."

"You just pop your tranquilizers and pray I'll go away, don't you?"

She didn't bother to deny it. The heavy meal sat like a warm rock in her stomach, more pleasant than she was willing to admit, the imported beer was strong and yeasty, and the scent of the ocean was all around her. She felt restless, uneasy, oddly threatened.

"I'm not going away, Carolyn."

"You did before."

"So you admit there's a possibility I really am Alex MacDowell?" he said lazily.

"No. I'm just not going to bother about it tonight."

"Very sensible," he said. "But then, you're a sensible young woman, aren't you? Loyal, smart, friendly, reliable."

"Man's best friend," she said. "You make me sound like a lapdog."

"Oh, I think you definitely have a bitchy streak."

She let herself smile. "No one in the family would agree with you on that."

"Maybe they don't know you as well as I do."

She stared at him in amazement. "You really do have an astonishing amount of gall. You think you know me better than people who've been around me for the past eighteen years?"

"They don't really look at you, Carolyn. They don't listen to you; they don't waste one moment thinking about you. You're part of the furniture to them."

"Maybe," she said, refusing to rise to the bait.

"I think about you, Carolyn. I look at you every chance I get."

"Yeah, and if I'm a piece of furniture to you, it's probably a bed."

He threw back his head and laughed, and the sound was soft and warm on the night air. "No one else sees this side of you, do they?"

"Nobody else threatens me."

"Why am I a threat? What am I going to take away from you? You think I'll take your place in Sally's affections? That now she has her son back she no longer has any need for you?"

That was exactly what frightened her, and she would have jumped off the roof before she admitted it to him. "Spare me," she said dryly.

"You don't need to worry. Oh, you're right—Sally's affections have certain limitations, but there's enough available for both of us."

"I don't really care," she said, an obvious lie. "I'm tired and I'm going to bed. I want us to make the first ferry out tomorrow morning."

"I already reserved a space for us. I figured you probably wouldn't be giving me a reason to sleep in."

"You figured right." She scrambled to her knees, moving past him to the open window that led into the front bedroom. "I'll see you in the morning."

She should have known she wouldn't escape that easily. He put his arm across the open window, barring her way, and she sat back on her heels, staring up at him in stony silence.

"Answer me one question, Carolyn," he said. "If you don't eat or drink or have sex, what do you do for fun?"

"I eat healthy things, I drink in moderation, and I have sex when I find someone worth sleeping with." She didn't bother to hide her defiance.

"But your standards are impossibly high, aren't they? How long has it been since you found someone you couldn't resist?"

"It hasn't happened yet."

Mistake, her brain screamed. He moved his arm away from the window, no longer barring her way, but instead he reached up and touched her face. His fingers were warm against her night-chilled skin, sliding over her cheekbone, into her wind-tangled hair. She didn't move, afraid to fight him. Afraid a struggle would just precipitate something she couldn't control.

"You look at me like I'm a rapist," he said, his voice a mere breath of sound as his thumb gently touched her lips. "You look like you're staring into the face of a murderer."

"Are you?" Her question was hushed, raw.

"Neither one," he said. "Will you let me kiss you?"

"Can I stop you?"

"No."

She didn't resist as he drew her down to meet his mouth. She told herself it wouldn't do any good to struggle. She told herself she wanted to see how his kiss compared to what was surely the most significant kiss of her entire life, when seventeen-year-old Alexander MacDowell kissed her in her bedroom the night he died. She told herself she was curious, she told herself . . .

His mouth was hot, wet, open against hers, unexpectedly intimate. She tried to pull back, startled, but she was off balance on the roof, and she tumbled against him.

For one brief moment she wondered whether she was going to fall off the porch onto the cement walkway below, but he caught her quite easily, pulling her across his legs, folding his long body around hers and cradling her on his lap.

"This is better," he murmured. "Now we can do it right."

"I don't want—" The words were caught between their mouths as he kissed her, his big hands cradling her face. She made no effort to pull away; she lay against him, letting him hold her, letting him kiss her. She closed her eyes to the moonlight, closed her eyes to the unsettling nearness of him, and simply let him kiss her.

It was nothing like that desperate, life-shattering moment in this very house, eighteen years ago. It was everything like it.

His mouth was open against hers this time, and when he used his tongue she didn't recoil in shock. She didn't want to breathe, to take his breath into her mouth, but she couldn't help it. He didn't just clamp his mouth over hers, he teased her lips, slowly, nibbling at them, as if he had all the time in the world. He slid his hand down her neck, covering her breast with a gesture so casual and so sure that she almost hadn't realized he'd done it. He kissed the side of her mouth, running his tongue over her lower lip, and then drew back, just a fraction of an inch.

"I can feel your heart pounding," he whispered. "Aren't you going to kiss me back?"

"No."

He laughed softly. "Then I guess I'll have to let you go."

It took a moment for his words to register. A moment to realize he wasn't going to kiss her again. His hand still covered her breast, and she could feel the pounding of her heart against his skin, but he made no further move on her. He just looked at her with cool curiosity, his wide, sexy mouth still damp from hers.

She didn't want to move, she realized with sudden dismay. His body was hot and strong beneath her, wrapped around her, and she could feel him, hard, beneath her hips. He wanted her, despite the calm expression on his face, wanted her quite badly. He just wasn't going to do anything about it.

Thank God, she told herself, not moving. Thank God he wasn't going to force any more kisses on her, wasn't going to put his hand inside her blouse, inside the thin lacy bra and touch her. Thank God he wasn't going to take her into the house, onto the double bed where he'd spent his teenage years, and do what she'd dreamed about when she couldn't control her dreams.

It wasn't him. No matter how much his slanted blue eyes reminded her of him, no matter how devastatingly sexy his mouth was, no matter how stupidly vulnerable he made her feel, he wasn't Alexander MacDowell. She had to remember that.

She scrambled away from him, practically falling through the open window into the narrow front bedroom that had once been Alex's. He made no move to follow her; he just sat back on the porch roof, staring out at the night sky.

She could taste his mouth. She could feel his hand on her breast. She could feel him, surrounding her, invading her.

"Run away, Carolyn," he said lazily from his vantage point. "I promise I won't come after you."

"Running away is more your style."

"Maybe," he said. "If I really am Alexander MacDowell."

There was a lock on the bedroom window. She could slam it down and lock it, trapping him on the roof for the night. It was cool now, but it would get a lot chillier before morning.

But she was a grown-up. A mature adult, immune to temper tantrums, immune to the insidious effect the imposter was trying so hard to have on her.

"At this point I really don't give a damn," she said wearily.

"Of course you don't," he said. And the amusement in his voice made her slam the window behind her.

THERE WAS A LOT to be said for self-discipline, he thought, stretching his legs out in front of him. For strength of character, for the ability to control one's raging appetites. Right now he couldn't think of a single thing in favor of it, but he was sure that sooner or later he'd be downright thrilled with his own restraint.

It was a funny thing about women, he mused. Some women were incredibly sexy, sure of themselves and their appeal, luscious and liberated and irresistible. They were his favorite kind of women, warm, welcoming, smart, and funny. Women you could laugh with, drink with, sleep with, talk with.

And then there were women like Carolyn Smith. At least, he presumed there were other women like her, though so far he'd been lucky enough to avoid running into them. She seemed to have no idea how exquisitely beautiful she was. In the few days in her company, he didn't think he'd seen her make a single natural gesture. It shouldn't have been the MacDowells who'd turned her into a repressed, rigid young woman—they didn't care enough to exert that kind of influence. But something had made her as earthy and lively as a statue.

He wondered if she ever laughed. If she even knew how to kiss. She wasn't a virgin. The information Warren MacDowell had gotten him had been very thorough, but as far as he could tell she'd never allowed herself to care for anyone but the goddamn MacDowells—who would abandon her at the first chance, if it suited their needs.

He'd been hoping to charm her, tease her into relaxing and accepting him. At least he'd hoped to get her to drop her armed warfare. He had too much going with the real MacDowells to spend his time being threatened by a poor almost-relation.

It had been a waste of time, but at least he understood her a little better. Knew just how hopeless it would be to try to seduce her into accepting him. She wasn't going to—it was that simple.

He smiled faintly, staring out into the night sky. Nothing was really hopeless, particularly when it came to sex. It just depended on how much energy he was willing to expend in relation to benefit gained. Carolyn Smith wasn't about to cause that much trouble, even if she wanted to. Her concern for Sally overrode her sense of justice. She wouldn't throw a monkey wrench into his complicated scheme unless she was certain he would harm Sally. He really didn't have to get her in bed to insure she'd be no threat.

There was, however, another very tangible benefit to seducing her. He just happened to have a case of unshakable lust—every time he looked at her, every time he heard her soft, clear voice, every time he smelled the clean, flowery scent she used. He wanted to shake her up. He wanted to see what Miss Priss looked like with her hair wild and loose and her cool eyes dazed with passion. He wanted to see what she looked like beneath those boring preppie clothes. He wanted to taste her skin.

He could hear the faint creak of the stairs, his ears preternaturally attuned to the sounds of the night. She hadn't gone to bed after all, unless she was planning on sleeping in the downstairs bedroom, which he doubted. That had always been Sally's palatial suite, and he sensed that Carolyn would never dare presume to sleep there, even with Sally in absentia, even if she wanted to get as far away from him as she could.

She was trying to be as stealthy as possible, but she wasn't that adept at sneaking around. He could hear the almost imperceptible sound of the door opening beneath him, and he held himself very still. If she'd had any sense, she would have used the back stairs, the kitchen door. Unless she wanted him to hear her, to follow her.

He doubted it. Carolyn was singularly unused to trickery and deceit, despite her years amidst the MacDowells. She was straightforward, honest, and honorable. Just about everything he wasn't. It was little wonder his very existence drove her completely crazy.

The moonlight had faded somewhat, but he could still see her quite clearly on the empty sidewalk in front of the house. She had an old cotton sweater pulled on for warmth, and she looked neither to the right nor the left as she crossed the street and headed down toward Lighthouse Beach.

She was walking slowly, steadily, a woman with a purpose. The beach was deserted, the tide was out, and a ring of seaweed and shells littered the sand. She walked all the way to the edge of the water, staring out over the inky vastness.

He couldn't see her expression—she was too far away. He could only watch her slim, straight body, the tension in her narrow shoulders, the determined set of her head. Why had she gone down to Lighthouse Beach? What was she remembering?

He was half-tempted to scramble off the roof and go after her. To grab her arms and force her to tell him exactly what she had seen on that deserted beach, long summers past.

It would be a waste of time. She wouldn't tell him, and if he put his hands on her he'd end up kissing her again. He could overwhelm her doubts and objections quite easily, but where would that get him?

He wanted to find out. He went through the window, down the darkened stairs, then froze. She was already back, opening the front door with belated stealth, closing it behind her.

"Have a nice walk?" he murmured from the landing.

She jumped. "Were you spying on me?"

"Honey, you left me sitting on the roof overlooking Lighthouse Beach," he drawled. "Am I supposed to ignore it when some stealthy creature sneaks out of the house and wanders down there like a lost soul?"

"You're supposed to pay attention to your own affairs and leave mine alone."

"What were you looking for?" He took a couple of steps down. She held her ground, but he could see the wariness in her eyes even in the darkened hallway.

"What makes you think I was looking for anything? I wanted some fresh air, and I wanted to be alone."

"You looked like someone visiting a holy shrine," he said. "Or maybe that's not entirely accurate. Maybe someone revisiting the scene of a crime."

He'd managed to break through her icy calm. "What do you mean by that?" she demanded.

"Just what I said. Did something interesting happen down at Lighthouse Beach? Did you lose your virginity to some studly local on a hot summer night? Or was it something else?"

She'd frozen up again, in control once more. "I happen to like the ocean," she said.

"There's no ocean in Vermont. Why do you live there?"

"Sally needs me."

"Not for long."

"Then I'll come back to the water. When she dies," Carolyn added, as if to prove that she could say the words out loud.

"Here?"

"No!" she said fiercely, blurting it out.

"Too many bad memories?" he persisted.

"The only bad memories I have are of Alexander MacDowell."

"And what bad memories are those, Carolyn?" he asked in a deceptively gentle voice. "Do you remember the night I left? What did you tell Sally and the others?"

He looked down at her, and knew. Without a doubt she was hiding something, some knowledge of what had gone on in this house the night seventeen-year-old Alexander MacDowell had disappeared, and he suspected she had never told another living soul.

"I went to bed while Alex and Sally were fighting," she said. "When I woke up the next morning he was gone. That's all I know."

"Sally said you were sick right afterward. That you were in the hospital with pneumonia, and that they were afraid you wouldn't pull through. She said she didn't know who she was more distraught about, you or me."

"She was more distraught about her son."

"Ah, but her son was gone. Run away like the spoiled little hellion he was. You were there, possibly dying. Don't you think she would have been more concerned about you? After all, as far as she knew her son was alive and well, just off raising hell someplace, and presumably he was going to show up sooner or later. You were near death."

Carolyn looked at him, not bothering to disguise the anger in her steady eyes. "I didn't die," she said. "But I don't remember much of what happened the night Alex left. In the first place, I wouldn't have been there; in the second, if I haven't remembered in eighteen years I doubt I'm going to remember now." He knew his faint smile was far from reassuring, but she held her ground. She was braver than the quiet little rabbit who'd spent her childhood in the shadow of the MacDowells. Warren had sorely underestimated her.

"Why did you walk down to Lighthouse Beach?" he asked again.

"To get away from you," she shot back, goaded beyond endurance.

He reached out and caught her shoulder, tightening his grip when she tried to squirm away. He wasn't going to kiss her again, much as he wanted to. And he wasn't going to get the answers he wanted, needed, from her tonight.

"Are you sure you really want to?" he asked.

But she had already wrenched away, disappearing into the back of the house before he could say another word.

Chapter Nine

HER DREAM CAME back that night, more vivid than ever, as she knew it would. It wasn't the sulky, teenaged Alex who came to her room; it was his imposter. The man with the same lost eyes, the same sensuous mouth grown older and more finely drawn, watching her, calling to her. In her dream she could see him lying on the beach as the water pooled around him and his murderer stood over him, the blood pouring from him, draining the life from him. "Why didn't you save me?" he said in a soundless voice. "Why didn't you tell anyone?"

But it was the imposter's voice, not the real Alex who called to her, and when she woke it was past dawn, and he was standing in the doorway, looking down at her.

"If you want to make the first ferry we have to leave in fifteen minutes," he said.

She'd slept in an oversized t-shirt and she wasn't about to jump from the narrow iron bed while he stood there watching her. "I'll be ready," she said. "If you go away."

He was leaning against the open door, looking disgustingly well rested. He hadn't been tormented by nightmares and memories of death. His dark blond hair was swept back from his face, damp from an early-morning shower, and he was dressed as usual in faded jeans and a dark green cotton sweater that turned his blue eyes greenish as well.

"Why are you sleeping back here?" he demanded lazily. "There are plenty of other empty bedrooms available. You don't have to be the little matchgirl anymore."

"It was the furthest I could get from you," she said with deceptive sweetness.

It didn't work. "Nice try," he said. "I think you sort of like the idea of being the poor little orphan, ill-used by her rich benefactors."

It was like a sharp blow to the stomach, so painful and unexpected in the shrewd truth of it that she couldn't say a word; she could only stare at him. "Bastard," she managed finally, with only a fraction of her righteous indignation.

"You deny it?"

"I don't deny any of your high-flown fantasies. We'll miss the ferry if you don't get the hell out of my room."

"I'll wait for you in the car."

"What about the house—?"

"I called Sally on the cell phone. Someone's coming in to take care of things after we leave. Get dressed, Carolyn, or maybe I'll go without you."

He would, too, she realized with sudden dismay as the door closed quietly behind him. There was nothing that would suit him better than to have Sally all to himself, without her interfering presence.

She threw back the covers and dressed quickly, grabbing her running shoes and heading downstairs in her stocking feet. Alex was leaning on the porch railing, a mug of coffee in his hands.

She would kill for a cup of coffee, but she would die before she would ask him for anything. "You ready?" he asked, pushing away from the porch. "The portrait's already in the car—I'm just waiting for you."

He had a second mug of coffee in his other hand, and he clearly hadn't missed the longing look in her eyes. "Want some?"

She wished she had the willpower to refuse. She didn't. She reached out for it, but he pulled it away. "You have to smile and say good morning first."

"You have to go to hell first."

His faint smile was absolutely infuriating. "A social pleasantry in exchange for coffee. That can't be so damned difficult, now can it?"

She gave him a sickly sweet smile. "Good morning, Alex. I hope you had a lovely night's sleep. Yes, I'd adore a cup of coffee; how thoughtful of you to offer."

If he'd pulled it out of her reach again, she would have knocked it all over him, but the imposter had a strong sense of self-preservation. He'd won this round; he was smart enough to settle.

"Get in the car," he said.

"I haven't finished my coffee yet."

"Bring it with you."

She couldn't come up with another argument. She drained the mug, set it down on the porch railing, and headed for the car.

If it wasn't a companionable silence, it was at least a relatively peaceful one, and she slid down in the seat, ready to nap her way northward.

He seemed willing enough to let her. Once they were parked on board the ferry, he reclined his seat as well, closing his eyes peacefully.

Carolyn's eyes flew open in the dimness of the ferry's belly. There was no way she was going to lie beside him and sleep.

But one small cup of coffee and a restless night's sleep proved too much for her. Up on deck she could have more coffee, lots of it, while she watched the island disappear into the mist. All she had to do was unfasten her seat belt and slip from the car.

She couldn't do it. She was just too damned tired. Alex seemed to have fallen asleep the moment he closed his eyes—his breathing was deep and even, and he seemed off in another world. He wouldn't bother her.

She was crazy to stay there. But she was too tired to do anything else. And for some inexplicable reason, trapped in a car with a liar and an imposter, she felt safe, at least for the moment. Safe enough to give in to the shades of sleep falling down around her. Safe enough to trust him. At least for the moment.

HE WATCHED HER. She slept like a baby, curled up on the front seat, half facing him, her hand tucked beneath her face. She probably sucked her thumb when she was a kid. He scoured his memory, but that piece of information eluded him.

All her life she'd been old before her time, a miniature adult, looking out for her adopted family. She'd been brought into the family at age two, and already she'd known she was living on borrowed time. She'd been a somber, well-behaved young child, and she was a somber, well-behaved adult. Except where he was concerned.

The teenaged Alexander MacDowell had always been able to rile her. The man who sat next to her in the car seemed to have the same wicked ability.

She needed to be riled more often. And he was definitely the man to do it.

But not right now. She was exhausted, with faint purple smudges beneath her eyes, and she didn't even stir when the ferry landed and he started the car engine. For a moment he wondered whether she was faking it, trying to shut out the necessity of making polite conversation.

But then, Carolyn didn't bother with manners as far as he was concerned. He suspected he was the only person she had ever been outwardly rude to, and it must have been absolutely liberating for her.

She shifted beneath the constricting seat belt, murmuring

something beneath her breath. He couldn't quite make out what she said, but he figured it didn't matter. He was oddly content to let her sleep as he drove northward through the thinning traffic. There was a certain amount of trust in her ability to sleep so soundly. She'd never admit to that trust, but he knew it was there, and it moved him.

Was she attracted to him? It was a strong possibility, despite her obvious hostility. He didn't know whether it was wishful thinking on his part, or whether he'd really tasted the beginning of a response last night on the porch roof.

Did he want her? Completely. And he had every intention of taking his time with her, spending long, slow, endless hours in bed with her, with no ghosts, no almost-family members breathing down their necks, watching them, as they always seemed to be watching.

It would make sense to wait until all this was over. Until Sally died, until everything was settled. Then there'd be nothing between them, no lies, no pretending, no family.

The problem was, he wasn't sure he had the self-discipline to wait.

They were within half an hour of home when she woke up, although she tried to pretend she hadn't, rather than have to make conversation with him. If he had a generous streak in his body he would have respected her reluctance. He didn't.

"Pleasant dreams?" he inquired.

She didn't move, obviously trying to decide whether she could fake it or not. She wisely realized it was a lost cause, and her eyes opened, still slightly dazed from her long sleep. "Pleasant enough," she said. "You weren't in them."

"It sounds as if I was before. Have you been dreaming about me? Erotic dreams?"

"Not likely," she said with an unflattering shudder.

He grinned. "Did you dream about me when you were a teenager?" He waited for her usual hostility, but she seemed too weary to bother.

"I used to have nightmares about Alex after he left," she said slowly. "They lasted for years, until I finally did something about them."

"What did you do? Have him exorcized?" He deliberately used the word "him."

"I saw a therapist in college. She helped me figure out what was fantasy and what was memory."

"And what did you remember? What haunted you?" His casual tone of voice was sharpening, but he could only hope she was still too sleep-drugged to notice.

She turned to look at him, and her eyes were absolutely clear and steady. "I dreamed he died. I dreamed I saw someone shoot Alexander MacDowell and throw his body into the ocean."

She'd managed to silence him. "Quite a dream," he said after a moment. "And you didn't do anything to stop it? You must have really hated him. No wonder you can't stand to be near me. Or is it a guilty conscience?"

"I couldn't have saved him."

"But you didn't try."

"But he didn't die, did he?" she countered with swift irony. "After all, you're here, alive and quite disgustingly healthy."

"But you saw me die. Did you see who killed me?" She was silent, and the smartest thing to do would have been to let it be, wait until she was ready to talk. But he wasn't feeling very smart, or very patient. "Did you?"

"No." She was fussing with her seat belt, her elegant hands nervous. "I'm still not sure what was memory and what was a nightmare."

"I thought your therapist helped you figure that out."

"She helped me let go of it. There was no way I could solve it, so the only thing I could do was put it away from me."

"And now I've brought it all back. No wonder you hate me."

She turned to look at him, and there was unmistakable surprise in her blue eyes. Eyes you could drown in, he thought absently. Light and dark, calm and stormy, all at the same time. "I don't hate you," she said. "I just wish you'd never come here."

They were coming up to the narrow turn onto the MacDowell's long, unpaved driveway. It was an unprepossessing entrance to the multimillion-dollar compound, low key on purpose. One could barely notice the state-of-the-art surveillance equipment. He yanked the wheel, started down the narrow, two-mile drive, and then pulled to a stop, turning off the car and swiveling in the seat to look at her.

She looked nervous, as well she should. "The snow's gone," she said, obviously trying to distract him.

"You want to tell me again that you don't hate me? I don't believe you, Carolyn. Why don't you unburden yourself and tell me what you really think of me?"

She rallied. "I'd think that would be obvious. I think the real Alexander MacDowell has been dead for the past eighteen years, and you're a very good, very smart imposter who's here to bilk Sally out of her money."

"And who's working with me? If I'm a phony I must have a partner in crime—I couldn't know so much about the family without inside help. Who is it—one of the servants? Maybe a business associate?"

"One of the family. You know too many intimate details. If I had to guess I'd say it was Warren. Patsy is too ditzy, her older children are too self-absorbed and stupid to carry something like this off, and Grace doesn't care about the money. Warren's got the brains and the nerve and the ruthlessness—though I can't figure out why he'd bother. The money will come to him and the others anyway—Sally's not going to change her will."

She was too smart and too damned observant. Warren wouldn't have given anything away, and neither had he. "Sounds to me like you're still caught up in a fantasy," he murmured.

"Alexander MacDowell is dead!" she said sharply. "I saw him die!"

"And never bothered to tell anyone? Not the police, not Aunt Sally, as she was mourning her lost child? You didn't even want to drop a clue that her wait was going to be in vain?" She couldn't come up with an answer. "Guilt," he said again. "You know, that's a lousy thing to have running your life for eighteen years. I'll tell you what—I forgive you."

"You what?"

"Forgive you," he said grandly. "For watching me die, and doing nothing to save me. Hey, you were a kid, and you probably didn't even believe what you were seeing. It's not your fault. Your therapist was right—let go of it."

She didn't look gratified. "You're an imposter," she said again. "And I'm not going to sit around and do nothing while you rob a dying old lady."

"Then prove it."

For a moment she looked startled, as if the idea had never occurred to her. "Why should I bother?" she said after a moment.

"Because it's driving you crazy," he said lazily, leaning back in the driver's seat. "I'll make a bargain with you. You prove I'm not the real Alexander MacDowell and I'll disappear. Without a whimper, without stealing the family silver. I'll just go away, and your safe little life will be yours once more."

"No!" she protested. "You can't do that! If the man she thinks is her long-lost son disappears again without a word it would kill her."

"Carolyn, she's dying," he said with great patience and no emotion whatsoever. "Make up your mind. Do you want to expose me as a fake or not?"

"I do. I just don't know if that's best for Sally."

"I can tell you the answer to that. She needs to believe her son has come back from the dead so she can die peacefully. I wouldn't think you'd want to deprive her of that, would you?"

There was confusion and real dislike in her clear blue eyes. He didn't blame her—he was giving her a hell of a hard choice. But he wasn't feeling particularly merciful that morning.

"You really are a bastard, aren't you?" she said bitterly.

"One more thing I have in common with the Alexander MacDowell you once knew and loved," he said lightly. "Why don't you busy yourself trying to find out who I really am, and who exactly it is who's been feeding me information? Once you have proof you can keep that knowledge to yourself as long as I don't harm Sally. Once she dies, which you and I both know won't be long, then you can trot out your evidence and I'll disappear in disgrace before they can throw me into jail."

"Very convenient. What do you have to gain from that?"

"A comfortable berth for the next few weeks or however long it takes. The personal satisfaction of knowing I'm making an old woman's dying days happy."

She snorted in disbelief. "And what about your accomplice? Will you let him face the police?"

"I don't think you'll call in the police, Carolyn. I think you just want to see me gone again. Don't you? So you don't have to deal with your guilt anymore, so no one takes your place with Sally, so no one threatens all that money you've worked so hard for all your life."

She looked at him with deceptive calm. "I lied," she said. "I do hate you."

"Sure you do, angel," he said easily. "And you can ease your guilty conscience by ferreting out the truth about me. Go for it."

She stared at him. "You're on," she said after a long moment. "I'll find proof you aren't the real Alexander MacDowell, and then I'll decide what to do with it. Maybe I'll just torture you a little."

"Kinky," he murmured. "Just be careful of one thing." She didn't look particularly interested in his advice, but he didn't care. "It might not be too smart to look into what happened to your childhood friend. After all, if he really was murdered, there's a good chance the killer is someone you know. Someone who was there at the house that night. If he or she finds out you saw them on the beach, you might be putting yourself in danger."

Her face paled in the bright light of midday. Clearly she hadn't considered that little notion, and he wondered if she was going to end up with a bullet in her back.

Whoever had shot the obnoxious teenage Alexander MacDowell and tossed him into the ocean had had eighteen years to get over his murderous tendencies. No other MacDowell had died an untimely death, or disappeared without a trace, or even suffered an unexpected accident. They were all safe and sound.

With Carolyn nosing about, that safety was likely to be threatened. And he was a selfish bastard to see her off on that particular tack.

"It's very sweet of you to be concerned," she said cynically. "I know perfectly well why you want me to find out what happened to the real Alexander."

"And why is that?"

"If I find out who killed him, you'll have someone to blackmail. You may not get Sally's money, but if someone in the family committed murder there'll be lots of cash available."

He looked at her with mock admiration. "I hadn't even thought of that. You *do* have a high opinion of me, don't you? And it doesn't bother you if I bleed money from someone else in your family?"

"Not in the slightest. Whoever killed Alexander deserves to suffer," she said flatly.

"I didn't know you particularly cared about him. He sounds like a spoiled brat and an absolute pain in the butt."

"He was."

"Then why do you care?" She kept her face averted, but he already knew the answer. "You were in love with him, weren't you?"

"I was thirteen years old!" she shot back. "Hardly of an age to recognize true love. And he was a brat who tormented and teased me. He had no time for me at all."

"That doesn't mean you couldn't have had a hell of a crush on him."

"Girls outgrow crushes quite easily."

"Not when they see the object of those adolescent infatuations murdered," he said blithely. "Too bad Alex never knew you had such a passion for him. I'm sure he would have enjoyed fulfilling your youthful fantasies."

"Who says he didn't know?" Her voice was icy cold. "You know, you don't seem to have any trouble talking about him in the third person," she said. "Are you admitting you're a phony? I can't prove it, at least not yet. Why don't you at least admit it."

"I'm not admitting anything, sweetheart," he said lightly. "That's for you to find out."

"And if I do?"

"I told you, I'll slip away quietly. With nothing more than a good-bye kiss."

And he watched with interest as the color left her face.

Chapter Ten

IN THE END, IT was really a very simple thing to do. So simple, in fact, that there was no way Carolyn could resist the opportunity. She told herself so as she pushed back any faint trickles of guilt.

The kitchen was deserted—Constanza had paused in the midst of her dinner preparations to serve tea to Aunt Sally and her son. It wasn't as if the others were deliberately excluded—Warren despised tea, Patsy was having her beauty rest, and her children had gone off in search of spring skiing. It was more subtle than that. Sally wanted time with her long-lost son, and Carolyn was too generous to intrude. But not too generous to resent it.

The filling for the seafood crepes sat covered, nestled in a bowl of cracked ice. The huge shrimp sat separately, far away from the filling, as if even proximity would contaminate it and endanger Alex.

It was a simple matter to shred one of the large, shelled shrimp into tiny pieces, to mix it in with the crab and sole filling so that no one would even see it.

And such a tiny portion would probably do absolutely nothing to even the most sensitive of allergies. If Alex even bothered to eat any of the crepes, his portion would be so microscopic that it would end up being no test at all. She had absolutely no reason to feel guilty, she reminded herself as she passed Constanza on the way out. After all, the imposter had challenged her to find proof. Sally might have ruled out DNA testing, but this was far simpler and more direct.

He ate three of the shrimp-tainted crepes. Carolyn sat across from him, toying with her food, watching, half-listening as Warren and Sally argued about politics and Alex flirted with the slightly boozed-up Aunt Patsy. For some reason she didn't have much appetite.

"You're not in a very talkative mood tonight, are you, Caro?" Warren said suddenly, fixing his pale eyes on her.

She almost knocked over her wineglass, catching it just in time. "I guess I'm tired from the trip."

"Alex said you slept the entire way back," Sally said, staring at her.

"Maybe you're coming down with something."

"Don't breathe on me!" Patsy said with a slurred shriek. "I can't afford to get sick. I hate illness of any sort. And don't let George know, whatever you do! He's got a pathological fear of infection."

"George is as healthy as a horse," Warren said with a snort.

"That doesn't mean he won't worry. I see too little of him as it is—he's always busy with his friends and his little club to spare time for his mother. I don't want him running back to New York because he's afraid he'll catch a sniffle."

"What kind of club?" Alex asked.

"Oh, heavens, I don't pay any attention," Patsy said with an airy wave of her hand. "He belongs to several, and they're all terribly expensive. Health clubs, nature-watching clubs, that sort of thing."

"George never struck me as the naturalist type," Alex said.

Patsy cast him a look of intense dislike. "You have no idea just how many interests a man like George has."

"No," he said, and there was a faintly edgy tone in his voice, "I don't."

"None of this matters, because I'm not sick," Carolyn said with barely controlled exasperation.

"How can you be certain? You're usually capable of decent conversation," Warren said with a faint whine. "Oh, do go to bed, Carolyn, and drink lots of orange juice. We can't afford to have you sick right now."

"No, Caro," Patsy chimed in. "You know how we all count on you during this sad time."

"I'm not dead yet," Sally announced in a wry voice. "And considering Alex is back, I don't consider it a sad time at all. I intend to go out with a flourish."

"Don't!" Carolyn said, pushing back from the table. "I don't want to hear about it!"

"I'm dying, Carolyn dear," Sally said quietly. "It's an inescapable fact."

"Let her be," Alex said unexpectedly. "She's had a rough couple of days."

"Not because of you, I hope?" Sally suddenly sounded quite stern. "I love you dearly and I'm overjoyed that you've come home, but I won't have you tormenting Carolyn the way you used to."

"The way I used to?" he echoed, all phony innocence.

"You may think I didn't know what was going on, but I did. You loved to tease Carolyn when she was younger. You must have made her life a living hell at times."

"Then why didn't you stop me?" Alex's voice was even, the question eminently reasonable. It sat in the room like a boulder.

Sally looked startled. "I . . . er . . . I tried. There was no controlling you at that age. You were such a devil, so headstrong! We tried everything, didn't we, Warren?"

"You were a hellion, all right," Warren said. "Besides, kids always pick on their little sisters."

"Carolyn wasn't my sister," he said softly, "because you never bothered to adopt her."

She jerked her head up to look at him. It was almost as if he were angry with them for not protecting her. Absurd, since he was supposedly the villain in the piece.

"Either way, I survived," she said, pushing back from the table. "And I'm sure you all have better things to discuss than my childhood, which was just fine, thank you very much. If no one minds, I'm going to bed."

"I told you she was coming down with something!" Sally said. "Sleep well, Carolyn, and don't worry about me. I've got Mrs. Hathaway and Alex to see to my well-being."

Carolyn summoned up a smile. "I'll be fine in the morning." She started toward Aunt Sally to give her a kiss good-night, when Warren's arm shot out to stop her.

"Don't you think you'd better keep your distance until we make certain you don't have something contagious?" he said sternly.

"Very wise idea," Aunt Patsy said, reaching for her wineglass.

Alex said nothing. But then, he didn't need to. He was just sitting there, peacefully digesting the shrimp he should have been allergic to.

Proof, she told herself as she paced around the library, trying to settle down enough so that she could sleep. It was enough proof for her, but she doubted it would hold up with anyone else. After all, it was only her word that she'd put a piece of shrimp in the crepes.

And for that matter, there'd been so little shrimp maybe it missed him entirely. It had been a stupid idea from the start, a random chance that she hadn't been able to resist.

It wasn't until she'd turned off the light that a sudden, unpleasant thought hit her. What if she'd been wrong and the shrimp had hit him later on, when he was alone in his room? What if he'd suddenly keeled over, passed out? What if he was alone and dying because of her?

"Ridiculous," she said out loud, into the darkened room. But the worry, once taken hold, wouldn't leave her, and by the time an hour passed she knew she wasn't going to be able to sleep until she made absolutely certain the imposter was fine.

She threw back the covers and pulled on a pair of jeans under her t-shirt. Besides, she didn't necessarily mind rubbing his face in the fact that he'd proven remarkably resilient to something that was purported to make him violently ill.

The house was dark and quiet. George and Tessa hadn't returned from their skiing yet, but Sally and her siblings had already retired. The stairs made no noise whatsoever as Carolyn climbed them, and by the time she reached the bedroom at the far end of the hall—the bedroom where she had once slept—she was feeling almost giddy with triumph.

She knocked on the door, quietly enough, then waited. There was no sound from the other side, but the light came from underneath. She knocked again, calling out his stolen name. Still no answer.

She started to turn away when she heard a thump on the other side of the door. The clicking noise as he fiddled with the lock. Maybe he wasn't alone in there, she thought suddenly. Maybe it was Tessa who'd brought him into this, and maybe she was in there with him, in his bed . . .

The door opened partway, shielding her view. He stood there in the shadows, looming over her, shirtless, almost threatening. "What do you want, Carolyn?" he demanded in a rough, slurred whisper.

For a moment she couldn't move. "Are you alone?"

He laughed, but it was a raw sound. "Yeah, I'm alone. Who did you think I was entertaining?"

"Your partner in crime?" she said.

"Fuck you." He started to close the door in her face, when she reached out and stopped him, amazing herself.

"Are you all right?" she asked.

He could have slammed the door—he was much stronger than she was—but he didn't. He simply stared at her out of narrowed eyes that were very bright and intense, shining in his pale face. "Why wouldn't I be?"

The guilt wouldn't leave her—she had to be certain. "Can I come in?"

His slow, mocking smile reminded her just how infuriating he could be. "Why, certainly, darling. Why didn't you say that's what you had in mind in the first place? I'm always willing to oblige."

He didn't open the door wider, though, and she knew the smartest thing would have been to walk away. She wasn't feeling smart. She pushed it open, and he fell back easily enough, letting her into the dimly lit room.

He stumbled over to the large, cushioned couch in front of the fireplace, the couch she had chosen for its enveloping comfort, and sprawled gracefully, looking up at her with a mocking smile. "Lock the door, sweetheart," he murmured, "and pour us both a drink." She did close the door behind her, rather than have any of the too-curious MacDowells overhear their conversation, but she made no attempt to lock it. "I think you've had enough to drink," she said coolly.

His grin was faint as he stretched out on the sofa. "Maybe," he said. "Maybe not."

Her eyes were beginning to get used to the dim firelight. She'd been trying to avoid looking below his neck—his body was undeniably disturbing—but now there was no looking away. He was tanned, even in the winter, and solid, the muscles a subtle definition beneath his flesh. The jeans rode low on his hips, and golden hair drifted across his chest, his flat belly.

Carolyn swallowed nervously. And then she noticed he was covered with a faint film of sweat, and his cool, mocking eyes were slightly glazed, and she told herself he was drunk, and she knew he wasn't.

"What's wrong with you?" she demanded.

"Nothing." He smiled sweetly. "Why don't you come over here and let me see what you're wearing underneath that baggy t-shirt?"

She wasn't wearing anything, and he knew it. She stayed put. "You're not Alexander MacDowell," she said sharply.

"You came up here to tell me that? No, you didn't. Why don't you take off your shirt and let me kiss you?"

She failed to understand how a man could entice and annoy her at the same time. The real Alex had had the same gift. "Why don't you sleep it off?" she said, turning away from him.

"I'll do just that," he murmured. "Aren't you going to tell me why you decided to honor me with a midnight visit?"

"I wanted to make sure you were all right."

"And why wouldn't I be, Carolyn?" The question was soft, ever so faintly accusing.

"Because . . ." The words stopped as she noticed the syringe lying on the table. She turned back in utter horror. "You're on drugs!"

He didn't reply, he just smiled.

"How dare you! How dare you come into this house and pass yourself off as Alexander MacDowell and inject yourself with your filthy drugs when no one's looking and—"

"They're very antiseptic," he murmured, half to himself.

"I'd smash it if I wasn't afraid of getting AIDS," she said furiously.

"Oh, you don't need to worry that I'll use it again. It's a one-shot measured dose." He seemed completely amused by her outrage.

"Pig," she said. "You're not going to die on us, are you? I don't think Aunt Sally could bear that."

"Why should I?"

"You must have injected some kind of stimulant. Cocaine, maybe? Your breathing is shallow and fast, and I'm willing to bet your heart is racing."

"Maybe my heart is racing because you're near, Doctor Carolyn," he mocked her.

"I'm going to find Mrs. Hathaway. I want a nurse to check you."

"Don't bother her; I'll be fine."

She looked at him, long and luscious and despicable on the couch she'd loved. "I'd like to murder you," she said in a cold, grim voice, turning and heading toward the door.

"Don't worry, you can always try again." She stopped, her back toward him, as a sudden, horrifying suspicion swept over her. She turned back, and without a word stalked back to the discarded syringe. It lay in a medical pack, and even in the dim light she could read the labeling. It was epinephrine, prescribed to fend off dangerous allergic reactions. Like a deadly reaction to shrimp.

She felt as if she'd been kicked in the stomach, as all the ramifications hit her. She began to shake, to tremble all over, and she hadn't even realized he'd risen from the couch and come up behind her. He put his arms around her, pulling her back against the chilled dampness of his skin, and she could feel his heart racing from the drug he'd taken to keep himself from dying.

"Don't look so stricken, Carolyn," he whispered in her ear. "I made it back here in time and no one noticed a thing. You're not the first person who's tried to kill me, and you probably won't be the last. At least you didn't really mean it."

"It's not possible," she said faintly. "You can't be."

"Anything's possible in this life. You've lived too long in the cocoon of the MacDowells or you'd know that. Just because you saw somebody shoot me eighteen years ago doesn't mean I have to be dead."

She couldn't bring herself to look at him. She wanted to pull away from him, from the accusing sound of his racing heart, but she couldn't. She hadn't realized how big he really was, how he could manage to enfold her, envelope her, dominate her with his size. "It's not proof," she said weakly, hoping to make him release her.

He didn't. "No, it's not proof. Lots of people are allergic to shrimp. Lots of people have blue eyes and look like me. Hundreds of people have a scar across their hip."

She'd forgotten. It was that simple, that obvious. Another guilt, so strong that she'd blotted it out.

She'd been nine, he'd been fourteen, pulling her long blonde braids, pinching her, tickling her, teasing her, until she'd finally turned around and socked him.

Unfortunately they'd been standing at the edge of the cliff overlooking South Beach, and he'd lost his balance, tumbling down that long, rocky incline in just his cutoffs. Mostly he'd had scrapes and bruises, except for the long gash across his left hip bone, enough to require a dozen stitches and hysteria on Carolyn's part. It didn't matter that Carolyn knew he was reveling in the attention and her guilt. She still felt like a murderess.

As she did right now.

"Scar?" she echoed numbly.

"From when you shoved me down the cliff."

That was another thing. He'd never told a soul that Carolyn had pushed him. He'd always insisted he was goofing around and tripped, and even though it gave him one more slice of power over her, Carolyn hadn't told the truth. No one knew about it but the real Alexander MacDowell.

Who was standing behind her, his arms holding her against his body as his heart still raced from the aftereffects of her crude attempt to test him.

"I don't believe it," she said.

"You don't want to believe it."

"Let go of me."

"Certainly." She hadn't realized his arms and body had been holding her up. When he released her she wavered for a moment, missing him. When she turned, he was watching her from a few feet away, looking oddly tired and smug.

"I want to see the scar."

"Doubting Thomas," he chided her. "If you don't mind, I don't either." He reached for the snap of his jeans, and she let out a shriek of protest.

He grinned, and moved his hand to his hip, tugging the loose jeans down over his lean hip bone. The scar lay whitely across the bone, just as she remembered it. Maybe too much like she remembered it.

"It doesn't look twenty years old," she said.

He let out a sigh of acute exasperation, and before she knew what he was doing, he'd caught her hand and yanked her toward him, placing it on his scarred hip, inside the waist of his jeans, and held it there. "You need to feel it to believe it, Carolyn?" he murmured, close to her, too close. "What else do you need to feel?"

She tried to jerk her hand away but he had no qualms about using force to keep her there. His skin was hot, sleek, smooth, the scar a rough ridge beneath her fingers. Suddenly the room was silent. She could hear the faint hiss and crackle of the dying fire. She could hear the racing thud of his heartbeat. She could hear her own pulse race.

And she knew the crazy, wild desire to sink to her knees in front of him and put her mouth against his scarred hip.

She kept her face down, certain he'd read that sudden, insane need and know everything. He'd always known her too well—how vulnerable she really was, what she wanted, what she needed. She could only be glad he'd disappeared for the most fragile of her formative years. The guilt and fear she'd lived with were a small price to pay for being out of his reach.

She was well within his reach right now. Her hand was trapped beneath his, his body was so close she could practically feel him touching her through the enveloping t-shirt, the loose jeans.

"Please, Alex," she said, not even sure what she was asking for.

"This is the second time you almost killed me, Carolyn," he whispered, his mouth hovering close to hers. "I'm not saying I don't deserve it. I think I like driving you to the edge of murder."

"That can be dangerous," she said in a hushed voice.

"Not really." His lips touched hers, so briefly she couldn't be sure there was actual contact. "I always know when to stop." He put his mouth against the side of her neck, where her pulse was racing wildly, and she felt the dampness of his tongue, tasting her.

"I don't believe you."

"You never do." He kissed the base of her neck, and all the time her hand was on his bare hip. "You're much safer believing that I'm a liar and an imposter, no matter how much the truth stares you in the face.

It's me, Carolyn, whether you like it or not. Your childhood playmate. Your juvenile tormentor. Your first love, come back to claim you."

She tried desperately to regain her scattered wits. "Dream on," she said.

"I am." He moved up the other side of her neck, tasting, biting, kissing her, and she found she was clutching his hip, wanting to pull him closer. "There's no escape, Carolyn. I'm your erotic dreams and your worst nightmares, all rolled up into one. Just pretend you're doing this as penance."

"Doing what?"

"Going to bed with me."

"I'm not . . ." His mouth caught hers in mid-protest.

And she knew, with a kind of numb, glorious despair, that she was.

Chapter Eleven

THERE WAS MUSIC playing—she hadn't realized that before. Something soft and slow and bluesy, curling through the air-like tendrils of smoke. She was frozen in place, in time, trapped by his blue eyes and her own adolescent fantasies. "I don't think—" she began.

He put his hand on her mouth. "Good," he said. "Don't think. I want you to close your eyes and forget about everything." His hands were sliding up under the loose t-shirt, cool on her bare back. He sighed, a sound of pure, animal longing, as he reached her shoulder blades and gently tugged her closer.

"You'll regret this," she warned him, her voice not much more than a whisper.

"I always regret the things I don't do, not the things I do." He began to pull the shirt over her head, slowly, and she knew she should stop him. And she knew she wasn't going to.

"This would be easier if I were drunk," she said in a choked voice.

"Too bad. I want you sober." The shirt went sailing through the air, and she was standing before him, wearing only an ancient pair of jeans, the firelight flickering across their bodies. She put her arms up to cover her breasts, but he caught her wrists before she could raise them, holding her arms down as he looked at her.

"You're not thirteen anymore," he whispered.

"No. I'm not."

His smile was slow, impossibly sexy. "Lucky for me." Still holding her wrists, he leaned forward and kissed her mouth with slow, exquisite care. For a moment she was merely a stunned, appreciative audience. The man knew how to kiss. He knew how to entice, tempt, worry, and then soothe a woman, all with the utter cleverness of his mouth, his lips, his tongue, his teeth.

He bit her lower lip, gently. "This time you're supposed to kiss me back," he said against her mouth.

"I'm admiring your artistry," she whispered.

"I've had lots of practice." He slid his hands up her arms, catching her shoulders and pulling her against him. The feel of his chest against her breasts was a shock. He was still chilled, and she could feel his heart racing beneath his smooth skin. But her heart was beating almost as quickly, and she didn't have the excuse of added adrenaline. It was all him.

She'd never realized a kiss could be so blatantly erotic. It had always seemed a necessary part of foreplay but never a particular enticement, something to be accomplished on the inevitable journey toward bed. But Alex kissed as if kissing were an end in itself, as if he found complete and utter pleasure in her mouth. The least she could do was kiss him back.

Her hands had somehow ended up around his neck, her fingers entwined in his long hair. She closed her eyes—she didn't want to look at him, didn't want to acknowledge the foolishness of what she was doing. She kissed him, clumsily, and he made a low, growling noise in the back of his throat, one of sheer animal arousal.

The sound made her wet.

He must have known. He slid his hands down and caught her hips, lifting her almost effortlessly, pulling her legs around his waist as he started toward the bed.

He pushed her down, following her, settling between her legs as if he belonged there. He was completely aroused, big and hard against her, and he loomed over her, rocking against her, slowly, insidiously, holding her hands trapped against the rumpled bed.

"Go ahead, Carolyn, close your eyes," he whispered. "Pretend it's all an erotic dream. It isn't really happening, it's just a fantasy."

She knew it was cowardice, but she did what he told her, afraid to look up into his Cossack eyes, afraid to watch his mouth, afraid to admit to what she was doing.

She was lying sideways across the bed where she'd spent so many nights alone. He pushed himself off the bed, looming over her in the darkness, and reached for the fastening of her jeans.

She caught his hand, trying to stop him, but he simply pushed it out of the way, unzipping her jeans and stripping them off her body, leaving her naked, stretched across his bed in the darkness. Vulnerable. Afraid.

He caught her hips and pushed her further up on the bed, putting his mouth between her legs. She jerked in protest, trying to get away from him, but he was too strong, and he dug his fingers into her hips, holding her still. "Don't be a baby, Carolyn," he whispered in the darkness. "Take what I can give you."

She threaded her fingers through his long hair, pulling at him, but he ignored her, using his tongue against her, and she wanted to weep. She hated this. She never let a man do this to her—it was too intimate, too demeaning, too overwhelming. She dropped her hands to the mattress, gritting her teeth, trying to shut out the feelings that were spiraling through her resentment. She was shivering, her hands catching fistfuls of loose sheet, and she bit her lip, hard, to keep from saying anything, asking for anything, bit it so hard she could taste the blood on her mouth, and she just wanted him to stop, wanted to crawl out of the dark, sweet smoke of tangled desires that were wiping everything out of her mind but what he was doing to her.

She was almost there when he pulled away, and she let out a cry of loss and despair, her eyes flying open to see him stretch out over her, his body hot now, burning hot, slippery with sweat as he caught her face with his hands, his eyes burning down into hers. "You sure you want me to stop?"

She stared up at him, unable to say a word. She was hot, trembling, shaking with a need more powerful than any she'd ever known. He touched her lip, and his fingers had blood on them. "You bit your lip," he said. "Bite mine." And he covered her mouth with his.

It should have hurt, but she was past the point of thinking about it. When he pulled away there was blood on his mouth as well, and his kisses were hot and wet along the side of her neck. She wondered if he left a trail of blood, like a vampire. She wondered if she even cared.

She couldn't breathe. When his strong hands finally covered her breasts she arched her back as a little convulsion washed over her, and she reached for him, trying to pull him down to her, needing him to finish this, finish her.

"Slowly, Carolyn," he whispered, pushing her back against the pillows. "No need to rush, we have all the time in the world."

"No," she said in a strangled voice. She opened her eyes, and she could see the firelight flickering over their bodies, dark, pagan, magical. "Don't make me . . . beg."

He slid his hands up her legs, pulling them apart. "Oh, angel, I don't want you to beg," he whispered. "I want to be the one to beg you."

She caught his shoulders, digging her nails into the smooth, sleek flesh. "You don't need to. I'll do whatever you want me to do."

"Maybe next time," he whispered. He touched her between her legs, and she jerked, fighting back a tiny scream. "Hold on tight, angel."

She braced herself, certain he was going to slam into her, hurt her. He didn't. She could feel the head of his cock, hot and hard against her, but he didn't move, he waited, patient, rigid, utterly still, until she thought she would scream.

"Now you can open your eyes, Carolyn," he whispered.

Her eyes flew open, and she stared up at him in breathless, heartless silence as he slowly, slowly pushed against her, stretching her, filling her with such fierce deliberation that she was shuddering before he'd even halted.

Her breath was coming in strangled gasps, and she could feel sweat and tears pour down her face. She gripped his shoulders so tightly her hands were numb, and everything was centered around his inexorable invasion, like nothing she had ever felt before.

It was too much, more than she could stand, and she tried to pull away, but he caught her hips with his hands, pinning her against the mattress. "Take me, Carolyn," he whispered. "You know you can. Don't be afraid of me. Take me."

She stopped struggling. She stopped breathing, her heart stopped beating, as he pushed the rest of the way into her, hard, shoving her back across the bed.

She had no idea what she screamed as the first convulsion ripped through her body. It wouldn't stop, wave after wave of shimmering, smothering, shattering delight that tore her from her body and dissolved her. He covered her mouth with his hand, muffling the noise, as he surged into her, again and again, until he went rigid in her arms, spilling into her tightly clenching body, and she knew she was totally lost.

It was a long time before he moved. His first word was a curse, as he pulled away from her and climbed down from the high bed. "Christ," he muttered, and through her fog Carolyn could sense his disbelief and sudden, inexplicable anger.

She waited until the bathroom door closed quietly behind him, and then she scrambled off the bed in desperation.

She almost collapsed on the floor, her legs like rubber bands. She caught herself on the edge of the mattress, taking a deep, steadying breath and forcing whatever stray reserves of strength back into her body.

She didn't have the energy to pull her jeans on. She simply grabbed her nightshirt and yanked it over her head, then headed for the door to the hall. If she ran into anyone she'd come up with an excuse. No one would ever suspect what she'd been doing. Even she couldn't believe it.

She had to escape, get away from him, away from this room, from the bed, from the sight and smell and feel of him. She felt broken, lost, and shattered, and she had no idea why. She only knew she had to escape before he touched her again.

ALEX STARED AT his reflection in the bathroom mirror. He looked like holy hell, like death warmed over, like the total son of a bitch that he knew he was. It didn't matter that she'd almost killed him just a few hours earlier. It didn't matter that he'd clearly given her the ride of her life. He looked in his bloodshot eyes and knew he'd made a grave, tactical error.

An error he was going to repeat, again and again, if he didn't get his crazy hormones under control before he left this bathroom. She would be asleep in that bed, curled up like a kid, maybe even sucking her thumb. There'd be dried tears on her pale face, and a smile on her pale mouth, and he wouldn't be able to leave her alone.

Jesus Fucking Christ, why couldn't he learn? That hadn't been a casual roll in the hay, guaranteed to screw her into complacent acceptance. It hadn't been a nice, lazy fuck to scratch an itch left over from adolescence.

That had been a major, Grade A, megaton, force five, point eight on the Richter scale act of sexual intimacy that was totally unlike anything he'd ever experienced before, and he had a pretty damned good idea it had shaken her even more than it had totaled him.

And he didn't know what the hell to do about it.

He knew what he wanted to do about it. Tie her to the bedstead, lock the door, and screw her until they were both too worn out to think or care or want. He wanted to fuck her so long and hard that by the middle of next week she was still climaxing. He wanted to take her every way he could think of, and even ways that hadn't yet been invented, and then walk away and never be tempted again.

It wasn't going to happen. But he was damned if he knew what was.

He couldn't remember what the hell he'd felt like at seventeen, but he could make a good guess that it was something pretty damned close to what he was feeling now. He was already hard again.

One day at a time, he reminded himself. One night at a time. Tomorrow, in the cold light of day, he'd figure out how to repair the damage the little episode would cause. With any luck, he could get rid of her, talk her into going away for a while, leaving him a clear shot with Sally and her family. If he played his cards right, she'd be too embarrassed to be anywhere near him, and that just might overwhelm her feelings of loyalty for Sally enough to get her to take a short vacation. Just long enough for him to do what he came here to do.

He had to find the truth about what happened eighteen years ago, when someone had put a bullet in his back. He wasn't going to find anything more from Carolyn—if she even knew any more, it was so deeply buried in her subconscious that nothing would ever drag it out.

He was going to have to redirect his efforts.

George and Tessa had been there that night, and George was someone who'd always been skulking around, watching. Maybe he'd seen something.

Warren and Patsy had been there, as well as Patsy's current boyfriend. Had there been anyone else, watching, waiting for a chance to put an end to the MacDowell hellion? He had to find out, to stop wasting his time with Carolyn Smith when she wasn't going to give him anything but the best sex of his life.

But it was only a little after two in the morning. They had hours before dawn, hours he could spend wearing down her resistance and getting her to do exactly what he wanted, with no more semivirginal protests or shyness.

Shit. He may have screwed Carolyn Smith with efficient thoroughness, but he had the unpleasant suspicion that he might have screwed himself and his plans even more effectively.

The fire had died down, leaving the large bedroom in darkness. He should lock the door—he'd been a fool not to take care of that little detail before he put his hands on her. Warren was entirely capable of showing up with a bottle of scotch and a tedious desire to go over things one more time. While Alex wasn't sure he would have minded, it might have put a damper on Carolyn's already shaky ardor.

He started toward the door and then stopped, suddenly aware that things had changed. The bed was empty. The room was empty. Carolyn had taken her clothes and bolted.

Relief, he told himself. He was feeling relief. She'd run away before things could get any more complicated. He was already far too vulnerable, too caught up in her clear blue eyes and pale mouth, in her long silky hair and her inexpert, absolutely lovely body. He had no doubt whatsoever he'd have been able to perform for the rest of the night with admirable inventiveness and still manage to keep himself aloof. But it was much easier not to be tempted.

So where had she run to? He doubted she'd gone back to the foldout bed in the library—right now she'd be scared shitless of facing him, and she wouldn't want to go anywhere he'd find her. She was probably in the shower, scrubbing all traces of sex from her pristine body. She was probably crying.

Of course, she wasn't the kind of woman who usually succumbed to tears. She cried when she came, when she had no control of her body or her emotions. The rest of the time her emotions were held coolly in check.

But he was willing to bet anything she was standing in a shower somewhere in this house and crying. And there wasn't a damned thing he could do about it.

He'd figure out how to deal with it tomorrow when he came face-to-face with her again. His instincts were practically infallible—he'd know how to handle it when he saw her. Maybe a faint leer and a pat on the butt would be the most effective way of getting rid of her. That, and he could tell Sally about it.

Sally wouldn't give a shit. She'd let the teenaged Alex MacDowell torment Carolyn without doing a damned thing about it. If it would keep her long-lost son by her side, she would be willing to sacrifice Carolyn a thousand times over. And Carolyn knew it, whether she admitted it or not.

Maybe Carolyn would already be gone. Maybe he'd wander down to breakfast and be greeted with the news that Carolyn had gone to visit college friends. He wouldn't be surprised. She was brave, she was strong, she was determined. But he'd ripped away every defense she owned.

He stretched out on the bed. He could smell the rich scent of sex and sweat and Carolyn. He wanted her back, wanted her with a need so powerful it made him shake.

Thank God she'd run away.

CAROLYN WAS IN the shower, crying. She was covered with the feel of his lovemaking, the marks he'd left. There were traces of blood on her neck and throat, from his mouth, from hers. She could see the marks on her hips where he'd held her. She could still feel him, inside her, and she doubted the feeling would ever go away.

No one could hear her. The shower was off of the exercise room that no one, with the occasional exception of George, ever used. She could howl to her heart's content, and no one would come looking for her. No one would worry about her.

She'd told herself when she turned twenty that she wouldn't feel sorry for herself any longer, and she'd kept that promise, until Alexander MacDowell had returned and reminded her of everything she wanted and could never have. A family. A real mother.

And the love of Alexander MacDowell.

She tilted her head back, letting the heavy streams of hot water sluice down over her face, through her hair, wanting it to wash the taste of him from her mouth, wanting it to wash her tears away along with the touch and the scent of him. Wanting it to swirl down the drain, out of her life, until she could pretend that it had never happened.

It wasn't as if she'd never had sex before. She had, occasionally, and usually enjoyed it. It wasn't as if she'd never had an orgasm before. She was a normal, healthy young woman, perfectly capable of seeing to her own needs if she wasn't involved with someone.

And yet it had been nothing, nothing, like what had happened tonight in the bedroom up under the eaves. It was compelling, frightening, a tantalizing taste of something so powerful and profound that she wanted to pull the covers up over her head and hide until he left.

The hot water was endless, pouring down over her, but there still wasn't enough to wash him away. She knew it, with a bleak desperation. He would cling to her skin, stay in her blood, until she had no choice but to run away from it, from him. And from the only family she had ever known.

She turned off the shower, standing motionless in the tiled stall as the steam settled around her in enveloping clouds. She pushed her hair back away from her face, squaring her shoulders. She'd figure a way out of this mess. If she had to leave, for a day or two, just to get her bearings back, then she would.

But she wouldn't let him touch her again. That had been a mistake of such monumental proportions that it still boggled her mind. She'd dreamed of Alexander MacDowell, willingly and unwillingly, for most of her life. There was just too much history between them to make sex a reasonable alternative.

She would have been much better off sleeping with an imposter. She'd been so certain he was lying, and she'd hated him, but she'd responded to him against her will.

Maybe she'd simply been reacting to the buried longing she'd always felt for Alex. Or maybe he simply knew how to be seductive.

It didn't matter. She knew, to her eternal regret, just how seductive he could be. How very dangerous. He'd told her she could consider it penance, for trying to kill him.

Surely penance wasn't supposed to be so painfully sweet?

She wrapped herself in one of the thick robes, stepping into the small, well-equipped gym. There was a low, padded table in one corner that had once been used for physical therapy when Sally had broken her hip. It would be comfortable enough for a few hours' sleep. No one would think to look for her in here, unless George decided he needed some early-morning calisthenics.

If he came anywhere near her he'd regret it.

She curled up on the foam mattress, pulling the terrycloth robe around her. Her wet hair spread out on the plastic cover, and she shut her eyes, tucking her hand beneath her face. She'd figure out how to deal with things tomorrow. For the rest of the night, at least, she was safe.

Chapter Twelve

CAROLYN GAVE UP trying to sleep at five a.m. The house was blessedly still and silent—the MacDowells as a rule slept late, and Constanza and Ruben didn't leave their apartment until after eight. She resisted the impulse to head back into the shower. If she hadn't washed Alexander MacDowell from her body, then it would only take time to wear him away. She could be patient.

She dressed hurriedly, finger-combed her tangled, still-damp hair, and went in search of coffee. The state-of-the-art machine was already set to do its thing, and within minutes she had a mug of rich Indonesian coffee.

She wandered over to the breakfast nook that no one ever used, looking out over the winter-dead gardens and the fields that sloped down toward the Connecticut River. The late-spring snow had vanished as suddenly as it had come, and there was even a blush of rose on the bare trees.

She drained her mug, then refilled it. She was going to need all the caffeine she could get this morning, and anything else that would help her get through the day. And figure out how she was going to deal with the reality of Alex MacDowell.

The house felt different. For so many months there had just been the four of them——Ruben and Constanza in their self-contained apartment; Sally in her hospital bed, slowly dying; Carolyn in the room upstairs, Alex's old room. Alex's old bed, which she'd finally shared with him.

Now there wasn't a spare room in the rambling house. Each bed was filled with MacDowells. Some she loved, some she tolerated, some she casually despised. There were too many MacDowells in the house, and she had to get away.

The French doors to Sally's rooms were shut, the curtains drawn. Carolyn didn't even bother to knock quietly. She opened the door, slipping inside, inhaling the unmistakable hospital smell as her eyes sought out the huddled shape of Sally MacDowell lying in her bed.

"It's about time you came in here," Sally said in a remarkably strong voice. "I heard the noise in the kitchen and I figured it had to be you. No one else in this family ever gets up before sunrise if they can help it. And none of them are capable of making their own coffee."

"It's past sunrise. The sun comes up early this time of year," she said calmly, moving closer to the bed, grateful for the subdued lighting. She couldn't have handled anything glaring at that moment. "And Constanza had the coffee set. All I had to do was push a button."

Sally snorted. "I doubt the rest of that bunch could do that much. Except maybe Alex. He would have had to learn to take care of himself during those lost years." She peered at her through the dim light. "Come and sit by me, Carolyn. I haven't seen enough of you the last few days. I can't sleep, despite all the damned drugs they keep pumping through my system. I need someone to talk to."

"You have a houseful of family," she said, taking the chair by the bed.

"It's your family, too. I suppose it's a waste of time to ask you to get me a cup of that coffee. It smells divine."

"You haven't been allowed caffeine for five years, Aunt Sally," she said.

"It's not my heart that's going to kill me—we all know that. I don't see why I can't indulge myself for the last few months."

Carolyn didn't quite see why either, but it was a waste of time arguing with the medical people. "Sorry," she said. "Maybe I'd better take it away . . ." She started to rise, but Sally's strong voice stopped her.

"You stay put, young lady," she said. She squinted at her. "You look like holy hell."

Carolyn laughed. "So do you."

Aunt Sally chuckled. "That's one of the many things I love about you, Carolyn. You'll always tell me the truth, won't you? The others lie to me, say what they think will make me feel better. But you're honest."

"For what it's worth."

"Anyway, I have every excuse to look like hell. I'm seventy-eight years old and dying. You're thirty-one, healthy, and beautiful. You shouldn't look like someone ran you over with a tractor trailer."

Instinctively she put a hand to her face. "I don't really, do I?"

"No. As a matter of fact, you look like a woman who's just spent the night with a lover. Did you?"

"No." It was an honest answer, even if it skirted the edges a bit.

"You're not still seeing Bob, are you?"

"His name was Rob," Carolyn said patiently. "And no, we broke that off months ago."

"That's good. I never liked him. He was too nice for you."

Carolyn found she could still laugh. "You don't think I deserve someone nice? Thanks a lot."

"You deserve someone strong enough to take you on. A lot of people think you're a sweet, shy young woman, but they don't know you like I know you. Deep inside, you have the heart of a warrior. You would have ended up eating Bob alive."

"Rob."

"Whatever. You need a real man, Carolyn. If you ever allowed yourself to find one, I'd give you my blessing."

"And what's a real man? One who'll keep me barefoot and pregnant? Or one that'll just slap me around when I get mouthy?"

"You're not going to end up trailer trash, Carolyn. You didn't come from it, you won't end up there."

Carolyn stared at her in shock. "Where did I come from, Aunt Sally?"

Sally closed her eyes. "You know perfectly well, Carolyn. I've never made any secret of it. You were the daughter of a Swedish woman who used to work for us. She left us, got pregnant, and died when you were still a baby. I was always fond of Elke, and I decided to bring you into the family."

"So you've always said. What about my father?"

Sally managed a fragile shrug. "I knew Elke, and that was enough. She was a sweet, graceful, lovely young woman who happened to make a mistake. She paid for it, but there was no need for her child to suffer as well. Do we really have to go over all this again?"

"What makes you think I didn't come from a trailer park?" Carolyn persisted.

"Breeding always tells," she said lightly.

"I'm sure the people who live in trailer parks will be thrilled to hear that."

"Oh, don't go all bleeding-heart liberal on me," Sally said in a querulous voice. "I'm not in the mood for a political argument. In this life there are the haves and the have-nots. You're lucky enough to be one of the haves."

"No," Carolyn said. "I'm lucky enough to be brought up by one of the haves."

Sally smiled faintly. "If you don't have a proper appreciation for the power of large amounts of money, then I didn't do a very good job."

"Money isn't everything."

"Famous last words. It's refreshing to have someone in the family feel that way, no matter how misguided," Sally said. "I'm sure you're the only one. The others have an abiding passion for it. Except, perhaps, for Alex." She looked at Carolyn with deceptive sweetness. "Tell me what you think about him."

Alexander MacDowell was the very last thing on earth that Carolyn wanted to talk about. "I need more coffee," she said, but Sally held up a restraining hand. She had an IV tube attached to it, something Carolyn hadn't noticed before, and she had to fight back her sudden panic.

"I can count on you to be honest, Carolyn. To tell me the truth. Tell it to me now. Do you think he's really my son?" Her eyes were faintly glazed by the painkillers, and there was always the possibility that she wouldn't even remember this conversation. It didn't matter. Sally was right—Carolyn told the truth no matter what the consequences.

She could also do her best to avoid a direct answer. "I didn't realize you had any doubts, Sally."

"I don't. I know exactly who and what he is. I just wondered about you. You're observant and far less self-centered than the rest of my family. You see things that others miss. Do you think he's my son?"

She wanted to deny it, but she couldn't. Not when she'd seen the truth so clearly. "He's the real Alex, Aunt Sally," she said after a moment. "I'm certain of it."

Sally's weary face creased in a peaceful smile. "I knew I could count on you, Carolyn. You wouldn't lie to me, and you wouldn't be wrong about something like this. When did you change your mind?"

"What do you mean?"

"I know perfectly well you thought he was an imposter when he first showed up. Even at dinner last night you were looking at him like he was some sort of serial killer. What happened between you in the last few hours? Does it have anything to do with the mark on the side of your neck?"

She'd missed that in her inventory of love bites. She couldn't even remember when he'd done it, but then, most of last night was an unsettling blur. "You think he seduced me into believing him?"

"No, you're far too willful for that."

"I'm not willful!" she protested.

"Of course you are. Otherwise, I couldn't bear to have you around me. And I doubt that he could have managed to seduce you if you still believed he was a fake."

"He didn't seduce me."

"You didn't sleep with him last night?"

She could deny it on a technicality. There'd been no sleeping involved. "Life isn't that neat or simple," she said instead. "He's your son—I have no doubt about it whatsoever."

For a moment it seemed as if Sally would push her further, but then she nodded. "Thank God for you, Carolyn," she said gently. "I don't know what I'd do without you."

"You'd be absolutely fine." Carolyn kept her voice brisk and unsentimental. "As a matter of fact, I was thinking of taking a little—"

"I don't think I've got much time left," Sally interrupted her with her customary ruthlessness.

Carolyn didn't move. "What do you mean?"

Sally smiled wryly. "You know perfectly well what I mean. The doctors said that at this point they could only make me comfortable. They're not even doing a very good job of that."

"I'm sure there's something we can do." She kept her panic under control. "Change your medication, see if there's some kind of experimental—"

"No. My time's running out. I know it, and my body knows it. I've faced it, and you need to, too. Don't make it harder for me, darling. I've had a better life than I deserve, and all I want is the people I love beside me. You and Alex."

You and Alex. Carolyn didn't flinch, but it was sheer willpower that kept her from reacting. "What about Warren? Patsy?"

"They've always been a pain in the rear and you know it. I don't think we can get rid of them, but at least you can keep them at a distance. I'm counting on you to protect me from them, Carolyn. I don't want Patsy's drunken weepings, and I certainly don't want Warren waxing philosophical. I need you here, Carolyn. I've never asked this before, I've always tried to urge your independence, but I'm asking now. Don't leave me."

There was nothing she could say. In all those years, Sally had given to her and accepted very little in return. If she wanted Carolyn by her side, she'd have her, even if she had to face Alex every day. "Of course I won't," she said.

Sally seemed to sink back into the mound of pillows, older, frailer than she had ever been before. On another woman the expression that drifted across her face might almost be smug, but Sally MacDowell never stooped to such petty levels. "And don't let Alex browbeat you. He's still a devil—anyone can see it. He's right—I should have protected you more when you were young. I should have put my foot down with him. As it was, I did too little, too late, and I lost him for half a lifetime. I've lived with the consequence of that mistake, paid for it. I won't let him bother you again. If he does, tell me."

"He's not a teenaged brat anymore, Sally," Carolyn said lightly. "He's not likely to play his old tricks on me."

"No," said Sally. "But he might have new ones."

The lighting in the room was too dim, and Carolyn could only hope that Sally couldn't see the color flood her face. "I won't let him bother me," she said. "And I won't leave you."

But Sally had already drifted into a drugged sleep, and Carolyn was trapped.

KEEPING AWAY from Alex turned out to be easier than she had ever expected. By the time she emerged, he was up and gone with George and Tessa, in search of the last good days of spring skiing. Warren had commandeered the smaller study where Carolyn usually did her bookwork, and she suspected he'd commandeered Sally's checkbook as well, but she couldn't bring herself to care. After all, it would all be his soon enough. She hadn't witnessed Sally's most recent will, but she knew full well what it contained. Generous bequests to Ruben and Constanza, and a small, healthy trust fund for Carolyn, enough to cushion some of the harder aspects of life. The bulk of Sally's vast estate was divided in half. One half to her son, the rest to her two siblings, a decision she'd held to even when Alex had been gone for more than a decade.

If Alex had been declared dead, the money went to Patsy and Warren, of course, after what would undoubtedly be endless legal wrangling. But Carolyn had always expected to be long gone by then, her ties to the family severed with Sally's death.

There was no lock on the library door, but she wedged a chair underneath the doorknob when she went to sleep that night, before the cousins returned from their day of skiing. She could only hope that Alex was just as appalled as she was by what had gone on between them. With any luck he'd be just as dedicated to keeping his distance.

Her luck held for three days. For three days Alex disappeared with his cousins, leaving early, returning home late. For three days Carolyn sat by Sally as she dozed, reading mysteries and trying to keep her mind off Alex. It was only on the fourth night, when they came back a little earlier, that she resorted to hiding.

It was stupid, weak, and totally instinctive. She heard his voice, low, sexy, and Tessa's provocative reply, and without thinking she dove into the darkened kitchen, rather than face him. Face them. Obviously, he hadn't given her a second thought from the moment she left his bedroom. For all she knew Tessa was sharing that bed now.

She really ought to find out, she thought with cool determination. After all, if Alex and Tessa were doubling up then that left a perfectly adequate bedroom where Carolyn could sleep, instead of camping out in the library.

She wasn't about to ask, any more than she was going to interrupt their jolly little party. George was in the midst of telling a mildly racist and not very funny joke, and she heard their voices trail away as they mounted the stairs.

She was smart enough not to jump to the conclusion that she was safe. Alex had a habit of checking in on Sally at odd moments—he was perfectly capable of going in to give her a good-night kiss. Now that she'd faced the inescapable truth, Carolyn couldn't resent him. If she had any sense at all she'd be angry with him for disappearing off to Killington to ski, but she couldn't go that far. Anything that took him out of the house, even if it was away from his mother, was a blessing.

She was hidden in the shadows of the alcove that held the breakfast nook. The moon was bright outside, letting in a fitful light, but even if someone decided they needed a midnight snack, they probably wouldn't notice her. As long as she stayed perfectly still until the last little creaks of the old house quieted, she would be safe.

Patsy came first, her gait unsteady, humming beneath her breath. She knew where they kept the Stolichnaya, and she'd come equipped with an extra shawl to wrap it in, just in case someone might see her and question her. It was a foolish conceit on her part—everyone knew just how much she drank, and no one seemed to mind, as long as she behaved herself. And Patsy, like the true MacDowell she was, was always a lady, even when she was shitfaced.

Tessa came next, dressed in a silk chemise and nothing else on her perfect body. She went for the freezer, found a pint of Ben & Jerry's Cherry Garcia, grabbed a spoon, and took it upstairs with her. She wouldn't need the ice cream if she was sleeping with Alex, Carolyn thought, leaning against the wall, praying for the occupants of the house to settle down. Knowing Tessa, she'd probably eat the entire pint and then make herself throw it up.

She was just about to emerge from the shadows when George came in. He was as scantily clad as his sister, in a pair of silk boxers, and his body was just as perfect. Unlike Tessa, he didn't go for ice cream. Constanza was required to keep freshly made carrot juice in the refrigerator at all times. George took the bottle, drank directly out of it, and then set it back with a satisfied belch.

Carolyn slid down onto the floor when he left, hugging her knees to her chest. *Go to sleep*, she ordered them all, as a new set of footsteps sounded on the stairs. *For God's sake, go to sleep and leave me alone.*

At least she was still spared Alex's disturbing presence. She could recognize Uncle Warren's measured tread, precise in his custom-made leather slippers, and she pulled further back into the shadows, closing her eyes for a moment.

"How's Sally doing?" His voice startled her into wakefulness, and for a moment she almost answered, certain he'd spied her huddled in the corner. And then she realized someone else had come into the kitchen.

"The same," Alex said, heading for the refrigerator. He bypassed the carrot juice and took a beer. She could see him far too clearly in the dimly lit kitchen, and she could only stay put, praying he wouldn't see her.

Warren was still out of sight, somewhere near the door. "I wanted to talk to you."

Alex turned and leaned on the counter, taking a swig of the Heineken. "What about?"

"Don't you think you should make more of an attempt to play the devoted son? Sally doesn't have much time left, and you've been gone every day, gallivanting with your so-called cousins. I would think a display of filial concern would be a wise idea."

"I've been spending time with her before I leave and when I get back, and she's told me she wants me to do things with the rest of the family. You're worrying about nothing—Sally's not having any second thoughts about who I am."

"It's not Sally I'm worried about. It's the others we have to convince."

"I'm busy convincing the others. George and Tessa have no doubts at all that I'm their long-lost cousin, and Patsy's usually too loaded to care."

"They're not the problem. It's Carolyn I'm worried about. She has a surprising amount of power in this family, and with Sally. If you can't manage to fool her, then we're in for some rough sailing."

"Stop worrying. Carolyn's been managed. She's totally convinced I'm the real Alexander MacDowell, and all she wants to do is keep as far away from me as possible. She won't put herself in a position to find out the truth."

"I hope you're right. I wouldn't underestimate her if I were you. She's the smartest one in the family, and the only one with any scruples. She's not going to stand by if she even suspects that you're not who you say you are."

"She's convinced, I told you," he said impatiently. "And I didn't know you even considered her part of the family."

There was a strained silence. "She's been with us so long she'd have to pick up some of our traits," Warren said finally.

"Well, don't worry about her," Alex said, draining his beer and setting it down on the counter. "I've got her completely fooled. At this point she'd swear on a stack of Bibles that I'm the real Alexander MacDowell."

"Good," Warren said. "Just make sure you don't do anything to jeopardize it." His footsteps faded away, that same, precise tread.

"Good night, *Uncle* Warren," Alex said in a mocking undertone. And he turned to follow him.

He froze, staring at Carolyn as she sat hidden in the darkness.

She rose, very slowly, not bothering to shield her expression. She moved past him, and he made no attempt to stop her. He could be a very dangerous man for all she knew, but she didn't care. If he touched her she could scream, loud enough to wake the entire house.

But he didn't touch her. He didn't say a word. He simply let her walk out of the kitchen, watching her with no expression whatsoever on his beautiful, remote face.

ALEXANDER WAITED until he heard the door to the library close. There was no lock on the door, though she probably wedged a chair beneath the handle. It didn't matter. He could get in through the French doors that led onto the terrace. Locked doors and security systems had never held any particular challenge for him.

But for the moment he couldn't move. Carolyn's expression haunted him. The shock, the pain, the hurt and anger.

And all he could think about was the last time he saw that identical expression. When he'd kissed her good-bye in the back bedroom of the house on Water Street when she was thirteen years old, and then gone out to die on Lighthouse Beach.

Chapter Thirteen

HE'D BEEN A hellion all his life, and he knew it. When he was a child, Sally had been alternately indulgent and absent, and no one had been able to ride herd on him. From the dubious vantage point of his thirties, he could look back and wonder where all that anger had come from. He'd had no father—Sally had always told him her husband had decided he didn't want to be married or have the responsibility of children, and he'd left, severing all ties, never wanting to see either of them.

But hell, other kids had it worse. He had a mother who doted on him, gave him everything he wanted. He had enough extended family to make him secure, he was smart and well-coordinated and too damned good-looking for his well-being, according to Sally.

But he had been a monster and a half as a kid, and he knew it. Had known it, even as he couldn't help some of the things he'd done. A vein of anger had run through him, so deep and unshakable that nothing he could do would drive it away.

Carolyn had gotten the worst of it. He could still remember the day Sally had brought her home, a solemn, enchanting child, not much more than a baby, looking around her with huge, oddly passive blue eyes, as if she already knew far too well that she was at the mercy of a capricious fate.

Odd, he'd never thought of her as a little sister, and Sally had never encouraged that perception. They had grown up together, with years and a gulf of anger separating them, and he'd always known deep inside that neither of them really belonged.

Maybe that was why he'd tormented her over the years, trashing her dolls, teasing her friends, taunting and torturing her when he had nothing better to do.

That, and the fact that she would look up at him with a mixture of adoration and hurt.

He didn't deserve to be adored, but nothing he did seemed to convince her of that. She was passionately loyal to the family, even though they never chose to make her legally theirs. Passionately loyal to

Sally and her devil-child, no matter how badly they treated her.

Not that Sally was ever deliberately cruel. She dispensed a distant, maternal air with democratic charm, and Carolyn had accepted it with pathetic gratitude. It used to piss him off, how she'd drop everything for Sally, putting her life, her interests, in the background.

It pissed him off to come back, eighteen years later, and find she was still doing it.

She deserved better than that. Better than the tepid kind of love Sally dispensed. Love on her terms. He had no doubt at all that Sally really did love her, as much as she was capable. But Carolyn Smith deserved to be loved with reckless passion. She needed to get away from this damned group of selfish bastards who had bled her dry in the name of family.

And he was one of the worst.

At least he'd been able to escape.

The damnable thing was, he couldn't remember much of what happened eighteen years ago. He'd stolen a car, and this time his mother was going to have a hard time buying him out of trouble. He could remember the row that night, Sally screaming at him, him screaming back. The house in Edgartown had been full—Patsy had just left her second husband, and she and her three children had taken up most of the second floor. Warren was there for the weekend, though he spent most of his time at the Yacht Club, away from the inconvenience of noisy children. He'd heard about Alex's latest fall from grace—it wasn't just any car he'd stolen, but the classic MGB belonging to a retired sportscaster. He could vaguely remember Warren's face, pale but splotched with rage, delivering ultimatums in a high-pitched voice.

This time he was going to jail, they told him. This time it was serious, and he was close enough to adulthood that he wouldn't be able to get off with a slap on the wrist. It was past time he learned his lesson.

So he'd left. Stalked from the house, he remembered that much. He'd walked for hours, until all the lights in the old house had dimmed, and then he'd gone back in looking for money.

His memory got vaguer at that point. He knew he'd ripped off Constanza, and he'd also known that Sally would immediately replace anything he took. He must have emptied Patsy's purse, then gone to Carolyn's room to see what she'd left lying around.

He could still see her face, watching him as he pocketed all of her treasures. She'd grown in the past year, and he'd been uncomfortably aware of her as female, rather than victim, for months now.

So he'd kissed her. He remembered that as well, the sweet shock of her young mouth, the incredible temptation of her body still warm from bed. It had haunted him over the years, and he never could figure out why. Maybe because that was the last thing he could remember.

He'd gone down to Lighthouse Beach—he'd figured out that much—even though he couldn't remember doing it. The Valmers' boat was moored there, and he'd have no trouble hot-wiring it and taking it to the mainland, disappearing from the only family he'd ever known.

Someone had been waiting for him down at the beach, and he hadn't the faintest idea who the hell it had been. In eighteen years that wide, gaping space in his memory hadn't filled in. Nothing had come back to him, and whether he pushed it or let it be made no difference. A big section was simply gone from his life, including his attempted murder.

One moment he was kissing Carolyn Smith and thinking he was a pervert and that she was jailbait.

The next, he was lying on a narrow bed in a house outside of Boston, looking at the man who'd once been married to Sally MacDowell. He'd had a hole in his back from a bullet, one that had been roughly extracted and bandaged, and no memory of how he'd gotten there. According to John Kinkaid, he'd just showed up at his doorstep the night before, looking half-dead, and Kinkaid had let him in.

Later, he'd been able to piece some of it together. The trawler filled with fishermen who weren't really interested in fish had hauled him out of the dark ocean and patched him up before dropping him off on the Massachusetts coast. He'd found a scribbled piece of water-soaked paper in his pocket with Kinkaid's address on it, and he could only assume he'd come across it when he'd been rifling his mother's purse. Either way, he was there.

He hadn't been expecting a touching, heartfelt reunion—he'd never been a sentimental kid—but the reality of it fell far short, anyway. He'd never seen pictures of his father, but it came as no surprise that Kinkaid was a good-looking man, even in his mid-fifties. No MacDowell would have settled for less than physical perfection.

He was tall, lanky, with a long face and brown eyes. Alex couldn't blame himself for not recognizing the significance of those brown eyes—at some point he'd hit his head and had a minor concussion to complicate matters. With a bullet hole in his back, he had no intention of going to a hospital emergency room or a doctor and have to answer questions. They'd just send him back to Edgartown.

Kinkaid fed him soup and ginger ale, even woke him hourly to make sure he was okay.

By the second day, he was giving Alex sweet black coffee, which he'd always had to sneak from Constanza's kitchen.

"Sally's worried about you," he'd said, sitting down opposite the bed.

Alex had proceeded to slop hot coffee on his jeans. "You told her where I was?"

"Relax, kid. She hasn't got the faintest idea. I'm not about to snitch on you."

"But she'll probably try to get in touch with you. She's smart—she'll figure out I might try to find my father."

An odd expression crossed Kinkaid's face. "We haven't been in touch in over seventeen years," he said. "I doubt she'll even think of me as a possibility. It's been too damned long."

"Since I was born," Alex said.

"Yes." The single word left no room for questions.

"She could find you. If she wanted to, she could find anyone," Alex said bitterly.

"If you think that, then why did you bother to run away? Or do you want her to bring you back?"

"I'll go back," he said. "When I'm good and ready. When I find the answers to a few questions."

"What kind of questions?"

Alex had snorted with adolescent contempt. "I wanted to meet my father, is that so crazy? That side of my life is a blank. Sally never talks about you; I've never even seen a picture of you. All I know is you walked out on us when I was born."

"And you want to know why?" Kinkaid lit a couple of cigarettes, passing one to Alex. He'd died of lung cancer ten years later, and Alex had given up smoking.

"I think I have a right to know," Alex said. "I have a right to know my father."

Kinkaid sighed. "Sorry, kid, but I can't help you with that one. I'm not your father." It should have come as a shock, but it didn't.

"Is that why you left her? Because she had an affair and got pregnant by another man?"

"Nope. The only time Sally got pregnant, I was the father. I have no doubt of that."

His head had been pounding for days—at Kinkaid's words the pain suddenly went into overdrive. "What are you saying?"

"That you aren't Sally's kid, either. Our baby was stillborn, and Sally never was a woman who took no for an answer. I don't even know where the hell she found you, though she must have paid through the nose for you. She brought you home and presented you as her newborn son, and if anyone had any doubts they were smart enough to keep their mouths shut."

"But not you?"

"Oh, I kept my mouth shut, all right. I just left. Our marriage had been a shambles for a long time, but I stuck around because of the kid. Once the baby died there was no need for me to get caught in Sally's lies."

"No, I guess not."

"Don't look at me like that," Kinkaid said with rough kindness. "It's nothing personal. I'm sure Sally loved you just as much as she would have loved a kid she gave birth to."

"I don't know if that's saying much."

Kinkaid shrugged. "As for me, it wasn't like I'd lost a puppy and could be happy with a new one. Once Sally lost our kid there was no reason for me to stay. You were her new toy, and she didn't need me around anyway." He sighed. "It was hard turning my back on all that money, though. Still, I don't regret it. I married someone else, we had a couple of kids, then went our separate ways. I see my daughters on weekends, and that's enough fathering for me."

Alex had stubbed out his cigarette. "I better get going," he said.

"Naaah, stay put," Kinkaid said, pushing him back on the bed. "In a way I feel like you're some kind of kin to me. Like a stepson or something. After all, you're my ex-wife's kid."

"No, I'm not."

"Listen, I'm sure Sally loved you like crazy. Just because she bent a few laws to get you doesn't make it any different."

"Am I even legally her son?"

"Hell, I don't know. I wouldn't worry about it if I were you, kid. She was willing to do anything to get you—she's not about to come out with the truth at this late date. She never liked admitting when she did something wrong."

"Do you think she did something wrong?"

"It's none of my business. She always used her money to get what she wanted. It just wasn't what I wanted."

"Yeah," said Alex, reaching for another cigarette from the pack lying on the table. "So that makes two of us."

"Two?"

"Me and Carolyn. She brought another kid home a few years later, a little girl. She just didn't try to pass her off as her own. She didn't bother to adopt her, either. She always said single women couldn't adopt, but I didn't believe her. Sally could do anything she set her mind to."

"If she spent enough money," Kinkaid said. "By the way, kid, what's your name?"

"Alex. Alexander MacDowell."

Kinkaid made a rueful face. "We were going to call our kid Samuel. Samuel Kinkaid."

"It's a good name," Alex said.

"Yeah."

And five weeks later, when Alex finally left, his name was Sam Kinkaid.

It had been surprisingly easy to disappear. John Kinkaid had drifted a long ways from the insulated propriety of the MacDowells, and he helped him get all the paperwork he'd need to start his new life. He passed no judgments, simply gave Sam a carton of cigarettes and a hundred bucks when he left, and the promise to be there if he needed him.

He hadn't. He'd never seen him again, but it hadn't mattered. He had his new life now. For the first time he was free.

He'd had a dose of reality quickly enough, with no one to bail him out of trouble, no money cushioning his every move. And he'd reveled in it, bumming around Europe, drifting, trying his hand at a variety of things. In the last eighteen years he'd been a car thief, a college student, a stockbroker, a ski bum, a gigolo, and a carpenter. He was strong and resilient, with his own admittedly twisted sense of honor, and he needed nothing and nobody.

Until he heard that Sally MacDowell was dying.

It was funny how the news came to him. He wasn't a fanciful man, but he couldn't keep from feeling that it was fate.

The MacDowell family, for all their money, kept a low profile. And Alex had deliberately kept himself from checking on them. That was his past life, over and done. He didn't care anymore.

Whenever he had spare money, free time, or any excuse at all, he found himself in Italy. Tuscany, to be exact. At one point in his life he wondered if he felt some kind of hereditary sense of belonging, but given his blond hair and blue eyes he doubted it. Whatever the reason, it felt like home as no place had during his years of wandering. It was only in Tuscany where he felt at peace.

He even owned a small, tumbled-down house up in the hills there. Not quite a villa, grander than a farmhouse, it was little more than a ruin, barely livable, surrounded by overgrown gardens where the air always smelled of roses, no matter what was currently blooming.

His friend Paolo had been helping him repair the roof, and when he'd gone home after lunch he'd left the wrappings from his sandwich behind. An elderly edition of the international *Wall Street Journal.*

The newspaper was old and faded, discolored from the sun. Why he should have chosen to read American financial news that was two months out of date still amazed him. But then, he was someone who always needed to be reading in his spare time—in the bathroom, while watching TV, when he was eating. He came across the news about the reorganization of MacDowell Industries when he was in the midst of a dish of cold pasta.

The article didn't say she was dying. It didn't need to—Alex could read through the journalistic lines easily enough. And he knew it was time to go home and find the answers to all the questions that had haunted him.

He couldn't exactly remember when the plan had hit him. At first he'd simply intended to go home and present himself to his loving family. Warren was the logical one to approach first—he didn't want to kill Sally from the shock of her prodigal almost-son returning.

But it hadn't been that easy. Warren was insulated from the hoi polloi, and several layers of secretaries and receptionists protected him from phone calls. His apartment in New York had an unlisted number, and if Alex had ever known it, he'd forgotten it long ago.

Finally, in annoyance, he'd left a terse message that Alex MacDowell wanted to speak to his uncle. He should have expected the swift response he got.

The MacDowells retained a large firm of lawyers. The return phone call from one of the junior partners was brief and to the point. Sally MacDowell's son was dead, and con men would be dealt with severely.

And that's when the idea had hit him. A little insurance, a little fail-safe. Years ago, someone had tried to kill him. One of the mighty MacDowells, probably. If they wanted him dead back then, they certainly wouldn't welcome him back now, when they'd gotten used to thinking all that lovely money was theirs. He had no idea what Sally's will contained, but he had little doubt that once he returned a large portion of her substantial wealth would devolve onto him. And Warren and Patsy MacDowell wouldn't like that.

It hadn't taken him long to find out the lay of the land, once he decided how he was going to deal with it. Alex had never been declared dead—his grieving mother had refused to allow it. Once she died the estate would be in disarray until they managed to come up with some proof. Anyone amoral enough and devious enough would welcome an effective imposter with open arms.

And if his memory served him, dear Uncle Warren was the perfect patsy.

It had been amazingly easy. He'd tracked Warren down to his men's club and simply sat near him in a quiet corner of the bar and waited. Warren's gaze had drifted past him with patrician lack of interest, then he'd frozen.

"Who are you?" he'd demanded in a hoarse voice.

Alex had smiled. "Your long-lost nephew?"

"He's dead."

"Maybe. It would be convenient if you could prove it. But you haven't been able to, have you?"

Warren reached for his dark amber drink, his perfectly manicured hand shaking. "What would you know about it?"

"I know a lot of things. I happen to look like a missing member of your family. I even looked like him back when he disappeared—the cops picked me up and questioned me when they were looking for him. With the right sort of help I could convince anyone I'm Alexander MacDowell."

"And why would you want to do that?"

"For money," he said lightly. "Oh, I'm not greedy. I wouldn't expect everything that MacDowell was going to inherit. After all, I'd need help if I wanted to pull this off. But think of the convenience. No delay in proving whether he's dead or not. No question about inheritance. We work out something nice and cozy, just the two of us, and once the old lady dies and there's a generous amount of disposable income, I'll take off and never be heard from again."

Warren had stared at him in disbelief. "And you think I'd trust you? You must be the con artist who's been trying to get in touch with my sister. I thought I had the lawyers take care of you."

"Don't be too hasty, 'Uncle Warren,'" he'd murmured. "You strike me as a smart man. You wouldn't want to dismiss an opportunity like this without careful consideration."

"Who the hell are you?"

"My name's Sam Kinkaid." He'd used the name deliberately, but Warren hadn't even blinked. Obviously, Sally's former husband had been erased from his memory banks.

Warren leaned back, looking at him for a long, thoughtful moment. "I could call the police."

"But you won't. You'll go back to your Park Avenue apartment and you'll think about this. You'll mull it over, thoughtfully, over a couple of scotches. You won't talk about it with anyone, because you're smart enough to know that a secret stretched three ways always breaks. And then, in a few days, maybe less, you'll call me."

Warren wrinkled his nose in fastidious disapproval. "You're very sure of yourself, aren't you?"

"It takes balls to carry off something like this. The question is, do you have any?" Warren simply stared at him, and Alex figured he'd set the trap well enough. He rose, towering over the older man. "It's up to you. Here's my phone number. I'll be waiting to hear from you."

"You can expect to hear from my lawyers," Warren said coldly.

Alex had only grinned at him. "Thanks for the drink, Uncle Warren."

His instincts told him when Warren would call, and his instincts were right. In less than a week he was being drilled privately in MacDowell family history, some of which was familiar, some of which was entirely new to him. He heard about Patsy's new marriages, her adult children; about Sally's illness and her devoted servants, Constanza and Ruben. And he heard all about Carolyn Smith, the foster child who was brought into the family and had never left.

He'd remembered that innocent kiss. The first and last taste of innocence in his wicked, self-absorbed life. And he'd looked up at dear Uncle Warren and smiled, knowing he was going to have a chance to taste her again.

Chapter Fourteen

SOME THINGS WERE better left in the past. Alex had never spent a
year in Vermont, so he had no idea when spring was supposed to come,
but surely by now it was long overdue. He'd be a lot happier breaking
into the library on a warm night than in the current frigid air.

She hadn't said a word when she walked past him in the
kitchen—maybe she was just going to spend the rest of Sally's life
ignoring him. He'd put her through the wringer quite effectively, but he
couldn't be sure he hadn't pushed her too far. He wanted her shaken,
unwilling to fight back. He didn't want her dangerous.

It would be warm in Italy tonight. The stars would glitter down on
his newly patched roof, and life would be peaceful. Once he had his
questions answered.

He'd already turned off the security system before he stepped out
onto the flagstoned terrace that led to the library door. It was a simple
enough matter to use his credit card and open the catch.

He was ready to move fast, in case she screamed, but she just lay
there on the sofa bed, watching him.

He was right—there was a chair wedged in front of the hall door.
She should have realized the outside door would be just as dangerous.

"Mind if I turn on a light?" he asked in a conversational tone as he
closed and locked the outer door. She wouldn't be able to escape that
quickly with the chair in her way. He could take his time.

"Yes." Her voice was flat, uncompromising.

"You prefer to conduct this in the dark?"

"Conduct what? I have a very loud scream."

"Most of the people in this house are deaf, either by choice or by
age. And I can move fast, even in the dark. I can stop you before you
even start."

"Why are you here?"

He moved closer. He could see fairly well in the dark, and she
looked pale, stubborn, angry. Which was good. He'd been half-afraid
he'd find her crying.

He wasn't usually susceptible to crying women, but somehow he knew he wouldn't be able to take Carolyn Smith's tears lightly. Especially if he'd caused them.

He'd caused her enough tears, years ago. He didn't owe her any more. "Mind if I sit?" He figured studious politeness wouldn't hurt.

"Yes."

He sat anyway, on the end of the mattress, near her body beneath the fluffy duvet. She moved out of his way as if he were an errant rattlesnake, and he almost reached out and caught her ankle beneath the covers. He resisted the impulse. He was in trouble enough—he didn't need to make it worse.

They sat in the darkness, in uneasy silence, for endless minutes. He wanted her to break it, but she was even more stubborn than he was. As stubborn as Sally herself, he thought, with a trace of annoyed admiration. If he wanted to accomplish anything and get to bed, he was going to have to be the one to push things.

"Don't you want to ask me anything? Yell at me?"

"Why should I bother? Yelling won't help. And I'm afraid all my questions have already been answered."

It was better this way, he told himself. Better that she believed he was an imposter, a charlatan, a cheat. He told himself that, but he didn't believe it.

"All right," he said lazily. "So I guess it's my turn to ask the questions. What are you going to do about it?"

"About what?"

"About your newfound certainty that I'm an imposter? I don't see you rushing in to warn Sally, but you may be waiting until morning. Or are you planning on going to the police?"

"I was considering the lawyers."

"Not your best choice," he murmured. "How do you know some of them aren't in it with Warren and me? And you know how ruthless lawyers can be. There's a lot of money at stake here. Warren MacDowell might not know any hit men, but I wouldn't be surprised if some of the MacDowell family lawyers weren't capable of digging someone up."

"Maybe they expect you to do the job."

He shook his head. "I'm a con artist, not a killer," he said. "If a deal falls apart I disappear. I don't try to force it."

"I don't see you disappearing."

"I'm not sure this has fallen apart. What are you going to do, Carolyn?"

She let out a tight breath of air. There was a slight catch in it, as if she'd been crying, but he knew she hadn't. "I don't know yet. That depends on a number of things."

"Like what?"

"Like what happened to the real Alexander MacDowell. Is he really dead?"

He knew she wouldn't see his wry smile in the darkness. "You tell me. You're the only witness to that night on the Lighthouse Beach."

"No, I'm not. Whoever tried to kill him knows what happened."

"But who says he or she is still alive? Maybe it was some outraged parent who finally had had enough of Alex tomcatting around his daughter and decided to blow him away."

"I don't think so."

"Do you think he's dead?"

She didn't answer. "Why are you still here? If you had any sense you'd get the hell out of here."

"I told you, I'm not sure this deal has fallen apart. You really want Sally to wake up and find her long-lost son has disappeared once more? It would kill her."

"She's dying anyway," Carolyn said, her flat voice betraying no emotion.

"Yeah, so she is. Maybe you'd just as soon hurry the process along. After all, you're bound to inherit a tidy little sum of money, and you won't have to deal with this family any longer. You must have gotten pretty damned tired of jumping every time they snapped their fingers."

"It wasn't like that."

"You mean Warren loves you like a niece?" he mocked her.

"Warren doesn't love anyone—you should know that. He's obviously been your source of information about this family. He's not big on sentiment, honor, or family feeling."

"No, he isn't."

"I haven't stayed for Warren and the rest of the family."

"I assumed you stayed for the money," he said.

"If that's all you can understand, then go right ahead and believe it."

He knew perfectly well it wasn't true. He wished, for her sake, that it was. If she were a coldhearted gold digger, or even a normal young woman with a reasonable amount of self-esteem and greed, she'd be much better off than she was now, prey to the emotional forces of the MacDowells.

"All right, you're devoted to Sally," he drawled. "You stayed with her out of love and gratitude, and you couldn't care less about your inheritance. So where does that leave you? Are you going to say the words that will destroy her last few weeks? Or are you going to sit by and watch a con man make a fool of her?"

She hesitated. "I don't suppose Warren hired you for Sally's sake," she suggested. "To make her last few months easier?"

"You really aren't that naive, are you, darling?" he said lightly. "Haven't you already told me that Warren doesn't have a sentimental, honorable bone in his body? He wants his inheritance unencumbered."

"And what are you supposed to do? Sign over all that money and disappear again? Don't you think that will be a little suspicious?"

"Who's going to question it?"

She leaned back against the pillows, her face still. "I could."

"But you won't." He moved then, and she made no effort to evade him. Maybe she knew it was useless. He loomed over her in the darkness, putting his hands on her shoulders. Small shoulders, delicate bones, beneath his strong hands.

She sat motionless, staring up at him, and he couldn't resist. He brushed his mouth against hers, lightly, just enough to tease. "You know what we can do about this little problem, Carolyn?" he whispered. "It's perfectly simple, and I don't know why I didn't think of it before. Your inheritance isn't that large—Warren showed me the will. You could do with a bit more to augment it. I'm sure I can arrange for Warren to shift some of Alexander's inheritance to you. Wouldn't that make life easier?"

He kissed her again, increasing the pressure slightly, and her lips were soft and pliant beneath his. The smart thing to do would be to back away, leave her tempted, wanting.

But the temptation was too much for him. With a faint groan he slanted his mouth across hers, pushing her mouth open with his, using his tongue.

She kissed him back. She couldn't help it, he could feel it in her mouth, in her hands as she reached for his shoulders, trying to push him away, and instead clung to him. She kissed him back, and it was almost more than he could bear.

And then she shoved him away from her, hard. He made no attempt to hold on to her, too shaken by her mouth, her touch, her scent. Too shaken by his own need.

"I'll make you a deal," she said in a rough voice. "You keep away from me. Don't touch me again, don't come anywhere near me. You can tell Warren that I still hate you from childhood, I don't care. As long as you leave me alone and you don't hurt Sally you can do anything you damned well please."

"What's the catch?"

"The moment you put your hands on me I'll call the police, and I don't care if the truth sends Sally into cardiac arrest. Do you understand?"

"Yes."

"And?"

He smiled wryly, hoping she couldn't see it in the darkness. It would give away too much. "I'm trying to decide which is more important. The money Warren's promised me, or fucking you."

"You've already had me," she said bitterly. "Go for the money."

It would have been so simple to tell her the truth. It would have been hard to get her to listen, to believe it, but he could make her. There were too many things only they knew.

But then, she thought he'd faked the scar, the allergy to shrimp. She might think everything was some kind of trick.

He wasn't quite sure what he wanted her to believe. What he wanted at all, apart from the truth of what happened that night. Once he had those answers, then the rest would follow. Then everything would make some strange kind of sense.

He was no closer to finding out the truth than he had been on his roof in Tuscany. The only difference was that now he was enmeshed in this family he'd left so long ago. Physically, emotionally enmeshed.

And with the child/woman he'd left so long ago. If he was going to find any kind of peace, he had to promise not to touch her.

The notions of peace and not touching Carolyn Smith were polar opposites, but right then he wasn't in any mood to figure it out. He was in the mood to pull the duvet back from her slender body and see if she still tasted as good as she had a few nights ago.

He wasn't going to. "I promise to keep my distance," he said. "For now."

She didn't look particularly gratified. "It's your call. I know perfectly well I'm not irresistible, so you might as well concentrate on ingratiating yourself with the rest of the family. But then, you've been doing that, haven't you? Once you disposed of me."

"I wouldn't have called it disposing of you," he said. "Are you going to tell me you didn't like it?"

"Get out."

He rose with a faint, deliberate swagger. "You want me to go outside or can I go through the house?"

"Go back the way you came."

"You don't want anyone to think we've been lovers?"

She was ready to snap, and he knew it, but somehow he couldn't stop from pushing.

"We weren't lovers," she said in a tight voice.

"Oh, yeah? What do you call the other night?"

"A serious mistake."

"And you don't make mistakes, do you, Carolyn? Perfect Carolyn, a paragon above reproach."

"I don't repeat my mistakes," she said.

"You will."

"I warned you—"

"And I promised. I won't touch you, sweetheart. I won't even breathe on you, much less kiss you the way you need to be kissed. I won't carry you off to bed and screw you senseless. Until you ask me."

Her laugh was strained. "Why stop there? How about I beg you on bended knee? That's about as likely."

"I'm not picky, Carolyn. All you have to do is ask."

If there'd been anything in reach she probably would have thrown it at him, but she had enough sense to realize a pillow fight wouldn't have accomplished anything. She simply sat there in bed, motionless, as he slipped back out the terrace door.

CAROLYN DRAGGED herself out of bed a little before six. The curtains on the library door were sheer, letting in the early-morning light, but even heavy drapes wouldn't have helped. Once Alex left she'd risen and shoved a chair under the outside door as well, but she couldn't convince herself she was safe from intruders. If the man pretending to be Alexander MacDowell wanted to get at her he could. He was relentless, and only his diffident promise and his admitted self-interest kept him at bay.

She showered in the exercise room, then stared at herself in the mirror. If she'd looked like holy hell a few days ago, it was nothing compared to the reflection in the mirror this morning. Her skin was pale, almost porcelain, except for the purple smudges beneath her eyes. She looked drawn, delicate; her eyes bleak and despairing; and her pale mouth was set in a thin, worried line.

Not the face to reassure a dying woman, she thought, reaching for her makeup. The results were far from miraculous, but at least the artificial pink in her cheeks looked only slightly feverish, and her worried mouth was a nice rose hue.

The sun was coming up over the mountains at the edge of the fields that stretched beyond the house, and suddenly she wanted to be free of the place, the trapped air of impending death, the lies and betrayals that ran rampant through the perfectly decorated hallways. She grabbed the leather coat that someone had left hanging in the gym, shoved her feet in an old pair of mud boots, and headed out into the early-morning garden.

It had been a frosty night, but the sun was warming the earth with greedy hunger, and Carolyn crossed the lawn, following the narrow path of crushed stone as she headed for the winter-stubbled fields. She reached the stone wall and paused, turning to look back at the house. The windows were blank reflections of the bright morning sun, staring back at her. They were all still asleep at this early hour, she assured herself. So why couldn't she rid herself of the sense that someone was watching.

She climbed over the stone fence, moving into the rough field, pulling the leather jacket around her. A stream lay just beyond this next stretch of field, and there was a fallen log she'd refused to let the gardening service remove. The stream would be swollen with melting snow, racing wildly, and she would sit on the log and breathe the cool morning air. And just maybe things wouldn't seem so bleak.

She never got as far as the river. She found the rabbit, lying in the stubble, sightless, staring, and she knelt down in sudden despair. There were wild animals all around—coyotes who hid in the woods and never showed themselves, but left carnage behind nonetheless. There were fisher-cats as well, and some even insisted that the catamount had returned to the forests of Vermont, though no one had yet sighted anything other than a suspicious pile of droppings.

Whoever had killed this rabbit had done a thorough, savage job of it, and Carolyn rose, unaccountably depressed. She heard the faint whirring noise as something flew past her head, and she batted at it absently. It was too early even for black flies, and whatever had flown past her was too small to be a bird.

She was no longer in the mood to visit the stream. She turned, and something sped past her again, with a high-pitched buzzing noise, and suddenly she knew what it was.

She threw herself down on the ground, sprawling onto the half-frozen earth, as another bullet raced past her and slammed into a tree. There was no sound of an explosion, but there was no other explanation. Someone was shooting at her.

It had to be some stupid kind of mistake. Someone must be poaching, must have thought she was some kind of animal. But that was crazy—the early morning was clear and bright, and she looked like no one but herself.

A hunter wouldn't use a silencer. She lifted her head, squinting in the distance. The house was too far away, and all the windows and doors were closed. No one could be sitting in a window using her for target practice.

They must be somewhere in the woods at the edge of the field. There were a dozen places to hide, and she couldn't even guess where the bullets had come from. All she could do was lie facedown in the stubble of cropped grass and hope whoever was trying to kill her wouldn't be brave enough to walk out into the field where he could get a clear shot at her.

As far as she knew, there were no guns at the house. Sally had always abhorred hunting, posting her expansive acres, much to the dislike of the locals. Warren was far too fastidious to evince any desire to tramp through fields in search of game. Alex, on the other hand, had always shown a typical boyish fascination with firearms.

But he wasn't Alex, she reminded herself. He wasn't anyone she knew—he was a cheat and a liar who had conquered her on every level. He could be a crack shot for all she knew. After all, he had the most to lose.

But if he was a crack shot, then he hadn't wanted to kill her. Maybe whoever it was simply wanted to scare her. A not so subtle warning, to keep out of the way and let Warren and his protégé do their thing.

She couldn't picture Warren at the other end of the gun. She couldn't picture Warren capable of murder.

She wasn't so sure of the man pretending to be Alex.

Would he cross the fields and put the barrel of that gun at the back of her neck and fire? She didn't want to die without knowing who wanted her dead. It had to be Alex—he had the most to lose.

So why couldn't she believe it?

The ground beneath her was hard and cold, the chill seeping into her bones. The sun overhead was bright, beating down on her, warming her, and she lay, half shivering, half sweating, waiting to die. The sense of déjà vu swept over her, and she was suddenly thirteen years old again, huddled in the cold on Lighthouse Beach, listening for the sound of a gun.

She lost track of time. She may have even fallen asleep—it was impossible to know. The sun moved higher overhead, and in the distance she thought she could hear voices, and she knew she couldn't wait any longer.

She tried to pull herself to her feet, but her legs collapsed beneath her, and she fell back onto the earth, half-expecting a bullet to slam into her head. No terrifying whirr, no unseen evil spinning past her. She tried again, and in the distance she could see the house, the shades pulled up, people moving behind the windows.

No one would shoot her now, in view of witnesses. All she had to do was walk back to the house, slowly, carefully, and she'd be safe.

Until whoever had tried to kill her decided to try again.

Chapter Fifteen

PATSY SAT IN splendid isolation at the head of the table, completely dressed, sipping pale coffee with her usual elegance. It was quite possibly the first time Carolyn had ever seen Sally's younger sister awake before eleven o'clock in the morning, and it was the one time she would have much preferred to avoid her.

"What happened to you?" Patsy sounded more fastidious than concerned. "You look as if you had a wrestling match with an alligator." She even sounded less fuzzy than usual, but then, she hadn't been up long enough to get a start on the day's drinking.

"I went out for an early-morning walk and I tripped." Until the words came out Carolyn had no idea that she planned to lie. If she had any sense at all she would have called the police, had them search the woods.

Except that she knew, instinctively, that they would find nothing. They wouldn't think she was lying, of course, but they'd have very strong doubts. And they would tell Sally, who wasn't strong enough to deal with this.

"What an extraordinary thing to do," Patsy said.

"Trip?"

"No, go for a walk." She shuddered expressively. "Communing with nature is greatly overrated, as you doubtless agree. Do you want coffee first or would you like to go change out of those clothes?"

Patsy's preference was more than clear from her expression, but Carolyn was feeling contrary. "Coffee, please," she said, taking a seat nearby and vaguely wishing she had had a close encounter with cow manure to make Patsy's morning complete.

Patsy wrinkled her nose but poured, passing her the cup with a perfectly manicured hand that showed not one trace of a tremor. "Suit yourself, dear."

"You're up awfully early today," Carolyn said in a casual tone.

"I couldn't sleep. Every now and then I wake up at the crack of dawn, absolutely unable to go back to sleep. I've learned the only thing I can do is get up and pretend it's the middle of the night and I'm simply behaving like a mad, decadent being." She yawned extravagantly.

"Is anyone else awake?" Carolyn tried to sound casual, and Patsy was too concerned with some vague inner working of her mind to notice the loaded question.

"I think I saw Alex wandering around somewhere," she said airily. "He looked dressed for outdoors. I'm surprised you didn't run into him during your little walk."

Carolyn set her coffee down very carefully. Patsy was far too self-absorbed to notice the effect her words were having, but Carolyn was used to protecting herself.

Who else would it have been? she demanded of herself. She'd caught him in a tangled knot of lies; she knew without a doubt that he was a fake, an imposter, a con man. She still had no proof—only her word against Alex's. And against Warren's.

She couldn't stop them, but she could make trouble. A hunting accident would take care of the problem quite nicely.

They couldn't have hoped to get away with it. But that would be a moot point if she were already dead. She wasn't particularly interested in vindication from beyond the grave.

"Where is he now, do you know?" she asked, reaching for a croissant and proceeding to shred it into tiny pieces.

"In with Sally, I presume." She turned her limpid gaze on Carolyn, the skin around her almost sixty-year-old eyes tucked and smooth and perfect. "Haven't you gotten over him yet?"

"I beg your pardon?"

"Surely you're too old to still be infatuated with him? You should have outgrown that years ago."

"I'm not infatuated with him."

"You certainly were when you were a child."

"I'm not a child anymore."

"No, you're not. I'm just afraid Alex might have noticed that fact as well. I remember we were always worried that Alex might decide to turn some of his hell-raising proclivities toward you. He didn't, did he?"

"Didn't what?"

"Molest you when you were thirteen?" Patsy said bluntly.

There was the kiss that had stayed with her for eighteen years. His strong young body pressed up against hers. But he'd been a child as well, much as he'd tried to cover it up.

"No," Carolyn said.

"I always wondered, you know. You went into that almost suicidal decline after he disappeared, and you were even more subdued than you had been before. I was afraid he might have done something, or . . . said something the night he left. You did see him, didn't you? Before he left?"

The lie had been told for eighteen years—it was automatic now. "No," she said. "The last time I saw Alex was that afternoon at the beach."

Patsy's gaze was remarkably clear-eyed. "You don't remember that horror scene at dinner that night?"

Carolyn shook her head. "I didn't even remember you were there."

"Well, I was." Patsy leaned back in her chair, fiddling with her coffee cup. "I've been thinking. Why don't you get away from here, darling?"

"I beg your pardon?"

"I mean it. You've devoted your life to my sister, and no one could doubt your dedication. But don't you think it's past time you had a life of your own? Sally's got her son back—she doesn't need you holding her hand anymore. Surely it's about time to make a break."

"I don't think it's going to be that much longer, Patsy," Carolyn said with great gentleness. Patsy had never evinced much grief or affection for her older sister, but Carolyn was always willing to assume it was simply a matter of covering up things that were too painful.

"True enough," Patsy said blithely, toying with one of the heavy silver forks. "I just thought it might be easier on you."

"It's sweet of you to be concerned."

Patsy's eyes met hers. "I know what you think of me, Carolyn," she said softly. "You think I'm a silly, frivolous creature who's interested in nothing but her own pleasure. But you're almost like family, I've known you since you were two years old, and I care about you."

Almost like family. Carolyn drained her cup of lukewarm coffee and gave Patsy her most dazzling smile. "It doesn't matter that Sally doesn't need me to be here. *I* need to be here."

Patsy nodded. "I understand, dear. We all need to be together during this sad time. I just . . ." Her voice trailed away.

"You just . . . ?" Carolyn prompted.

"I just hope that you're . . . careful."

Carolyn froze. "What do you mean?"

Patsy waved a hand airily. "Oh, heavens, I don't know what I mean.

I suppose it's my maternal instincts coming to the fore. I just worry about everyone."

As far as Carolyn could see Patsy's maternal instincts had never surfaced for anyone but George, and her sole worry seemed to be reserved for herself. Either Patsy knew something, or suspected something. And she was far too cagey to admit what it was.

For some reason Carolyn wasn't expecting Alexander MacDowell, or the man pretending to be him, to walk through the breakfast room door and take a seat at the table with all the insouciant charm of someone who really belonged there.

"We were just talking about you," Patsy said in a silky voice.

"Were you?" His rich, beautiful mouth curved in a generous smile, and if there was a trace of wariness in his blue eyes, she couldn't see it. He looked totally at ease, as if she wasn't capable of bringing his whole masquerade tumbling down. "And what were you saying?" He took the cup of coffee Patsy offered him and began spooning indecent amounts of sugar into it.

"She was warning me to be careful," Carolyn said.

His eyes met hers, full of mockery and an I-dare-you glint. "What does she think you need to be worried about? Surely not me? I'm completely harmless, aren't I, Aunt Patsy?"

"Completely," Patsy said with no trace of irony. "Actually, my telling her to be careful had absolutely nothing to do with you, of course. She fell while she was walking today, and banged herself up a bit. I just warned her to watch where she was going. We don't want two invalids on our hands."

His eyes had narrowed, all amusement vanishing. "What happened?"

You know perfectly well what happened, she wanted to scream at him. *You either tried to kill me, or to scare me off.* "I tripped over the rough ground and went sprawling," she said instead. "Just clumsiness on my part. I won't make that mistake again."

If his mockery had been unsettling, the strange expression in his eyes was even more so. "Patsy's right," he said abruptly. "No one wants a nasty accident."

"There won't be one," she said, unable to keep the edge out of her voice.

"Actually," Patsy said, "I was suggesting that now that you were back among the living, Carolyn ought to give herself a little break. Get away from this place for a while, away from responsibilities and death.

After all, Sally has her son back. She doesn't need Carolyn anymore." Carolyn might have almost suspected Patsy of deliberate malice in that last statement, but Patsy was too obtuse for that kind of thing.

"It's nice to know you think I'm all things to all people, Aunt Patsy," Alex drawled. "But I'm afraid my arrival doesn't cancel anyone else out, particularly Carolyn, who's been a far better daughter to Sally than I've been a son."

"Yes, but whether a child is dutiful or not has nothing to do with how much a parent loves them. Of my three children Grace is by far the nicest, most generous, sweetest tempered. And she bores me to tears. Whereas George is fully as self-centered as I am, and I adore him." Patsy yawned indulgently, then bestowed a blithe smile on the two of them as she rose from the table. "I do wish you two would learn to get along, though. You never did, even when you were young. It would make life so much more pleasant if you could put away your battles for the time being. Either that, or one of you should leave."

The last thing Carolyn wanted to do was be left alone with Alex, but she couldn't very well race after Patsy without causing more unwanted questions. And she wasn't about to let him know just how nervous he made her. Doubtless he suspected, doubtless he was doing everything he could to make her uneasy. But she wasn't going to do or say anything that would give him proof of his power over her.

"Why is she trying so hard to get rid of you?" he murmured lazily.

"How do you know she's not trying to get rid of you? She just said one of us should leave."

"She knows I'm not leaving. That leaves you."

"She was asking me about the night the real Alex died." She changed the subject deliberately.

He winced. "Would you mind not bandying that 'real Alex' stuff about? You never know who might be listening."

Carolyn smiled sweetly. "No, we don't, do we? Are you going to tell your partner in crime that I know?"

"Which one? Oh, you mean Warren? No, I thought I'd leave that up to your discretion. If I were you I'd keep him out of it entirely and just deal with me."

"And you're so much less of a threat?"

"Count on it."

She stared at him across the wide expanse of the table, letting her eyes slowly assess the man who'd tricked her, lied to her, seduced her. Was he also a man who'd tried to kill her when she'd found out too much?

He was almost indecently beautiful, with his Cossack face and his erotic mouth. F's blond hair was wet from a morning shower, pushed back away from his face, and he looked like a lost Russian prince, come to claim his throne.

Except that he was a pretender, in more ways than one.

"Are you going to leave?" he reached over and poured himself another cup of coffee, and she had the dubious pleasure of admiring his lean, elegantly muscled body as he stretched. She remembered more about it—the phony scar, low on his hip. His skin, hot, smooth . . .

She jerked herself away from the erotic reverie. "You'd like that, wouldn't you?"

"It would probably be easier. But I'm not trying to force you to go. I'm just curious."

"Nothing will get me out of here until Sally's gone," she said in a terse voice. "No matter what you do."

"And what do you think I'd be doing?" he countered. "You already said you'd call the police if I touched you again without you asking."

"And I told you that would be a cold day in hell—"

"Children, children." Warren strolled into the room, looking disgustingly pleased with himself for a man involved in a criminal conspiracy to defraud his dying sister. "Are you two squabbling again? I swear the two of you have been at each other's throats since you were infants. I told Patsy you hadn't grown out of it, but I wish, for the sake of the peace of the household, that you could put your differences aside for the time being."

"No," Carolyn said, pushing back from the table.

"No 'good morning' for your Uncle Warren?" he asked plaintively, when he was the least avuncular creature in the world.

"Talk to your 'nephew,'" she said pointedly, and left the room, no longer caring whether it looked like she was running away.

She was.

"WHAT WAS THAT all about?" Warren asked, taking Patsy's vacated spot at the head of the table and reaching for the coffee.

Alex merely shrugged. "You know Carolyn—she tends to get a bit emotional over inconsequentials."

"Actually, that's not the Carolyn I know at all. She's always been a very reserved, quiet young lady. A perfect MacDowell, in fact." There was an odd trace of smugness in his voice that Alex couldn't begin to fathom.

"Interesting that the perfect MacDowell isn't a MacDowell at all," he said lazily, waiting to see how Warren would respond.

But Warren was an old campaigner, a wily creature with the soul of a politician and the morals of a businessman. He wasn't about to let anything out that he wasn't ready to share. "Life is full of interesting quirks," he said. "She's become much more volatile since I last saw her. I assumed it was the stress of Sally's impending death. She's always been devoted to her, you know. But now I'm wondering whether you might be the cause of this recent snappishness of hers."

"Maybe I bring out the worst in her," Alex suggested.

"Don't. We can't afford to make any enemies we don't have to. If Carolyn has any doubts as to your identity she could make a very great deal of trouble. Nothing we couldn't deal with, of course, but I want this whole thing to run as smoothly as possible."

A nasty suspicion had been niggling at the back of Alex's mind, formed from Patsy's seemingly random words and the slightly rumpled state of Carolyn's clothes. "How would you deal with it?"

"I said 'we,' didn't I? We're in this together, I presume?" Warren said sharply.

"Of course."

"If you couldn't seduce her into being quiet we could always try bribery."

"I suspect that wouldn't work any better than seduction."

"You're probably right," Warren said gloomily. "Well, assuming she begins to suspect, we could arrange a little accident."

Alex froze. "What kind of accident?"

"Oh, nothing fatal. We could work something out. Something to put her in the hospital a few days to get her mind off her suspicions. Or I could do something with Sally's checkbook. Carolyn's been handling it, and I could probably manage to cook up an unfortunate discrepancy which I'd have to bring to Sally's attention."

"You're a real sweetheart, aren't you, Warren?" Alex said wryly, keeping the distaste out of his voice.

"Takes one to know one, my boy. Actually, the real Alex was a little shit. I wouldn't be surprised if he'd turned out worse than either of us if he'd lived."

Alex took a careful sip of his sweetened coffee. "What makes you think he's dead?"

"Isn't it obvious? When there's this much money involved there's not much else that could keep him away," Warren said easily.

"You sounded more certain than that, dear uncle," he said lightly. "You sounded as if you had specific knowledge of whatever happened to Sally's son."

Warren laughed. "You're imagining things. Don't get spooky on me, boy. We're headed into the homestretch. Sally's on oxygen, and I don't think she'll be coming off it. If we can just keep our nerve we should do fine. As long as Carolyn doesn't start having any bright ideas. I'm not about to give it up at this late date."

"You think she's the only one we have to worry about?"

"Absolutely. You've done a hell of a job ingratiating yourself with George and Tessa, and Patsy doesn't bother to look past the nose on her face. If she did, she wouldn't care, as long as she's taken care of in the style to which she's become accustomed. Carolyn's a danger because she has nothing to lose. And because she's got an annoying puritanical streak that wouldn't flinch at destroying everything for some stupid ethic."

"A concept you're not overly familiar with, Uncle Warren."

"Don't push me, boy. I'm not in the mood for games."

"If Carolyn's the quintessential MacDowell, how come she's so burdened with defects like honor and decency?"

Warren glared at him. "You don't have much cause to be self-righteous. You're the one who came to me with this little scam."

"And you're the member of the family who jumped at it," Alex reminded him coolly.

"So we're both tough, ruthless human beings with a lousy sense of right and wrong. No one ever got rich worrying about ethics."

"I didn't think you had to worry about getting rich. You're a MacDowell, aren't you?"

"You know what they say—you can never be too rich or too thin. In this volatile market it's only wise to guard your assets to the best of your ability."

"Even if they're not your assets," Alex observed wryly.

"Don't tell me you've suddenly developed a conscience? It's a little late for that. Remember, this was your idea."

"You already reminded me of that." He looked at his uncle with a steady gaze. "And don't worry about my conscience. I've got it well under control. As long as we get one thing straight."

"You're dictating to me, boy?"

"There'll be no little accidents. Not to Carolyn, not to anyone. Is that understood? I'm a con man, not a killer." He had to admire the utter smoothness of his statement. In fact, it was the truth. He was conning all of them, just not in the way they thought he was.

Warren shrugged. "I'll just leave it up to you to keep Carolyn in line. Make sure she doesn't start suspecting anything, or I might be forced to take a hand."

"If you take a hand I'll cut it off."

Warren looked at him as if he'd suddenly grown two heads. "I thought you didn't believe in violence? You sound positively savage! If I didn't know better I'd be worried for my safety."

Alex gave him a positively beatific smile, one displayed for the sole purpose of terrorizing Warren. "It never hurts to be afraid, Uncle Warren. Life is full of little surprises."

Warren stared at him in blustery dismay. "It would take a lot to surprise an old warhorse like me. I doubt there's anything you could say that would shock me."

Alex drained his coffee cup and set it down in the saucer in utter silence. "You'd be surprised, Uncle Warren."

Chapter Sixteen

ALEX SLAMMED THE door shut behind him, not caring if it woke his sleeping cousins from their beauty rest. He was edgy, frustrated, tormented by the sense that something was very wrong in the MacDowell house. Something even worse than an ancient attempt at murder.

He'd had more than one reason for avoiding his bedroom the last few days, but right now there was no place else to go. He couldn't get rid of the memory of Carolyn, the stricken expression in her eyes when she saw the hypodermic needle and realized she'd nearly killed him, that she'd been wrong all along. The unmistakable fear that underlay the very real sexual desire he could feel emanating from her, when he held her hand against his scarred hip. The faint, sobbing noise she made when she came.

He spent his nights in that same bed, remembering laying her across it, tasting her. She was gone, and he could still feel her there, just out of reach.

He never thought he'd come back to his old life just to become prey to an adolescent sexual obsession. It served him right, he thought wryly. He'd always been a bit too Machiavellian for his own good. Now he was getting distracted when his goal was very clear.

He'd come back for one reason. To find out who tried to kill him, and why. So far he wasn't much closer to that knowledge than he had been living in Italy.

At least two people knew the answer to that question. One was Carolyn Smith, but the secrets were locked deep inside her brain, where even she couldn't unearth them. She had seen what happened that night, even if she'd blanked it out.

Just as he had. Of course, he had an excuse for not remembering. He'd had a head injury on top of the trauma of being shot, and injuries like that were tricky things. Whoever had tried to kill him was probably counting on that.

Unless the third witness, the murderer, was certain he'd been successful in the first place.

Warren was the logical culprit. He'd never, for one moment, questioned Sam Kinkaid's identity, or worried that the real Alexander MacDowell would show up. He claimed it was simple common sense—no one would leave all that potential money unclaimed.

But Alex knew far too well just how simple it was to turn your back on millions of dollars. He'd done it once, and never regretted it. He had every intention of doing so again.

It wouldn't do him any good to try to prove who he was, even if he decided that was a good idea. There were no dental records, and DNA testing would show absolutely nothing. He had been bought and sold in infancy—whoever had bred him had dismissed him years ago.

He could work some more on Carolyn. She was the only definite source of information—maybe he could get her drunk, get her mad, drug her, anything to jar her recalcitrant memory. Maybe he could convince her to try hypnosis, drug therapy, convince her that unless she dredged those memories from her brain they'd haunt her for the rest of her life. It wouldn't take much pressure, and he knew it.

But he didn't want to do it. He'd upset her life too much already, and she looked at him as if he were a cross between Ted Bundy and Brad Pitt. Surely he could find the answers without dragging her back into it.

Of course, it wasn't entirely noble on his part. She was already making him crazy, invading his sleep, tormenting his waking hours, so that he was far more concerned about her than about an ancient murder attempt eighteen years ago. He was much better off keeping his distance from her, at least until he found out the truth about his past. He wasn't at all sure what would happen next. Maybe he'd just disappear, back to Italy where no one could find him.

Or maybe he'd take Carolyn with him.

He still thought of Sally as his mother, no matter what laws she had to bend or break to get him. She was sleeping, her color an ashen gray, the oxygen tubes threaded into her patrician nose.

He sat by the bed, watching her as he had for so many hours since he'd returned. Trying to understand her.

"So?" The sound of her voice was so quiet he almost thought he'd imagined it. She opened her eyes then, turning to watch him with grim amusement.

"So what?" he responded lightly.

"Smart ass," she muttered. "Are you waiting for me to die?"

"No."

That startled her. "I thought that was why you came back. To say good-bye to your dear old mother, to ease her passing into the next world."

"There's that," he agreed.

"But you had another reason for coming? Apart from the money, of course?"

He didn't bother to argue with her. She trotted out his inheritance any time she felt threatened. She was obviously feeling threatened right then, and he didn't want to make it worse. But he wasn't going to let her go without answers.

"Where did I come from?"

To her credit, she didn't even blink. "You mean you've reached the age of thirty-five and no one's explained to you about the birds and the bees? It serves you right for taking off before I could acquaint you with the facts of life."

"I've known about sex since I was twelve years old, maybe younger." He put his hand on her fine-boned, blue-veined one, and it was frail and birdlike beneath his. "I want to know where I came from. Who'd you buy me from?"

She let her eyes drift closed. "I don't know what you're talking about, Alex, and I wish you wouldn't try to confuse me. I tire very easily nowadays. Why don't you let me get some rest and then you can explain your ridiculous—"

"John Kinkaid told me your baby was born dead, and you went out and returned with me in its place. I want to know where I came from. For that matter, I'd like to know whether I was legally adopted or not."

"Kinkaid," Sally muttered in a voice of deep loathing. "He should have died years ago."

"He did."

He'd managed to startle her, and this time she didn't bother hiding it. "Then how did you find out?"

"He told me. I ended up at his place when I ran away, and he didn't believe in fostering illusions. I've known for eighteen years that I'm not really your son."

"You are, damn it!" she said in a raw voice that was little more than a whisper. "You're the son of my heart and soul, even if you don't happen to be the son of my body. And you know it, even if you're in the mood to deny it."

"I know it," he agreed softly. He still had his hand on hers, and she turned hers palm upward, holding it. "I still want you to tell me how you found me."

Her sigh was so faint he could barely hear it. "I would have thought you'd learned by now that everything has its price. Thirty-five years ago unwanted babies were surprisingly easy to come by."

"So you just walked into an orphanage and picked me out?"

Sally's smile held no humor whatsoever. "If only it were that simple. I'm a careful woman, and I plan for eventualities. I was over forty when I got pregnant, and that didn't augur well for success. Even if the birth went well there was always the possibility that the baby would have Down syndrome, and I'd have to find a replacement."

He should have been appalled. Part of him was. Part of him knew her too well to be surprised at her calm ruthlessness. "So how did you manage it?"

"I heard about a girl who was pregnant, due around the time I was. She was from a good family, and the father was equally well-bred. He'd died in a car crash, and she was trying to hide the pregnancy from her parents. I helped her."

"In return for her child. What if your baby had survived?"

"Then I would have had the child put up for adoption, as the young lady wished."

"The young lady," Alex said softly. "My birth mother. Who was she?"

"It doesn't matter—she's dead now. Her family never even knew of your existence—they're dead as well. It's too late for touching family reunions."

"How did she die?"

Sally's eyes met his. "In childbirth."

"So I killed her."

"No, dearest," Sally said in a low voice devoid of regret. "I'm afraid I did."

CAROLYN MOVED away from the window, letting the curtain fall. Alex had slammed out of the house, and she had watched in silent surprise as the gravel spurted beneath the tires of his rusting Jeep as he tore down the driveway. Something must have set him off—he was an actor, a man in perfect control of his reactions. It had to have been something extraordinary to elicit such a reaction from him.

She leaned against the wall and closed her eyes, wondering if she'd imagined the incident out in the field that morning. She'd never seen a bullet, she'd never even heard the sound of a gunshot. She hadn't slept well in over a week, not since the prodigal son had returned to his happy home—it would be no wonder if she was beginning to get paranoid.

Maybe he realized that he didn't have anything to fear from her. She wasn't about to destroy Sally's last few weeks on this earth. And afterward, she didn't give a damn what happened to the money. If Warren wanted to commit felonies in order to get rapid access to it, then that was his business. She didn't even care about the small legacy Sally had told her she'd arranged for her. She just wanted to be away from the MacDowells for the rest of her life.

She'd always thought of them as her family. A not very close-knit, not very loving family, but family nonetheless. The last week had shown her all too clearly how wrong she'd been.

Odd, that didn't ignite the usual feelings of desolation and abandonment. Suddenly freedom loomed, in all its uncertainty, and while a small part of her was frightened by its vastness, she was past ready to go.

All she had to do was avoid being alone with the man pretending to be Alexander MacDowell.

Patsy had retired back to her room; Warren was sitting in the small library, going through the checkbook and looking both bored and impatient. Tessa and George were nowhere around, which left Sally.

The room was warm and dark, utterly still except for the sound of the various medical monitors. Carolyn stood in the door, watching her, trying desperately to distance herself from the old lady who had been her only mother, who was still the only family who cared about her.

And she was dying. In the last few days she'd seemed to shrink, draw in on herself. The first two days when she thought she had her son back, Sally had had more life and energy than Carolyn had seen in months. But she was paying for that burst of false health, moving further down that road toward death.

She was asleep, as she usually was, her pale, waxy face still in the shadows. The chair that usually resided by her bed had been pushed out of the way, as if someone had left in a rage and hadn't cared what he trashed as he went. A wastebasket lay spilled on the floor, a glass lay broken and crushed on the carpet.

Sally opened her eyes. It took her a moment to focus on Carolyn, and the disappointment was clear.

"I'll get someone to clean up this mess," Carolyn said softly, turning to go.

"No!" Sally's voice was nothing more than a raw hush. "Sit by me, Carolyn. I need to talk to you."

The pale white tracks of dried tears were almost indistinguishable on Sally's papery skin. But they were there, and Carolyn had never seen Sally MacDowell cry.

"Of course," she said, pulling the chair back beside the bed. She put her hand on Sally's trembling one. "Are you in a lot of pain? Should I try to find Mrs. Hathaway?"

Sally shook her head. "I don't think morphine will help this time. I'm paying for my sins, Carolyn. It's not that I don't deserve to. But let me tell you—I'm not enjoying myself."

"I can't imagine your sins have been that great that you have to suffer for them," Carolyn murmured.

"And I always thought your imagination was one of your strong points." Sally managed a faint smile. "I've done more wicked, selfish things than you can even begin to guess. Don't worry, I'm not about to make a deathbed confession. You don't need to hear about it, and there are some things I'd rather take with me to the grave."

"Maybe you'd feel better if you talked about it."

"Maybe. And maybe I don't deserve to feel better." She sighed, seeming to shrink back into the pillows.

"Alex is upset with you." It was a reasonable conclusion.

"As he should be." Sally glanced over at Carolyn. "I've done only one thing in this life that I can be proud of, Carolyn, and I'm afraid I've come very close to destroying that as well."

"You haven't destroyed Alex."

"That's not what I'm talking about. I can't take credit for the good things that Alex is, only the bad things. I'm more than responsible for that. No, the best thing I've done in my life is be your mother. Even if I was never able to adopt you, at least I brought you up with love and security. The sort of things you wouldn't have had . . ." Her voice trailed off, either from weariness, or the sudden knowledge that she'd said too much.

"You've been the best mother in the world to me," Carolyn said softly.

"Hardly that. But I tried." Sally sighed. "Stay with me, Carolyn. I'm afraid to be alone."

Sally MacDowell had never been afraid of anything or anybody in her entire life. "Of course I'll stay," she promised. "I'll be here as long as you want me."

I KILLED YOUR mother, she'd said. The woman who'd raised him, spoiled him, loved him, betrayed him.

Alex slammed his foot down on the accelerator, oblivious to the tall pines that flew by. He hadn't believed her. He'd even laughed at Sally's flat confession, certain it was some kind of sick joke.

"Sure you did," he'd said. "What did you do, hire a hit man just to cover up your tracks?"

And Sally had stared at him from bleak, sorrowful eyes. "My baby was premature, Alex. He died inside me, three weeks before he was due, and the doctors had to deliver him or I'd die. And I had to have a baby.

"It was easy enough if you had enough money. Easy enough to find the doctors to agree, easy enough to make that poor girl agree. They induced her, at my instructions. And when you still wouldn't come, they did a cesarean on her to get you out, and she bled to death. There were complications, and they couldn't stop the bleeding, and if she'd just been left to deliver on her own, when her body was ready, she would have been fine."

"You can't know that." He couldn't recognize his own voice.

"That's what the doctor told me. Of course, he was wanting a larger payoff, so maybe he was exaggerating. It didn't matter. In the end I was responsible. Playing God, trying to make everything go my way. They were buried together, you know. My baby and the woman who died giving birth to you. I used to wonder if she took care of my baby in heaven." She sighed. "These damned drugs. I can't keep my mouth shut once they start working. But I can't bear the pain. Maybe I should, as payment for my sins."

"What was her name?" Alex didn't bother to soften the cold anger in his voice. "Where was she buried?"

Sally had turned to look at him, her eyes glazed and drugged. "Dear boy, I had her buried in a pauper's grave under a phony name. I don't even remember which one."

And he'd gotten up and left her, knocking things over as he went.

Funny, he thought bitterly, he hadn't realized what a sentimental streak he still possessed. He'd always had the notion, in the back of his mind, that he'd find the woman who'd given birth to him. She had to be younger than Sally—chances are she was in her mid-fifties at the most. Sally was dying, and he hadn't wanted to cause her pain. He figured he could trace the woman who'd borne him after she died.

But there was no middle-aged woman waiting to welcome him. She'd died, died at the hands of a ruthless woman and incompetent doctors. Died giving birth to him, whether it was his fault or not.

He was twenty miles away from the MacDowell house before he pulled off the side of the road and turned off the motor. His hands were shaking, he noticed absently. He didn't ever remember his hands shaking before.

He should have stayed in Tuscany instead of returning to dig up a past better left buried. Sally would have given up on him long ago; his murderer had probably never given him a second thought.

There were some questions better left unanswered. But he'd come after those answers anyway, and now he was paying the price.

The best thing he could do was to keep driving. He didn't want their damned money, and had no intention of claiming it. He wanted to see the expression on Warren's face when he found out that he'd been duped by the real Alex the whole time, but apart from that, he had nothing left to accomplish. Whoever had tried to kill him had probably had very good reasons. Maybe it was the retired sportscaster whose car he had stolen that summer night eighteen years ago. Maybe it was a serial killer.

He didn't think so. Some member of his loving family had shot him in the back and dragged or thrown him into the ocean to drown. And for some reason, he no longer gave a damn. Some mysteries were better left unsolved.

If he went back he'd have to make his peace with Sally, and he wasn't ready to even look at her. If he went back he'd have to come to terms with Carolyn Smith, another mystery. If he went back . . .

He'd spent most of his life running. Running away from home, from responsibility, from family, from commitment. He was a loner, happier that way. He had acquaintances, he had a few close friends, but he always prided himself on needing no one.

But he was afraid he was going to start needing someone. Not just anyone. Carolyn.

He was too young to be going through a midlife crisis. Maybe it was simply a reaction to the idea of losing his mother. Losing two mothers in short order, he thought grimly. It was no wonder he was screwed up.

He couldn't stay a spoiled kid forever. Maybe it wasn't midlife, maybe it was simply the long-delayed inevitability of growing up. He couldn't run away. He could leave, but he had to make his peace with them before he left.

He had to face Sally and forgive her. No matter what she'd done, she was his mother, despite legalities or honor or blood ties.

And he had to face Carolyn Smith, or she'd haunt him the way she had for the last eighteen years. She was a woman, a quiet, bewitching, complicated woman, but only human. He'd never needed or wanted anyone in his life before. He wasn't going to start with a piece of his past.

He'd leave them both, but he'd say good-bye first.

And then he'd be free.

Chapter Seventeen

IT WAS MIDAFTERNOON when he drove back up the deceptively narrow drive to the MacDowell house. A light rain had begun to fall; the silver-gray bark on the maples had a faint blush to them. Spring was finally coming to the frozen reaches of Vermont. But Alexander MacDowell was tired of waiting.

He could hear voices in the living room, and the clink of glasses. It was early for cocktail hour, but Patsy was always one to start drinking as soon as she had the chance. He should go in, pour himself a stiff single-malt scotch and be pleasant. There were things that couldn't be changed.

Instead, he took a sharp right to Sally's suite of rooms. She was sleeping, her color even worse in the filtered afternoon light, and he stood at the end of her hospital bed, watching her, searching for anger, searching for forgiveness.

She was his mother. It was that simple, that basic. No matter what she had done, no matter who she was. Whether she regretted her selfish sins or not, she had always loved him to the best of her ability. And he loved her—he could accept that now. Just as he could accept it was time to let her go.

She wasn't alone in the room. He hadn't even noticed Carolyn in the shadows, curled up in the overstuffed chair, sound asleep. In the shifting shadows she looked ethereal and delicately beautiful. Odd that she had no idea how lovely she was. It seemed as if she'd done her best to negate any effect her beauty might have on people. It was simply a fact about her, like her blonde hair or the smattering of freckles across her elegant nose.

The room was still and silent, only the quiet whirr of the machines filling the air, a soothing white noise that blotted out the world. He took the chair at the end of the bed, folding his long limbs into it, and watched the two women who were so powerful in his life.

It was strange, almost dreamlike, as he let his gaze travel back and forth between the two of them, their faces blending, one old, one young, one aged and dying, one practically flawless. The elegant nose, the wide-set eyes, the same generous mouth. One old, one young. The same face. The same patrician, MacDowell face on both women.

He was too stunned to move, to react. How could he have missed it before? How could anyone have failed to see the powerful family resemblance? Once noticed, there was no way it could be ignored, and yet Carolyn had no idea, of that he was absolutely certain. She went through life as an outsider, one who was with the MacDowells on sufferance. She had no notion that she had more right to be here than he did.

But where did she come from? Sally would have been in her late forties when Carolyn was born—there was no way she could have been her mother. Tessa was only a few months older than Carolyn, which left Patsy out.

There were a few distant relatives, of course, but in truth the MacDowell lineage had proven surprisingly weak in the last few generations, and except for Patsy's brood, seemed likely to die out.

Which brought him to Warren. When he was a snotty teenager he used to wonder whether Warren was gay, and whether the elegant, well-bred women he occasionally dated were simply a smokescreen. It had seemed incomprehensible that a man could find other things more interesting than sex and passion.

But quite obviously sex and passion had ruled his life for at least a short time thirty years ago, or Carolyn Smith wouldn't exist.

He could be wrong. Warren had never evinced the slightest bit of paternal interest in Carolyn—he seemed to view her as a cross between an intrusion and a convenience, nothing more. When he'd briefed him on how to impersonate Alexander MacDowell, he'd dismissed Carolyn as a minor family retainer, of no possible interest or importance. As a matter of fact, if his memory served him properly, Warren even complained about the small trust fund Sally had set aside for her, saying it was totally unnecessary.

Maybe Warren wasn't Carolyn's father at all. But Alex wasn't putting any money on that possibility. Warren was the least paternal, least sentimental creature he'd ever met. He was willing to dupe his older sister on her deathbed in order to get his hands on more of her money. He probably wouldn't think twice about abandoning a daughter.

It was one too many shocks reeling through his mind, and Alex rose abruptly, silently, unwilling to face either woman with their secrets in his soul. He needed that drink after all, even if he had to face Aunt Patsy and

Uncle Warren to get it. He needed to get royally loaded, as drunk as he hadn't been in more years than he could remember.

"HOW'S YOUR MOTHER, dear boy?" Warren greeted him affably, the picture of expansive bonhomie.

"Dying," Alex said shortly, pouring himself a tall glass of straight scotch.

Warren winced. "We know that, Alex."

"Then why ask?" Alex took his drink and moved over to the French doors, turning his back on his loving family.

"In this family we believe in polite conversation, darling," Tessa purred, coming up behind him. She smelled of Poison, a remarkably apt perfume that had always turned his stomach, and she slid her hand up his arm.

"I've been on my own for too long," he said, taking a stiff drink of the whiskey. "My values have shifted."

"Values?" Patsy echoed with a slightly high-pitched laugh. "What are those?" She turned her overbright eyes toward her son. "Fix me another drink, would you, Georgie?"

"Don't call me Georgie," George snapped, his eyes pale and watchful.

"We're all getting a bit testy," Tessa murmured in Alex's ear. "Why don't you and I go someplace where we can be alone?"

He turned to look at her with an assessing gaze. "Is that a come-on, Tessa?"

She smiled a catlike smile. "Are you feeling queasy because we're cousins? Part of your 'values'? Don't worry about it, darling. Marriage between first cousins is perfectly legal in this state."

"I'm not planning to marry you, Tessa," he drawled.

"Actually I had other things in mind as well," she purred.

He considered it. For a long, lazy moment he looked down into her pampered, perfect face, down her elegant model's body, and wondered whether he could fuck Carolyn out of his system by screwing her first cousin.

He didn't think so.

He could see the resemblance between the two of them, of course, when he'd never noticed it before. They had the same long, elegant body, though Tessa was sporting a heroin-chic skinniness that was hardly conducive to lust. The same bone structure, though Tessa's mouth was thinner despite her collagen-puffed lips, less generous; and her eyes held an opaque glitter unlike Carolyn's eyes, which reflected her healthy, clear emotions.

No, he didn't want her. He didn't want any of them, or their money, or their lies. He wanted the truth, and then he wanted to get the hell out of there and never look back.

And he could only hope Carolyn would manage to escape as well.

He put his hand over Tessa's thin one and carefully removed it from his arm. "Thanks, but no thanks, Tessa," he said. "I'm not in the mood for recreational sex."

"Then what are you in the mood for?"

"Getting drunk."

"That never solved anything, Alex," Warren intoned. "I know you're grieving the imminent loss of your mother, and feeling tremendous guilt over the long separation between the two of you, but I assure you—"

"Go to hell, Uncle Waldo."

Warren's carefully groomed, artificially tanned face paled in sudden shock. "I'd forgotten you used to call me that," he said in a strangled voice. "I hadn't thought of that in over twenty years."

It had been a stupid, rebellious move on Alex's part, and he should have known better. "It suits you," he said. He grabbed the bottle of Glenlivet and another glass from the tray and headed for the door. "If you'll all excuse me, I think I'll join my cousin in a deathwatch."

"Your cousin? Which one do you mean?" George demanded. Patsy was sitting in the corner, humming to herself, glassy-eyed and vague, and Warren was still staring at him in horrified shock.

"Carolyn," Alex answered. "Dear, sweet, loyal Cousin Carolyn."

"She's not our cousin, Alex," Tessa said sharply.

"Isn't she?" He glanced at Warren, who looked as if he was ready to vomit. "Maybe you're in for a few surprises."

Carolyn stirred sleepily when he walked in, opening her eyes to watch him in surprise as he poured her a drink and set it down on the medicine-littered table beside her.

"I figured you'd need this," he said, retaking his seat at the foot of the bed.

She made no move to touch the glass. "I don't think Aunt Sally needs you in here drinking yourself into a stupor," she whispered.

"Aunt Sally wants him here, drunk or sober," came a voice from the bed.

It almost sounded like a voice beyond the grave. Sally didn't open her eyes, didn't move, but she reached out her hand for him.

"Then I'll leave . . ." Carolyn started for the door, but Alex stopped her before Sally's voice could.

"I need you both," Sally said. She opened her eyes then, and the effort to focus on them seemed to take all her strength.

He wasn't about to release Carolyn so that she could run away. He had no guarantee that her love for Sally would overpower her feelings about him, and he was taking no chances. He led her back to her chair and pushed her down lightly, then put the drink in her hand.

"We're both here, Mom." He hadn't called her that since he'd been a little boy, eschewing it as far too sentimental. Sally's eyes filled with sudden tears.

"Are you my best boy?" she whispered, an old litany from his earliest memory, a last attempt at asking forgiveness.

"Always," he replied, leaning over and kissing her cool, papery cheek, granting it.

And he retook his seat at the end of the bed and poured himself another drink.

He'd learned years ago that he had a real problem in holding his liquor. The problem was, he had an almost endless capacity for it and he never passed out. At three in the morning, with Sally stabilized, he left the room and went in search of a cup of coffee and a shower. At five in the morning he went for a walk in the icy mist. At six in the morning he found Carolyn in the hallway, her narrow shoulders shaking with silent sobs.

He looked past her into the sickroom. Sally lay propped against the pillows, almost smaller than she had been before. He moved quickly to the bed, but Sally looked up at him with calm determination. "Take care of her, Alex," she whispered.

"I don't think she wants me to."

"She wants you. Take her away and let me get some sleep. Please." There was a faint, almost beguiling smile on her face, one he knew too well. He knew what she planned, he knew how she wanted it, and he wasn't going to be the one to stop her.

He kissed her good-bye, very gently, and she smiled up at him. "You take care of her," she said again. "Promise me."

"I will."

He closed the door behind him with silent deliberation. Carolyn looked up, startled, her face streaked with tears, but he didn't waste any time. He simply pulled her into his arms, pressed her face against his shoulder, and held her.

She fought him, so he kissed her. She punched at him, and he simply scooped her up in his arms.

He didn't know where to take her. Carrying her upstairs was too melodramatic; besides, she was likely to scream the house down. There were no beds downstairs except for Sally's, and he doubted if anyone had made up the folding sofa in the library. It didn't matter. He carried her in there, dumped her in an overstuffed chair and proceeded to jam chairs under the various doorways.

"What do you think you're doing?" The words were barely audible, muffled in tears and outrage, and he ignored them as he pulled out the sofa. The bottom sheet was still on the mattress, but he had no idea where the pillows and the covers were. He didn't need them.

He came over to her, and she'd already risen from the chair, prepared for battle. He was calm, predatory as he reached up and began to unbutton her shirt. She slapped at his hands in a vain attempt at stopping him, but he simply ripped the pale silk shirt open.

"I thought you weren't going to touch me until I asked you?" she said in a furious whisper.

"Ask me." He pushed the shirt from her shoulders, then reached for the waistband of her jeans.

"Go to hell," she said, and kicked him in the shins.

He caught her face in his hands, holding it still, tilting her mouth up to his. "Ask me," he said again, his mouth hovering inches from hers.

She stopped struggling. Her face was wet with tears, she looked lost and broken and so damned sweet.

"For what?" she whispered.

"For anything you want."

"What about the truth?"

"I don't know if you really want it," he said.

He expected her to deny it, to explode in a rage. She surprised him, as she often did. "Maybe you're right. Maybe there are things I don't want to know." She closed her eyes, and her eyelashes were wet with tears. "Kiss me."

He was too startled to move. "What?"

"You said any damned thing I want," she said in a small, tight voice. "I want you to kiss me. I want you to lie in that bed with me and make me forget everything. Forget what a liar you really are, forget that Sally's dying, forget that someone tried to kill me. I want to see if you're good enough to distract me."

He slid his hands down to the lacy white bra covering her small, perfect breasts. "I'm good enough," he said in a low voice.

"Prove it," she said. "Do it."

He looked down at her, at her face full of anguish and need. If he were a good man, a decent man, he would simply lie on the bed and hold her. But he'd never been a good man, his sense of honor was nil, and he needed to lose himself in the sweetness of her body just as much as she needed it.

The room was dark, shadowed, only the early-morning light coming in from the uncurtained windows. Her face was shadowed as well, but it didn't seem to matter. They lived in shadows, the two of them, with secrets and lies surrounding them.

But what lay between them was real. And that was all that mattered.

He kissed her then, a slow, deep, claiming kiss, and her fingers dug into his shoulders and she trembled. He'd never made a woman tremble before, but Carolyn was different from all the women he'd had over the years. He was through fighting it—he had too many other things to fight. He could lose himself in her body, in her soul. And he wanted it.

"You ran away the last time," he whispered against her mouth. "Are you going to run away again?"

"No."

"Even though I'm a cheat and a liar and a con man and a thief?"

"Are you?"

"Do you care?"

"No," she said in a fierce little voice. "I want you. I don't care who you are, I don't care what you are—none of it matters. I need you."

He hadn't realized he'd been holding some sort of rein on his emotions. Her words broke it, broke through the formidable self-control he'd built up since he was a child.

She didn't want to think, and neither did he. He took a step away from her. "Take off the rest of your clothes," he said hoarsely, pulling his sweater over his head.

For a moment she hesitated. Her eyes never leaving his, she reached for the snap of her jeans. She skinned them off, but she was still wearing plain white underwear and a pair of socks. There was something ridiculously beguiling about those socks, and he didn't want her to take them off.

He shoved his jeans off, stepping out of them, but she still kept her eyes on his. They'd made love before, she hadn't been a virgin, and yet she was still shy about bodies. His and hers. "Get on the bed," he said.

He could see her uncertainty, and he knew he couldn't force her. "Change your mind?" he asked quietly.

She didn't move. "Have you?"

"Look lower and you'll get your answer." Her gaze dropped to his erection, then jerked away. "We already agreed I'm too crude for you, Carolyn," he taunted. "You can still run away. This is your decision this time. I'm not going to force you, not going to make it easy for you. If you want to get your clothes back on and leave, go ahead."

"I'm afraid," she said in a very quiet voice.

"I know you are. And I can't figure out why. We've already done it once and you didn't suffer any Victorian trauma. You know I won't force you, you know I won't hurt you. What's the problem?"

She stood very still. "I'm afraid I'll fall in love with you."

He didn't know what to say to that. And then a faint, reluctant smile curved his mouth. "Well, you can't say I haven't been doing everything I can to keep that from happening."

It started a laugh out of her. "True," she said.

"Listen," he said. "I know all about you. About your relationships, about your weaknesses. Warren had very thorough notes on everyone in this household. You don't make stupid mistakes when it comes to men. You get involved with decent, sensible men. You don't fall in love with bad boys. I'll just be a temporary fluke."

"I was in love with the real Alex."

He could only hope she couldn't see his reaction. "You were thirteen when he left," he said roughly. "Thirteen-year-old girls don't know anything about love. And he was a selfish, spoiled brat who didn't care who he hurt."

"I loved him."

He wanted her to stop saying that. He wanted her to say it again. She was very calm now, as if she'd made up her mind, and he was willing to let her go.

"Listen, babe," he said with a deliberate drawl. "It's getting light, and sooner or later the family's going to start bustling around. Do you want to do it or not?"

He waited for her to grab her clothes and storm from the room. She looked at him slowly, letting her eyes move down the length of his body, dancing across the white scarred line across his hip, then moving to his cock.

That was one major problem with being a man. You couldn't

pretend disinterest if you were standing there naked, with a half-dressed woman watching you. And not just any half-dressed woman. But Carolyn—sweet, tart-tongued, fiercely loyal Carolyn. He wanted her without lies, he wanted her every way he could take her. He wanted her whether she wanted him or not, but he wasn't going to make a move.

He didn't need to. She crossed the room, and before he realized what she was planning to do she sank to her knees in front of him and took him in her mouth.

He climaxed immediately, half in shock, unable to stop himself, and she held his hips with her strong hands, taking him, as he struggled vainly for control that was lost the moment she put her mouth on him. And then she sat back on her heels and looked up at him out of calm, knowing eyes.

They didn't make it to the bed. He shoved her down on the rug, following her down, yanking the rest of the clothes off her in savage haste. He was still hard, and she was completely aroused by what she'd done, and he slid deeply into her, pulling her hips up higher so that he could fill her.

She convulsed around him, and he knew a fierce satisfaction in it, as he put his mouth over hers and drank in her strangled cries of completion.

Her climax was endless, shuddering, and he almost came again before she finally stilled, panting, her eyes glazed. He pulled away from her, and she reached out for him in sudden desperation.

"Turn over," he said. "I want you that way."

He half expected her to object. She didn't. She did what he wanted, and her strangled cry of pleasure when he pushed back inside her almost finished him.

He wanted, needed to make it last. To take her every way he could think of, and more, so there would be no more secrets between them, no more lies. She was even tighter from this angle, and he tried to think of something else, to slow himself down, but he couldn't, all he could think and feel and hear was Carolyn, the soft, desperate little cries she was making, the rich scent of sex in the air, the silky smoothness of her back, the deep, clenching tightness of her.

He reached between her legs and touched her, and she exploded, her scream no longer muffled, a sobbing cry of complete surrender and savage, ultimate pleasure.

And he gave himself up to it, filling her with everything he had left, pouring into her.

He wanted to throw his head back and howl in animal triumph. He wanted it to last forever, feral and real and all encompassing. Time seemed to stop, an endless, surreal moment, where only the two of them existed in the universe.

And then he looked up, and saw the faint shadow of someone watching them through the French doors.

Alex leaned over and wrapped his body around Carolyn's, protective, covering her. She was drenched with sweat, trembling, and he knew she needed to collapse as much as he did. He glanced back at the window, but whoever had been watching was now gone, vanished, and there was no way he could tell who it had been, man or woman.

He rolled to his side, taking her with him, moving surreptitiously out of range of the windows. He wasn't about to tell her someone had been watching, but he wasn't going to give any pitiful voyeur another chance. She was shivering, trembling, but there was nothing he could grab to throw over her, he could only try to warm and calm her with the strength of his own body.

Slowly she stilled, her breathing returning to normal. He almost thought she'd fallen asleep, wrapped up tight against him, when he heard her voice. "I lied to you," she whispered.

"Did you?" The floor wasn't the most comfortable spot in the world, but it made no difference. He had no interest in moving. "About anything important?"

"You remember when I said I was afraid I might fall in love with you?" He could feel the shaky breath vibrate through her body. "It may be too late."

And he lay there, wrapped around her, afraid to tell her one more lie.

Chapter Eighteen

THE EARLY-MORNING sun had begun to pour in through the French doors that led onto the terrace, mercilessly bright. Merciless was a good word, Carolyn thought, trying to make herself as still and small as she could with Alex's body enveloping hers. There was no hiding from the glare of the clear morning sunshine as it moved across the carpeting to the spot where they lay, entwined.

She had no illusions that he might be asleep. Fate hadn't been particularly kind to her in the last few days, and she doubted she'd be granted that particular dispensation. She was simply going to have to gather any remaining shreds of dignity left to her, pull herself out of his arms and somehow manage to get dressed.

She'd made a fool of herself on every level, and to top it all off she'd made the ultimate, idiotic confession. She should have known she'd tell him, sooner or later. She'd never been particularly sensible or self-protective when it came to those she loved, and the man pretending to be Alexander MacDowell had somehow become one of the select few, whether he deserved it or not.

Of course he didn't deserve it. He was a fraud and a cheat. But he'd been genuinely loving with Sally—she couldn't fault him for that.

She needed to get away from him. She needed to check in on Sally. She started to pull away, and for a moment his arms tightened around her, as if he were reluctant to let her go. And then he released her, rolling onto his back, and she knew he was watching her as she sat up.

"Keep out of range of the windows," he said in an unexpectedly prosaic voice. "You never know who might be wandering around out there."

Her bra was in reach, and she grabbed for it, struggling into it with her back turned to him. She searched around for the rest of her clothing. Her jeans and shirt were halfway across the room, but she had no idea where her panties were.

"Looking for these?"

She had no choice but to turn back to him. He was holding the wisp of white cotton in one of his large hands, and his expression was absolutely unreadable. She snatched them away from him, pulling them on over her sticky body with as much dignity as she could muster, which was just about nil. With that much clothing on she felt slightly better, and she turned to look at him, ready to tell him to get out of her life, forever, when she noticed something.

He had turned away from her, looking out the window, and she saw the scar on his shoulder, one she hadn't noticed before. It was oddly round, with rough edges, shiny. It mesmerized her, like the eyes of a cobra, and without thinking she reached out toward it.

He turned back, his eyes meeting hers, and he didn't move, didn't flinch as she touched the ancient scar with delicate fingers. "What is that?" she whispered.

"What do you think it is, Carolyn? It's an eighteen-year-old scar from a bullet."

Someone was trying to force the door, and she whirled away in sudden panic, but the chair Alex had stuck beneath it held. "Carolyn, are you in there?" George's voice sounded surprisingly intense. "You'd better come out, fast."

She scrambled to her feet. "I'll be there in a minute, George," she called. "Is Sally worse?"

"Have you seen Alex? We can't find him anywhere."

Alex had already stood, yanking on his jeans with a complete disregard for his nudity and her watching eyes. Alex. The real Alex. The lying, deceitful, very real Alex MacDowell.

Carolyn was buttoning her shirt as she pulled the chair away from the door and opened it, uncaring whether George or anyone else knew what she'd been doing. "What is it?" she demanded.

But Alex had already come up beside her, taking her arm, moving her away from George before he could answer.

She considered struggling, then stopped, as the enormity of what was happening hit her.

Patsy and Warren were in the dining room, arguing loudly, their voices carrying through the downstairs. In the distance Carolyn could hear Constanza sobbing.

And Sally's body lay empty and abandoned in her hospital bed. A bottle of pills lay scattered on the table beside it, and some littered the starched white sheet. But obviously, even in her weakened condition, she'd managed to take enough.

Carolyn stood, unmoving, as Alex walked past her. They hadn't even closed her eyes as she stared sightlessly toward the ceiling, or removed her oxygen. Vaguely she wondered where Mrs. Hathaway was, then dismissed the thought. It didn't matter. Aunt Sally had been ready to go, and she was never a woman to sit and wait when appropriate action could be taken.

She watched as Alex gently closed her eyes, then removed the oxygen tube from her nose and set it on the table, turning off the machines with calm efficiency. And then he turned and looked at Carolyn, and his Cossack eyes were very calm. "Do you want to say good-bye to her before the others start fighting over the spoils?"

"Aren't you going to fight, too? Isn't that why you came back?"

He shook his head. "I came back for her. I came back for the truth. She's gone, and it doesn't matter now. I'm ready to leave."

She nodded, her emotions frozen. She walked past him, taking the seat she'd abandoned a few hours earlier. "Did you know she was going to do this?"

"I guessed."

"And you didn't try to stop her?"

"Would you?"

"No." She curled her feet up underneath her. "Good-bye, Alex."

He left her without a word.

SHE HAD MORE time than she would have imagined. Sally's family kept their distance, though the raised voices that echoed back left little doubt about the subject of their cantankerous discussion. It didn't matter. Carolyn sat in the shadows by Sally's bedside, keeping a vigil that would mean nothing to anyone but herself.

She didn't want to leave her alone, even though the Sally she'd loved and protected had already left. She had little doubt someone had seen to the formalities, and someone would come to take away the body before long. In the meantime, Carolyn wasn't going to leave her unattended. It was ridiculous and old-fashioned, but she couldn't stop from feeling she needed to honor her dead.

It must have been hours before Mrs. Hathaway came in, flustered, tearful, anxious. She cast a nervous glance at Carolyn before she swept away the spilled pills, the remnants of painkillers that littered the tables beside the bed. "I'm sorry I wasn't here," she said in a low voice. "Mr. MacDowell insisted I take the night off, that he'd stay with her. If I'd had any idea I never would have left."

"Alex can be very persuasive," Carolyn said in a dull voice.

"Oh, no, it was Warren who sent me away," Mrs. Hathaway corrected her. "He said he wanted time with his sister."

Carolyn just shook her head. Sometime during the last few hours her mind, her emotions, had overloaded, and she'd gone into a blessed state of numbness. It didn't matter who said what. It didn't matter who was who. All that mattered was that Sally was gone, and for good or bad, Carolyn's life would never be the same.

"It's not your fault," Carolyn murmured. "She was more than ready to go."

The arguments from the living room seemed to have died down a bit, and she could hear the sound of a car pulling up in front of the house. She glanced outside and saw the local undertaker's hearse. A Mercedes, only the best for the MacDowells. She rose, touching Sally's hand in a final farewell.

"She was a good lady," Mrs. Hathaway said with a sniffle.

Carolyn didn't bother to argue the point. She had loved Sally dearly, but Sally Aylebourne MacDowell was too strong, stubborn, and ruthless to be called a good lady. "I'll go see if any of the others want a moment or two alone with her before they take her away."

"You do that, Miss Carolyn," she said. "I'll just make sure the poor lady is tidied up."

It was a waste of time, and Carolyn knew it the moment she stepped inside the library. Warren and George were in the midst of some heated discussion and barely noticed her presence, Patsy merely smiled dazedly, and Tessa didn't bother with any civilities.

"They've come to remove Aunt Sally's body," she said baldly. "Did any of you want a last moment alone with her?"

"Don't be macabre, darling," Tessa said with a dramatic shudder. "I don't care for corpses."

"Who's come to remove the body?" Warren demanded, looking up. "I didn't make any arrangements."

"Someone must have called the funeral parlor," George said. "Someone high-handed."

"It must have been Alex," Tessa said, with a faint, smug smile on her artificially puffed mouth. "After all, it's his mother."

There was no missing the dark look that passed over Warren's face. "I don't think any of us need to see her," he said after a moment. "After all, she's gone."

"So she is," Carolyn said in a deceptively calm voice. "If no one minds, I think I'll go for a drive. I'd like to get out for a bit."

"But we might need you—" George objected, but Warren immediately overruled him.

"We don't need Carolyn's help, son," he said. "I think we're more than capable of handling this."

Carolyn didn't even blink. "I'll be back in a while."

"Er . . . which car were you thinking of taking?" Warren demanded. "I'll be needing the Mercedes, and I'm not certain—"

"I'll take my car." At his perplexed look, she swiftly amended it. "The Toyota."

"It's in your name?"

"I bought it, Uncle Warren. Out of my own money. And I'll be taking it with me when I leave," she said matter-of-factly.

"Of course you will," George said heartily. "We wouldn't suggest anything else."

"Anything else," Patsy echoed, her eyes bright. With unshed tears for her sister, or with something else, Carolyn couldn't be sure.

She hadn't driven her car in days, even weeks. Not since long before Alex had shown up. It sat in a corner of the huge garage that had been built to look like a carriage house, small and unprepossessing among all the more expensive cars belonging to the extended family of MacDowells. Except, of course, for Alex's rusty black Jeep.

She'd lost the feel for her car, she decided, as she started down the long, narrow driveway toward the tiny village of Stanton. The brakes felt spongy beneath her foot, the accelerator sluggish, even the steering seemed unusually recalcitrant. She wasn't planning on staying with the MacDowells for a moment longer than she had to—just through whatever memorial service they planned for Sally, and then she'd be out of there. But she'd better take the car in for a once-over before she embarked on any kind of long drive.

The car was picking up speed, hurtling down the narrow, hilly drive with dangerous enthusiasm. She tapped the brakes, but the car barely responded, gathering speed as she neared the sharp corner that led down the last stretch of driveway to the main road.

She stomped hard, only to have the pedal go straight to the floor. She tried to shift down, but the gearshift wouldn't move, and the speedometer was moving higher and higher.

She didn't stop to think. Unfastening her seat belt, she opened the door and rolled out, landing in a clump of dirt as her car continued on without her. She lay in the rubble, trying to catch her breath, barely conscious of the great crashing, rending noise of her car as it crashed into something up ahead.

She struggled to sit up. Her hands were cut and bleeding from her fall, her ankle was twisted, and her tiny, beloved car was gone.

She was shaking, past tears. She struggled to her feet, barely able to put her weight on her left ankle. The house was more than a mile away—it wasn't much further to the main road, where presumably she could hitch a ride. She could just disappear, go away and never be seen again. Turn her back on the small trust fund Sally had set up for her, turn her back on the family who had never been hers.

Turn her back on Alexander MacDowell.

Except that her purse was back at the house, with all her identification, credit cards, and cash. The idea of disappearing without a trace was hypnotic, but the reality of it was far too difficult. Maybe a seventeen-year-old rebel could do it, but not a sensible, thirty-one-year-old woman.

She was halfway back to the house when she heard the car coming up the road. She knew who it was immediately—that noisy rumble was unlike any of the MacDowells' well-tuned luxury cars. Even if she hadn't recognized the sound of the Jeep, she knew full well who would bother to come after her.

Maybe the man who had sabotaged her car in the first place? The man who had shot at her in the woods, the man who was determined to get rid of her.

But now that Sally was dead, why would any of this matter? She stood her ground, watching as he turned the corner, wondering whether he'd plow into her while she stood waiting.

The Jeep ground to a halt inches away from her, and he slammed open the door, looming up over her like the wrath of God. She could pride herself on the fact that she met his onslaught calmly. She didn't even flinch.

"Are you trying to get yourself killed?" he demanded, grabbing her arm roughly and dragging her out of the road.

"It wasn't my idea," she muttered, not bothering to struggle.

"Where's your car?"

"Crashed somewhere on the road ahead. My brakes failed so I jumped out." Her voice didn't even shake.

He halted, staring down at her. There was no reading anything in his expression apart from complete fury. "Your brakes failed?" he echoed. "What the hell is that supposed to mean?"

"One of two things. Either I don't have proper maintenance done on my car, or someone is trying to kill me. I vote for the latter. And I vote for you."

He looked at her in utter astonishment. "You think I'm trying to kill you? Why?"

"You were out yesterday morning when someone shot at me. As far as I know everyone else but Patsy was still asleep."

"When did someone shoot at you? I don't remember you saying a word about it!"

"I didn't think anyone would believe me."

"So you thought you'd just wait around till someone tried it again. Very wise. And what makes you think I'm the one who'd most like to kill you? Though right now I wouldn't come up with much of an argument. I'd like to strangle you."

"You have the most to lose," she said with icy certainty.

"Why? What do I have to lose?"

She opened her mouth to answer, then stopped, disconcerted. "Sally—" she began.

"Sally's dead. And I don't give a shit about any inheritance—I'm planning on getting out of here before someone decides to use me for target practice as well. I don't have any reason to want you dead, apart from the fact that you do your best to annoy me. And I've given up murdering people who annoy me in my old age."

"Then who tampered with my brakes?"

He knew. She could tell by the sudden, odd expression in his face that he had a very good idea exactly who might have tried to kill her.

"Get in the car," he said abruptly.

"I'm not going anywhere with you."

"Get in the goddamned car, Carolyn, or I'll tie you up and throw you in," he said in a low, dangerous tone of voice.

She wasn't going to get away from him. His grip on her wrist was iron hard and painful, and with her twisted ankle she'd have no chance of outrunning him.

"All right," she said at last.

She'd managed to startle him. "You've decided to be reasonable? How novel."

"No," she said. "I just decided if anyone was going to murder me I think I'd prefer it was you."

"Bitch," he said genially, opening the door for her.

She climbed in, casting one last, longing glance toward escape. And then she noticed the suitcases in the back seat. Including her own small one.

He was already behind the wheel. "Fasten your seat belt," he said, putting the car in gear.

"What are you doing with my things? Where are we going?"

"We're getting the hell out of here. You may be willing to face death like an early-Christian martyr, but frankly I'm not interested in dying young. I did it once already, and it's highly overrated."

He'd shocked her into silence. She fastened the seat belt around her with shaking fingers, then clutched the door handle as he tore down the narrow road at breakneck speed. They passed her car smashed up against an outcropping of rock, but he made no attempt at slowing down, he just kept driving. She looked away, shuddering.

She waited until they'd reached the main road. It was deserted, and she realized with dismay that it was already late afternoon. She'd lost all track of time, she hadn't eaten in what seemed like days, and she was being kidnapped by a criminal. Or was she?

"Who the hell are you?" she said finally.

"Who do you think I am?" He kept his eyes glued to the road.

"I've given up trying to figure it out. Why don't you be original and tell me the truth for a change?"

He still didn't look at her. Instead he reached into his jeans pocket for something. "Hold out your hand, Carolyn."

She did so, expecting God knew what. Anything but the tiny pile of gold he placed in her palm.

It was her gold charm bracelet. The one he'd stolen from her the night he left, the one thing she begged him not to take. It was still there—each delicate charm that Sally had chosen for her over the years was intact. She stared down at it in disbelief. It had been eighteen years since she'd last seen it—she'd almost forgotten how precious it had once been.

It was a while before she found her voice. "Why do you still have it?"

"I'll never forget your face that night," he said, his voice distant. "You looked so bereft, and I couldn't figure out if it was because I was going or because I was taking your most precious possession. I knew you had a massive crush on me back then. I used to think if I could bring you back the bracelet, if I could keep from pawning it, then when I brought it back to you you'd tell me I was more important than a goddamned piece of gold."

"I didn't care that it was valuable. I cared that it came from Sally. She brought me here, took care of me, loved me—"

"You still don't get it, do you? The MacDowells don't do anything out of selfless motives."

"Sally loved me—"

"Maybe. She always loved to be surrounded by pretty things, and you know it. But she didn't just happen to pick you up off a street corner, you know. It was no accident that she brought you back here."

"What are you talking about?"

"Haven't you ever wondered why someone like Sally MacDowell would bring home the bastard child of a former servant? She who usually kept her charity work at arm's length?"

"Don't!"

"Didn't you ever ask? Don't you want to know where you came from? Why she brought you home to be part of the family?"

"Stop it!" Her voice rose to a wild edge. He was silent for a moment, concentrating on the road. He glanced over at her for a moment, then back.

"Well, when you're ready to know the truth, you can ask me," he said.

"You haven't impressed me as someone with an intimate acquaintance with the truth."

"I know it when I see it. Whether I like it or not."

A sudden suspicion entered her mind, filling her with such sick horror that she couldn't push it away. "You aren't going to tell me you're really my brother, are you?"

He threw back his head and laughed. "Wrong. Trust me, Carolyn, we have no blood relationship at all. Not even a whiff of incest."

"Then if we're not related, what's the big secret?"

"I'll tell you when we get where we're going."

"Where are we going? And why?"

"I'm saving your life, Carolyn." Then he added, almost as an afterthought, "And mine."

Chapter Nineteen

SHE LOOKED LIKE holy hell. He didn't want to take the risk of stopping on the way south, but she looked like she was at the very end of her endurance, so he pulled into a diner by the Massachusetts border and practically force-fed her something from the all-day breakfast menu. She ate automatically, refusing to look at him, her hands bruised and bloody, her face scratched, her demeanor frighteningly calm. He considered taking her to a hospital to get her ankle x-rayed, then decided against it. She wasn't limping too badly, and the sooner they reached their destination the better.

He should have realized they would have missed the last ferry by the time they reached Woods Hole. She sat in the car passively enough as he made a reservation for the first boat over in the morning, saying nothing when he drove into a nondescript motel and got them a room for the night.

She went straight into the bathroom, and he could hear the shower running full force. He'd already checked—there was no other way out of the room, so he knew there was no way she could escape, if she suddenly had the crazy need to. The motel didn't come with room service, but he found a place that delivered Chinese food and called in a huge order. By the time she came out, looking like a pale, drowned rat in a baggy t-shirt and oversized jeans, he was setting the cartons out on the table.

"Don't bother telling me you're not hungry," he said, forestalling her instant protest. "You need to eat, and if you don't cooperate I'll tie you to the bed and pour fried rice down your throat."

A faint, answering smile would have been too much to hope for. Instead she simply sat on one of the hard little chairs and reached for the can of soda he'd gotten from the machine outside.

There were no plates, so he simply shoved the carton of lo mein at her, along with a pair of chopsticks, then started in on his own beef and broccoli. "You can have the egg rolls," he said, breaking the silence. "They have shrimp in them."

That broke through her numbness. She jerked her head up to look at him, and her eyes were bleak. "Why are we here?"

"We missed the last ferry."

"That's not what I mean and you know it. Why did we come here? Why are we going back to the Vineyard?"

"Unresolved business. I want to know who shot me. No one seems to be able to pry that information out of your brain, and I'm not comfortable letting go of it, particularly now that someone's started using you for target practice. I thought I could just forget about it and get on with my life, but I guess I'm not as forgiving as I thought I was. Particularly since someone seems to be up to his old tricks."

She picked at the lo mein with a complete lack of interest. "What do you mean?"

"Whoever shot at you, whoever tampered with your brakes, is presumably the same person who thought they'd killed me eighteen years ago. At least, I'm assuming it's the same person. They were all in the Vineyard the night someone shot me, and I'd hope there aren't two would-be murderers in the MacDowell family."

"Why would they want to kill me? I have nothing to do with you." There wasn't even a trace of defiance in her flat voice.

"Isn't it obvious? We both happen to be a singular inconvenience to anyone interested in inheriting the bulk of Sally's estate."

"My trust fund isn't going to make a hell of a lot of difference in the scheme of things. Not when you consider how much Sally left. Besides, the trust fund is already in place—my death wouldn't change it." She pushed the carton of food away from her.

"Well, maybe our busy little murderer doesn't realize that. Or maybe he knows perfectly well you could have a much greater claim if you chose to exert it."

"What are you talking about?"

"Eat your dinner."

"I'm not hungry, and I'm not going to eat another bite until you explain yourself." Anger had finally begun to splinter through her unnatural calm. Anger, and a trace of fear. She didn't want to hear what he was going to tell her. She didn't want to know the truth.

"Haven't you ever wondered where you came from?" he said, putting his own carton of food down on the Formica-topped table. "Didn't you ever bother to ask, ever think about why Sally would bring you home to live with us? She certainly didn't make a habit of picking up strays." He couldn't keep the cynicism out of his voice, remembering his own origins, but Carolyn took it wrong.

"You don't need to remind me," she said bitterly. "I don't belong. I was here on sufferance. I have no right to be among the MacDowells."

"Didn't you ever ask where she found you?"

"I know where she found me. No one's ever made any secret of it. I'm the illegitimate child of someone who used to work for her."

"Nice of Sally."

"She hasn't been dead for twenty-four hours, Alex," she said sharply.

"That doesn't make her a saint, and she'd be the first one to tell you so."

"You know the story as well as I do. Sally was always fond of the woman, and when she died Sally decided to see that I was taken care of."

"She could have just written a check every month. And don't tell me that wasn't Sally's style. You know perfectly well she preferred her charity long-distance. What made her bring you into the house?"

"Obviously, you have some theory," Carolyn said, her icy calm vanishing. "Why don't you share it?"

He tipped his chair back, surveying her with a remote air. "You're a MacDowell," he said flatly.

She didn't blink. "Sure."

"Haven't you ever noticed the resemblance? You and Tessa could be twins."

"You're out of your mind. My mother was a Swedish nanny—"

"She might very well have been. But your father was Warren MacDowell."

All color left her face. She stared at him with a kind of sick shock. "No," she said flatly.

"Yes. There's no other explanation. Sally was too old, and Patsy had just had Tessa. The bloodlines in the MacDowell family have run very thin these last few generations. Too much inbreeding, I'd guess. The only other living MacDowell is an ancient great-aunt in a nursing home in England and a second cousin who's both too young and gay. No one else."

"I'm not a MacDowell."

"You know you are," he said. "And that's always been the problem. Deep in your heart you've known you belong."

"You're crazy," she said, but he could see the dawn of doubt in her eyes that were so like Tessa's.

"Why don't you ask Warren?"

She pushed away from the table in sudden fury. "I'm not asking

Warren a goddamned thing. Now that Sally's gone I don't care about the rest of your sick family. If Warren happened to have fathered me I'm sure he knows it was the worst mistake of his life, and he's not about to admit it. And I don't want to know. I don't want to see or talk with any MacDowell ever again in my entire life." She was looking around the room in desperation. "And that includes you."

"What are you looking for?"

"My shoes. I'm getting the hell out of here."

"No, you aren't," he said with deceptive calm. "I told you, you aren't safe."

"And I told you I don't want to spend another minute with any of the MacDowells."

"Fine. I'm not a MacDowell."

Instantly he realized that was a tactical error. She was a strong, resilient woman, but she'd been through too much in the last few days, culminating in Sally's death that morning. She picked up a chair and threw it at him.

He managed to knock it out of his way and leap up after her. She'd opened the door, halfway out, barefoot or not, when he caught her arm and dragged her back in, slamming the door shut behind her and pushing her up against it. His own tenuous hold on his temper had snapped as well, and he didn't care. He loomed over her, trapping her, holding her there, as she fought against him, her strong fists pounding against his chest, her bare feet kicking his shins, as a litany of pathetically lame curses came from her mouth.

He caught her shoulders and shook her once, hard, shocking her into momentary silence. Tears were pouring down her pale face, the tears she hadn't shed since Sally's body had been found. "Someone needs to teach you how to swear," he muttered.

She took a deep, shuddering breath. "Who the fuck are you?" she demanded hoarsely.

A small, reluctant smile cracked his face. "That's better. I'm Alexander MacDowell, and you know it."

"Which would supposedly make you my first cousin," she said bitterly.

He shook his head. "The only person in this room with MacDowell blood is you. Sally's only child died before he was born—she managed to find another baby boy to substitute for her own."

Carolyn stopped fighting. She leaned her head back against the door, staring up at him. "You're crazy!"

He shook his head. "Why do you suppose Sally was so dead set against DNA tests? She knew nothing would be proved. I'm the changeling in the family, Carolyn. Not you." She looked up at him in shock, and he couldn't resist touching her face, the silky smooth, pale skin. "Not you," he repeated softly, leaning his forehead against hers. "Not you."

HE LEFT HER alone. After she pushed him away he stepped back, and made no move to touch her again. She could be grateful for that much, Carolyn thought in a blinding daze of pain. If he touched her again she would crumble, and she couldn't afford to let that happen.

She was cold, so cold. She'd lost track of the time, but it didn't matter. She crawled into one of the queen-sized beds and pulled the covers up tight around her face, shutting out the world, shutting out the man who seemed to have been the harbinger of everything disastrous in her life. If she could sleep then maybe it would all go away.

When she woke the room was filled with an eerie light, and the bed was moving. She lay in the odd stillness, disoriented, knowing something was terribly wrong and not able to remember it. The bed was shaking, and it took her a moment to realize it was her body, wracked with shivers, that was making it move.

Alex lay stretched out on the other bed, asleep. The blue light of the muted television set filled the motel room, and Carolyn watched the screen for a moment. He'd been watching The Weather Channel when he fell asleep. She had no idea whether he was expecting a natural disaster or he was just a weather junkie. She didn't care.

All she cared about was getting warm. It was 3:47 a.m. according to the digital clock, and the room was like a freezer. She expected to see her breath mist in the frigid air. The pile of blankets lay on top of her like layers of ice, closing the cold in around her, and Alex lay in a t-shirt and jeans, seemingly oblivious to the cold. His bed was stripped down to the bottom sheet—he'd piled them on top of hers, and she felt a dizzy sense of gratitude. In this ice cave he was willing to risk freezing to death for her sake.

She'd read somewhere that freezing to death wasn't a bad way to go. You got numb, and then you fell asleep, and that was the end of it. But the numbness wouldn't come, no matter how badly she needed it, the cold was sharp and painful, and she bit her lip rather than cry out. All she could do was lie in the cocoon of covers and shake.

She tried to hit him when he climbed onto the bed beside her, but her arms were trapped beneath the pile of blankets. He made no move to get under them, he simply lay on top of them, wrapping his body around hers. He was hot in the icy room, burning hot, and she thought he must be dying. She didn't care. She needed his heat.

He was talking to her, she realized. Soft, meaningless phrases, as he warmed her body with his, and one hand gently stroked her face. Her tears were made of ice as well, but the heat from his hand melted them, so that they ran down her skin, burning her.

His whispered words made no sense; she knew that. "Hush, Carolyn. It'll be all right, I promise. I won't let anything happen. Just take a deep breath and let the heat surround you. I won't leave you. I promise I'll take care of you."

From somewhere deep inside she wanted to laugh. She didn't need anyone to take care of her. She had learned early on to be strong, to take care of herself.

And besides, everyone always left her, sooner or later.

What other silly things was he saying to her? It didn't matter. His feverish body was warming hers, and she could feel herself draining him. She'd leave him a cold, frozen husk if she weren't careful. She should bring him under the covers, share the warmth with him. She should tell him she didn't need him. She should do a thousand things.

But all she could do was sleep.

ALEX CONSIDERED making her eat cold lo mein for breakfast, then decided he couldn't be that cruel. The room was stifling hot, and when he finally woke her she was logy, covered with sweat, limp with heat and exhaustion.

"Five minutes for a shower or we'll miss the first ferry, and I don't know how hard a time we'll have getting a space on the next one."

She stared at him with blank incomprehension. He wondered if she remembered anything about last night. Probably not, and just as well. It would take a long time to get past her distrust—knowing she'd been vulnerable enough to cling to him and weep in his arms would be hard for her to accept.

He was willing to give her all the emotional space she needed, as long as she stayed close. His first and foremost task was to keep both of them alive. Getting past her formidable sense of betrayal and anger would have to wait.

She was out of the shower and dressed in five minutes flat. He'd already packed up their meager belongings and stowed them in the car, and he was waiting by the open door when she came out. "We can get coffee and something to eat on the ferry," he told her.

"I'm not hungry."

"If you tell me that one more time I'll strangle you," he said calmly. "I don't give a shit whether you're hungry or not. I'm not hungry either. Our lives happen to be in danger. It would make sense if we managed to eat something."

"Wouldn't it make more sense if we didn't go to Martha's Vineyard? Assuming you're right and someone wants to kill us, wouldn't Edgartown be one of the first places they'd look? They're bound to find us."

"I want them to find us. I want to flush him out. I want to see the face of the person who shot me eighteen years ago. I want to look into his eyes."

"His?"

"Or hers. Get in the car, Carolyn, or we'll miss the ferry."

"Maybe I want to miss the ferry."

"Then whoever's trying to kill you will simply find us in Woods Hole."

She climbed in the car, maintaining a stony silence until they were safely onboard.

He half hoped she'd continue to ignore him. He didn't want to deal with questions when he wasn't sure of the answers. And a wrong guess would be fatal.

The moment they were parked she left the car. He let her go. There was no way she could get away from him on a boat, and for the time being they weren't in any danger. If she needed half an hour away from him he was willing to grant it.

The last thing he expected was to see her reappear at the car with a carrier holding two cardboard cups of coffee and a couple of muffins.

She climbed back into the passenger seat and held out the tray. He glanced at it warily.

"Any shrimp in the coffee?" he asked.

"I could spill it on your lap," she offered sweetly. "I'm trying to make a peaceful gesture. At least you could meet me halfway."

He looked at her pale mouth, set and determined. She was even stronger than he'd realized. She sat beside him, calm, composed, and shattered inside. And for some reason he found her dignity even more devastating than her vulnerability.

He took the cup of coffee. It was overpoweringly sweet, just the way he liked it. "So we've got a truce?"

"For the time being. Have a cyanide muffin."

He managed a smile. She was bundled in several layers of sweaters, including one of his, and her long blonde hair was damp from her morning shower, hanging in a windswept tangle down her back. She was still wearing the faded jeans, and he'd never seen anyone look less like a MacDowell. It was all he could do not to jump her.

"Are you going to tell me who you think it is?" Her prosaic question made only a slight dent in his erotic fantasies.

He took another gulp of his coffee. It was too hot and he didn't give a damn. "I don't know."

"But you must have some suspicions."

"It could be almost any of them. Patsy, Warren, Ruben or Constanza. Hell, even George and Tessa might have something to do with it."

"Tessa was fourteen when you left."

"And you were almost fourteen. If you'd had a gun, don't you think you could have shot me?" he countered.

"Easily. But why would Tessa care?"

"I don't know," he said. "I don't know why anyone would want to kill me."

"I don't know why anyone *wouldn't* have wanted to kill you back then," Carolyn replied. "The question is, how does that tie in with now? And what makes you so sure someone wants to kill you? Or me, for that matter? I might have been wrong about the gunshots. It might have been some idiot hunter. And brakes do fail."

"Brakes do fail," he agreed. "But seldom with such exquisite timing. You want to go back to the bosom of your family and give them a chance to try again? Just to make certain someone really is murderous?"

"Isn't that what we're doing by coming to the Vineyard? You're trying to lure them, to get them to try again. I don't know why we bothered to come here. We didn't have to drive two hundred and fifty miles just to get someone to attempt murder—we could have stayed home and saved a lot of time. Why waste the gas?"

"Because here we have the upper hand."

"Do we?" She wasn't bothering to hide her cynicism. "It's an island. Doesn't that limit most avenues of escape?"

"He'll be coming. And we'll be ready for him," Alex said calmly.

"There's that 'he' again. You think it's Warren, don't you? Dear, doting Uncle Warren, out to kill his nephew and his daughter." Her voice was brittle. "How very . . . MacDowell of him."

"I don't know who it is. He's the obvious choice. He knows you're a threat to the inheritance. He doesn't think I am. That's why you've been the target up to now."

"And now?"

"Now I think he'll want to hedge his bets. I don't know what they're thinking up in Vermont. Probably that we've gone off for a few days of hot, unbridled sex. Except the murderer will know better. He'll know why we've run."

"And what if they don't guess where we are? Maybe it's not as obvious as we think."

"Then I'll call and tell them," Alex said. "Just to help things along."

Carolyn was silent for a moment, surveying the crumbled remains of her muffin. "All right," she said finally. "But just one thing."

"Yeah?"

"We're not having hot, unbridled sex on the Vineyard." She sounded very certain.

He wasn't about to disabuse her of the notion. One battle at a time. "Whatever you say."

Chapter Twenty

THE HOUSE ON Water Street was spotless—during their absence someone had come in and cleaned up any trace of their last visit. Fortunately, the power and water were still on, and this time the phone was working as well. Carolyn listened to the dial tone for a moment, then put the receiver down with a faint frown. There was no one she wanted to call.

"Phone working?" Alex stood in the hallway, holding their suitcases.

"Yes."

"Don't answer it if it rings."

"I thought you wanted them to know we were here."

"I do," he said. "But I don't want to have a cozy conversation with them." He started toward the stairs.

"I can carry my own suitcase," she said. "I'll be sleeping in my old room."

"No, you won't," he said flatly. "I'm tired of you playing Cinderella."

"Fine," she snapped. "Then I'll sleep downstairs in Sally's room and wallow in luxury."

"Sorry," he said, sounding not the slightest bit repentant. "You're sleeping with me."

She glared at him. "I told you, I'm not about to sleep with you ever again."

He was unimpressed. "You look just like my mother did when she was being haughty. I'm amazed I never noticed the resemblance before."

"I thought you told me she wasn't your mother."

"She didn't give birth to me. But she was my mother, nonetheless."

"I'm still not sharing a bed with you."

"You don't have to. You just have to share a room with me. Haven't you gotten it through your stubborn head that you're in danger? Someone wants to kill you. Someone who thinks you stand in the way of a tidy inheritance. This old house is too big for you to be wandering about without someone looking out for you."

"You really think Uncle Warren is going to show up here with a gun?" She couldn't think of him by any other name. "I don't see the point. Why would he think I'd be a threat? Up until last night I didn't know I had any connection to him, and now that I do, I'd just as soon put as much distance between us as possible. He doesn't need to kill me. He's repudiated me all my life—I'm not about to go asking for anything now."

"Maybe you want revenge for his rejecting you."

"I'm not the revenge kind of person," she said flatly.

"I know that. I'm not sure Warren is as observant. He doesn't look much past the nose on his face. His abiding interest is the MacDowell money, and he can't comprehend why someone else wouldn't be equally obsessed. Anyway, we don't know that it's Warren. He's the logical choice, but there's no proof. Maybe Patsy isn't as big a space cadet as she seems."

"Maybe not," Carolyn said in a quiet voice.

"We'll be sleeping in the front room—"

"The hell we will," she said. "There's only one bed there."

"At least it's a double. Don't worry, angel, I'll drag a mattress in and sleep on the floor. It's got the best location. We can hear anyone coming up the stairs, we have a view of Water Street, and we can always escape off the porch roof."

"What about the back stairs?"

"The floor in the hallway creaks. So does the double bed in the front room, for that matter. If you change your mind we'd better do it on the mattress and not on the bed."

She just stared at him. "You're awfully cheerful for someone who just lost his mother and is convinced someone is trying to kill him. Or is it the thought of all that nice money you've just become heir to?"

The look he gave her was chilling. "Why, it's the thought of all that money, of course," he said affably. "Why else would I have been hanging around for the last eighteen years, living off the fat of the land? Isn't it obvious?"

"Sorry," she muttered.

"Frankly, I'll be damned glad to get the answers to questions that have been haunting me for almost two decades. I want this over with, and I want to know what's behind it. We're going to find out, and then I'll be out of your life and you can go back to being the perfect little

MacDowell, secure in the knowledge that you really are one."

She stared at him. He'd paused on the landing, and his voice was cool and bitter. "Where will you go?" she asked, unable to keep the wistful note out of her voice.

If he heard it he ignored it. "Wherever my nice fat millions will take me, babe," he said, and disappeared up the stairs.

It was a sunny day, with a cool spring breeze blowing across the island. Carolyn opened the windows, letting the wind blow through the old house, following her as she walked from room to room, looking at it all with fresh eyes.

More than any other residence, including the Park Avenue apartment and the compound in southern Vermont, this house was the MacDowell house. It was filled with family treasures, portraits of MacDowells, furniture handed down for generations. This house of ancient lineage, where she'd never really belonged, should have changed. Now that she knew she had a right to be here, she should have had a sense of homecoming.

She didn't. She looked up into the painted eyes of the man who was, in fact, her grandfather, and felt no kinship. Commodore MacDowell had been a ruthless, formidable old man, and his oldest daughter Sally had taken after him in many ways. Carolyn looked into his eyes and felt nothing.

She sat in the Stuyvesant chair, one that had belonged to her ancestors, one that she'd never dared sit in before. It was just an old wooden chair, rickety and uncomfortable.

She'd been given exactly what she'd always wanted, a real family, just as the one person she'd loved had been taken away. And the damnable thing was, once she'd gotten it, it meant nothing. She didn't need to be a MacDowell. After all these years she didn't need to be anyone but herself.

The phone rang, and she started to reach for it automatically, then stopped herself. It should have been Sally on the other end, but Sally was dead. Was it Patsy, her voice slurred and faintly anxious? Or Warren, pretending concern or not even bothering. What would he do if she called him "daddy"? She could just imagine his horror.

Whoever was on the other end of the phone line wasn't about to give up easily. It stopped ringing, then started again two minutes later. The phone had a particularly shrill tone, one that would reach clearly through the rambling old house, and Carolyn stared at it with acute dislike, willing it to be still. They tried a third time, and then the phone was mercifully silent.

She heard him come clattering down the back stairs, but she made no move to find him. She could see the bay from the windows, and more than anything, she wished it were twenty years ago, before Alex had died and been reborn, before she found out too many secrets.

She heard the slam of drawers, the rifling of papers, but she still didn't move. Maybe if she closed her eyes she could will herself back in time. Or at least pretend, for a short, peaceful while.

Except that it hadn't been that peaceful on the island all those years ago, she knew that full well. Patsy and her latest lover had been there, and both Warren and Sally had disapproved. Apparently he had criminal connections, but Patsy had been radiant, completely smitten, and unwilling to listen to anyone's warnings.

George and Tessa had been there as well, come to think of it. Tessa had run with her own social crowd down at the club, basically ignoring Carolyn, despite the fact that they were the same age. And George had been a pompous, perfect, stuffy teenager, always watching, always judging, always ready to report on Alex's latest transgressions, or anyone else's misdeeds that he happened to catch.

And then there was Alex himself. How could she have thought that was a happy time, when she was so plagued with adolescent misery over him? She'd longed for him with an intensity she could still remember, even to this day. She could summon up those feelings, the ache in the pit of her stomach, the fluttering in her chest, the dreamy possibilities of his mouth.

She laughed in sudden bitter recognition. It was no wonder she could easily conjure up her adolescent passion for him. She'd never outgrown it. Living out her fantasies, eighteen years later, had only intensified it. She'd been a fool to let herself give in, when she was usually so careful, so defensive. She should have guessed the power he still had over her.

He appeared in the doorway, a sheaf of papers in one strong hand. "What's so amusing?"

"I am," she said shortly. "I never realized quite what a fool I could be." She wasn't about to elaborate, especially when the steady gaze made her feel particularly foolish. "What are you looking for?"

"Information. Clues, hints, proof."

"Of what?"

"Where I came from. My birth mother's dead, and her family never even knew she was pregnant. But she summered on the Vineyard, I know that much."

"Why do you care?"

He shrugged. "Curious, I suppose. I've known I wasn't Sally's birth child for the last eighteen years, but I never even thought of who gave birth to me."

The Stuyvesant chair was uncomfortable. She rose and wandered over to the corner window seat. "Are you going to tell me what happened to you?"

He didn't move from the doorway. "Are you going to ask?"

"I'm asking."

A cool smile curved his mouth, and he dumped the papers on the table. He ignored the revered chair—when he was a child he only used to sit in it to annoy Warren, but Warren wasn't around. He sank down in a wicker chair, and it creaked in protest. "Unfortunately, I don't have the answers, and I never have. I remember getting caught boosting that car. I remember Sally and Warren screaming at me. They were already having a fit about Patsy's new boyfriend, and my latest transgression was the final straw."

"Why did you steal a car? Sally would have bought you one."

"I only borrowed it for a while," he protested lazily. "Just for a short joyride. I had every intention of returning it to where I got it, with no one the wiser. Unfortunately, we had a stool pigeon in our midst."

"You don't have to tell me," she said. "George."

"George the Pig," Alex agreed. "He hasn't improved much with age, has he?"

"He's very good-looking," she offered halfheartedly.

"I'm not talking about his looks. He was a perfect angel and a complete snitch. He was always sneaking around, watching people." An odd expression crossed his face, as if he suddenly remembered something. "I wonder if he still does."

"Still does what?"

"Watches people," he said absently. "Anyway, I decided to take off, I remember that much. I waited until everyone was asleep, then I came back to the house and emptied every purse I could find." He frowned. "It seems there was something more, but I can't quite remember. Something about Patsy." He shook his head. "It doesn't matter. I'm sure Patsy didn't come sneaking down to Lighthouse Beach and put a bullet in me."

"Who did?"

"I don't know. I remember coming up to your room. I was half-tempted to take you with me, you know," he added. "You were very tasty back then, and you did adore me so. Teenage boys need to be adored."

"Teenage boys need to be beaten," she said, ignoring her immediate, treacherous response.

He laughed. "I made do with kissing you good-bye. If you'd been a couple of years older I would have taken you to bed, but I guess even I had some sense of morality back then. I still hoped that kiss would ruin you for any other boy. At least until I got back."

"You took too long," she said.

"So I did. I wasn't expecting to get shot. I wasn't expecting to find out my parentage was a lie." He paused, staring out into the bay.

"You still haven't told me what happened."

He shook his head. "I told you, I don't remember. I walked down to Lighthouse Beach. I was going to steal the Valmers' boat, I remember that much. Someone came after me, someone shot me. But I can't remember any details."

"Why not?"

He shrugged. "Head injuries can do that. Apparently, I got a concussion as well."

"I don't understand—why aren't you dead? I saw someone shoot you." She shuddered. "And I did nothing to stop it."

"You would have been shot as well," he said prosaically. "I don't blame you—you were just a scared kid at the time. I survived—you probably wouldn't have."

"But how did you survive?"

He grinned. "Thank God for drug dealers."

"I beg your pardon?"

"I ended up in the water—I assume whoever shot me must have dragged me in. I was somewhere out there, clinging to a piece of driftwood, when a group of nefarious types fished me out. I didn't bother to ask what they were doing, and they didn't bother to tell me, but they knew how to treat a gunshot wound and shock. They dumped me off near Cape Ann and I made my way to my so-called father."

"I didn't know you knew how to reach him."

"I didn't. When I went through Sally's purse I found my father's address tucked in one of those tiny compartments. I figured it was a sign."

"What did he think about his son being shot?"

"He told me I wasn't his son," Alex said. "After the initial shock I took it pretty well. But I decided then and there that I had no reason to ever go back to the MacDowells. No matter how much I wanted to see what happened to you when you were a few years older."

"Stop it!" she snapped, pushed beyond endurance. "I don't want to hear your lies about spending eighteen years wandering the world, dreaming about me. I don't believe it for one moment."

"I still had the charm bracelet, didn't I?"

There was absolutely nothing she could say to that. The possibilities were too frightening. "I'm going up for a nap," she said sharply, rising. "I don't need your company for that, do I?"

"Not unless you want it."

"I don't," she said flatly. "Call me if a crazed murderer appears."

"You don't sound worried. If you don't believe we're in danger why did you come with me?"

"You didn't give me much choice."

"Bullshit," he said with a slow, knowing smile.

"Bullshit to you, too," she said, heading upstairs.

He was right, the double bed creaked alarmingly when she climbed on it, pulling a duvet over her. She didn't care. She left the shades open so that she could stare out at the bay. And then she closed her eyes and dreamed. She would have been better off awake. She dreamed strange, erotic dreams, where she had slow, deliciously depraved sex while all the MacDowells watched with thunderous disapproval. And she didn't care. All that mattered was the silky smooth texture of his skin, the creamy taste of his flesh, the dark fever in his blue, blue eyes.

When she woke it was dusk, and she was ravenously hungry. The house was dark and quiet, and she wondered if Alex had gone out someplace. Or whether their supposed murderer had come stalking and claimed his first victim.

She still couldn't believe it. Murders weren't a part of her safe, neat little world, despite the fact that she thought she'd witnessed one so long ago. The memory of that night had been such a trauma that she'd shut it out of her mind. Nice people, good people, rich people didn't kill. They didn't shoot wild teenaged boys; they didn't try to kill sensible young women.

But as much as she wanted to deny the reality of it, she couldn't. She still had scrapes and bruises from having to ditch her brakeless car. She could still remember the whine of the bullets flying past her in the woods. And she knew perfectly well just how much money Sally was leaving her heirs. For some people, it was more than enough to kill for.

She found him in the music room, a drink in his hand, a distant expression on his face. The room looked like a bomb had hit it—papers and photos scattered everywhere. She knelt down and began to scoop them up automatically.

He watched her, making no effort to help. "Do you know the Robinson family?" His voice was slightly rough.

She rose, dumping the papers on the table. "The ones who live up island, by the cliffs? I vaguely remember them. Nice old couple, friends of Sally. They both died in the last few years, and I don't think they had any children."

"They had a daughter named Judith."

"I remember now. They had pictures of her at their house. She died a long time ago."

"Thirty-five years ago, to be exact." He took a deep drink of his whiskey. "Care to join me in a toast to my long-lost mother?"

"Not particularly. I think we need to eat," she said briskly.

"What about your own mother?" He pushed it. "Don't you care about your past?"

"Not particularly. As you said, Sally was my mother in every way that counts," Carolyn replied evenly. "Just as she was yours."

"Sounds like incest to me," he said lazily, but she wasn't fooled. She was confronted with a little boy who was hurting, and she was good at soothing hurts.

"I'm not worried about it."

"At least Sally didn't lie to you about everything. Your mother was Elke Olmstedder, the nursemaid she hired from Sweden to take care of me. I guess Warren knocked her up and Sally kicked her out when she found out about it."

"Do you remember her?"

Alex shook his head. "Sorry. I was too young."

Carolyn nodded, dismissing it. "Why don't I see what we have to eat in this place—"

"Don't you care?" he broke in. "Don't you want to know how you ended up here?"

"Not particularly," she said calmly. "But obviously you want to tell me."

"Your mother died when you were two and I guess Sally must have had a belated attack of conscience. Either that, or Warren talked her into finding you."

"I doubt it. Warren's always found me an inconvenience. At least now I understand why. It must have been Sally's idea. I bet she decided you needed a little sister to torment."

"And after all, you were a MacDowell," he said in a silky voice. "I'd say she was hedging her bets. Sally was good at that."

She came over to him and took the drink out of his hand, and surprisingly enough he didn't resist. "I'd say Sally loved us both, no matter what her other motives. And that's what we need to remember."

"Incest," he said again, looking up at her out of sleepy, sexy eyes.

"Fuck you," she said without any real heat.

"Yes," he said. And he rose, coming toward her, slow and sexy and determined.

Chapter Twenty-one

SHE WAS RUNNING away from him. No sooner had Alex risen to his feet than Carolyn turned and left the room. "I'll find us something to eat," she called over her shoulder in a brisk voice.

She'd have to be a fool to think he wouldn't follow, and Carolyn Smith was no fool. He was in no particular hurry, and he arrived in the kitchen in time to see her pouring his half-full drink down the sink.

"I wasn't finished with that," he said mildly.

"Yes, you were." She was already poking her head into the refrigerator. "There's nothing to eat."

"We could always get fried clams," he said.

"No!"

"What about pizza? I bet I can even find delivery."

"I thought you told me everything was closed down off-season?" she said. "It's only been a week since we were here."

"A lot can happen in a week," he said lightly. "Besides, I may have exaggerated the situation before. After all, the island has a fairly large year-round population."

She wasn't happy with him, but then, that was nothing new. "What else have you been lying about?"

The fact that he wasn't going to let her sleep alone in the double bed, he thought, but didn't bother to tell her that. "I've told you so many lies I've lost count of them," he said. "At this point I think everything's out in the open, but I can't guarantee it."

"What else would you be lying about?"

How I feel about you, he thought. Maybe dragging her down here wasn't the smartest idea in the world, but he couldn't leave her behind. It was simply too dangerous.

He seemed to be totally incapable of ignoring the effect she had on him. She moved around the kitchen, setting water on to boil, moving with calm grace, and all he wanted to do was ease her down on the hardwood floor, strip off her clothes, and put his mouth between her legs. He was worse than when he was seventeen. Then he was impartially obsessed by all females, including thirteen-year-old Carolyn.

Now all that lust was channeled directly toward one woman, and he was having a hell of a time keeping it under control. She had her back to him, and was busy rifling through the cupboards, and he could no more resist the impulse than he could stop breathing. He moved across the room, coming up directly behind her, not quite touching her, so close he could smell the soap from the cheap motel, smell her skin and her shampoo and her faint, erotic, female scent, and he put his arms to either side of her, trapping her against the counter.

She didn't turn in his arms to face him, much as he wanted her to. She froze, keeping her back to him. "What do you think you're doing?" She would have sounded bored if it weren't for the faint quiver in her voice. The faint tremor that washed through her body.

She didn't realize he found her back as erotic as the front of her. She'd braided her silky blonde hair in one thick braid, exposing the nape of her neck, and he wanted to bite her, like a mating cat. She stood straight and still within the prison of his arms, and he wondered if he would ever be capable of making her laugh. Right now it didn't seem likely. Right now it didn't seem as if either of them had much reason to laugh.

He gave in to temptation, putting his mouth against the back of her neck, kissing her there, slowly, letting his tongue touch and taste the warm, soft skin. She shivered, taking in a deep breath, and he pressed his hips against her buttocks, wanting her to feel him.

"Don't," she said in a strangled voice.

He moved his mouth to the side of her neck, tasting, teasing. "Why not? Are you going to tell me you don't want me?"

"I don't want you."

"Liar."

She turned in his arms then, a major tactical error on her part. He allowed her enough room, then moved in closer, so that he could feel the soft fullness of her breasts through his t-shirt, pressing against his chest. He could press up against her thighs, nestle there, where he belonged, knowing she could feel it too. She wanted to escape from him; he knew that full well. She also wanted him to kiss her.

He brought his mouth close, so close that he could feel the soft puffs of her breath against his lips. But he didn't close the gap. "Do you want to kiss me, Carolyn?" he whispered.

"I want you to let me go," she said in a dull voice.

He dropped his arms to his side, no longer imprisoning her. "But do you want to kiss me?"

She raised her eyes to look at him, and there was anger and betrayal in their cool depths. "Yes," she said. "But I'm not going to."

He smiled then. "Maybe not now," he agreed. "But sooner or later."

She didn't dispute him. "Arrogant bastard," she said. "I'd prefer later."

"I wouldn't." He leaned closer, savoring the sweet temptation, when the shrill sound of the phone jerked him out of his erotic reverie.

He stepped back, reluctantly. "Do you want to get the phone or shall I?"

"I'll get it." She dashed from the kitchen, and he resisted the impulse to follow her. She was more than capable of handling any of the MacDowell clan, and at the moment he trusted her composure more than his own.

He waited as long as he could, then followed her out into the living room and the one downstairs phone that Sally would allow. She was sitting in a chair, a lost expression on her face.

"Who was it?"

"Uncle Warren."

"I don't suppose you called him 'daddy,' did you?"

She roused herself. "I barely thought about it," she said, an obvious lie, but he decided to let it pass. "He's been looking for me, he said. They found my car and they were worried. Patsy's in the hospital. Some kind of drug reaction, apparently."

"I can imagine," he drawled. "Did she OD?"

"I don't know. Warren said her children are with her."

"And where is your dear papa?"

"Don't call him that!" She shuddered. "He's in Vermont, I assume. He's trying to make funeral arrangements for Sally, dealing with Patsy's hospitalization, and mad as hell that I'm not around to take care of the details." She glanced up at him. "He didn't ask about you."

"Interesting. Either he no longer cares, or he already knows."

"What did you two plan on doing when Sally died?"

Alex chuckled mirthlessly. "He was supposed to pay me off handsomely and I was supposed to disappear."

"How much?"

He shrugged. "I don't really remember, since I had no intention of taking it. Somewhere in the mid-six figures, I think."

"Wouldn't he be worried that you were planning on blackmailing him? Unless he's figured out that you really are Alex."

"Warren's not that smart. Are you sure he was calling from Vermont?"

"How could I be?" she said in a cranky voice. "The phone is ancient."

"Exactly. In this life you can't be sure of anything."

"Especially in this family," she said bitterly.

"Of which you are well and truly a member. Finally," he pointed out.

"I don't think so."

She'd managed to surprise him. "What do you mean?" He almost sounded affronted.

She looked at him. "I mean you're well and truly a MacDowell, aren't you, Alex, despite the fact that you have no blood tie to them. You're a ruthless, handsome, self-centered liar, willing to do anything to get what you want in this life, no matter who you hurt. Sounds like the quintessential MacDowell to me."

It shouldn't have stung, but it did. "And you're Miss Pure-as-the-Driven-Snow?"

"No. But I don't put my wants in front of everybody else's, and damn the cost. And I don't lie."

"You don't lie? I guess we can add self-delusion to your list of sins as well," he said. He didn't trust himself to move any closer to her—leaning against the doorjamb in the back parlor kept him from touching her.

"I don't lie," she said fiercely, making the mistake of rising from her chair and coming toward him, too angry to realize her danger.

"What do you think of me?"

"Why bother to ask—you know perfectly well what I think of you."

He managed an extravagant yawn. "Yeah, I know. You despise me, you think I'm lower than dirt, I'm a liar and a cheat and I didn't even have the decency to tell the truth about being an imposter. I'm as rotten as I ever was, the bane of your existence, and you wish whoever had shot me had had better aim. Does that about sum it up?"

"That about covers it." She came right up to him, a major mistake. "Except for one thing."

"And what's that?"

She had the absolute indecency to smile at him, a to-hell-with-you, in-your-face kind of smile. "When you figure it out, let me know," she said sweetly, walking past him before he could put his hands on her.

THE HOURS IN THE old house dragged. There'd been a time when Carolyn had loved the house on Water Street with a wistfully possessive passion, wanting it with a deep, shameful longing. The house was like a prize in the MacDowell family—passed down through generations, it sat on North Water Street in elegant majesty, its wide porch overlooking the bay and Chappaquiddick Island, its graceful lines and history-rich furnishings a symbol of the grace and privilege of being a MacDowell. The siblings had fought over it, and even though Sally hadn't been there in the last ten years, she'd never relinquished an ounce of her financial interest or control in the place.

Now it would be Patsy's and Warren's. Or possibly Alex's, if he wanted it. He said he had no interest in his inheritance, but the man had been known to lie, she thought wryly. And who could turn down an inheritance of such magnificence as this house?

She could. She realized it with a sudden, liberating shock. She could turn her back on this huge, stuffy old house in Edgartown, with its history and its perfection, where even as a child she was told to behave herself, never to make too much noise, not to make a mess, do nothing to mar its pristine beauty. It was a huge house, built by a sea captain for his half-dozen children, but no child's voice had rung out in the halls for generations, even when Alex and the rest of them were little. It was a dead house, and Carolyn found she could let go of it as easily as she'd let go of the MacDowells. It was a hard lesson to be learned in this life, and she was lucky she'd learned it by the age of thirty-one and not years later. The things you most longed for in life quite often turned out to be worthless and shallow.

She glanced across the room to Alex. He was stretched out on the wicker chaise, a remarkably uncomfortable chair in Carolyn's opinion, though he didn't seem to mind. His eyes were closed, but she had no illusion that he was sleeping. Still, it gave her the time to look at him at her leisure, and she knew with dark certainty that this might be the last time.

Worthless and shallow. Most certainly he was, as well as beautiful and dishonest and pathologically self-centered. He was also what she had longed for most in this life, more than family, more than to be a real MacDowell, more than this perfect mausoleum of a summerhouse.

She still wanted him. Ached for him, like a stupid, hormone-riddled adolescent. She looked at his long, lean body, his ripe mouth, his Cossack eyes, and she burned.

He wasn't ever going to know it. Oh, he might guess. After all, he was an intelligent enough man, and wise in the ways of women. He knew perfectly well she lusted after him, just as he knew she could keep her lust firmly under control.

What he didn't know was that she still loved him, deeply, passionately. And most likely always would, since time and the harsh truth and sorrow couldn't touch her feelings.

She wasn't about to end up a bitter old woman, mourning a lost love—she had too much sense for that. Once she broke free of the MacDowells she'd get on with her life, find someone kind and good to marry. She'd have babies, babies that she'd never give up to a rich old woman willing to pay the price. And only on certain hot summer nights, or maybe on cool, crisp autumn ones, would she think about Alexander MacDowell and remember the man she loved.

"Do you ever get the feeling that someone is watching you?" Alex's voice drifted toward her, startling her. He hadn't bothered to open his eyes, but he must have been far too aware of her perusal.

"So sue me," she said.

Then he did open his eyes, looking at her with veiled amusement. "I didn't mean you. Of course you watch me, just as I watch you. Whether you admit it or not, we're both suffering from a case of terminal, mutual lust, and even if we manage to keep our hands off each other, we can't stop watching."

"Terminal lust," she echoed. "What a charming way to put it."

"Do you deny it?"

"Lust is not how I'd describe my feelings for you," she said dryly.

"I won't bother arguing with you about it. I was talking about this house. I've always had the feeling that someone was watching me. Maybe it's all the windows looking out over Water Street."

"It's off-season. No one's walked by in hours, and the traffic is minimal."

"So why do I get the feeling someone is spying on me? Or am I being paranoid?"

"You're probably being paranoid."

"Probably?"

"I'm feeling it, too."

He sat up swiftly, the ancient wicker chaise creaking. "Maybe they've gotten here sooner than I thought."

"Who?"

He shook his head. "I don't know. We can rule out Patsy, I suppose, since she's in detox."

"And her children, since they're by her side. Which leaves Warren."

"Maybe," he said. "Maybe not." He rose. "I'm going outside to see whether we might have any unwanted visitors."

"And leave me alone in here? Forget it."

"You mean you expect me to protect you? I'm touched, Carolyn. I didn't think you were about to accept anything from me."

She glared at him. "You're a pain in the ass, you know that, Alex?"

"I know that. Why don't you go upstairs and lock the door while I scout around and make sure the house is secure?"

"How could it be? This is an old place—if anyone was determined to break in I'm sure they could with very little difficulty."

"There's also a state-of-the-art security system I can turn back on."

"Which any member of the MacDowell family could easily circumvent."

"Not if I change the password," he said airily. "A simple enough matter if you know what you're doing. Go upstairs and wait for me. I won't be long."

"You want me stripped and bathed and properly scented?" she said in an acid voice.

He didn't rise to the bait. "I want you any way I can have you."

She didn't bother with a response. She stomped upstairs, making a great deal of noise as she went, just in case some murderous intruder had managed to get in through the back way. She wasn't in the mood to confront anyone at that moment, least of all Alexander MacDowell and his lust.

A week after their last visit the moon was waning, but still bright over the water. The trees were covered with leaves now, obscuring a great deal of the street, and already there were more lights across the bay. By early May the place was beginning to come alive.

He'd already dragged a mattress into the front bedroom, pushing the double bed up against the windows to make room for it, though he hadn't bothered with anything as civilized as sheets. She wasn't about to make it up for him, either. She stripped off her jeans and climbed into bed, keeping her bra and panties on underneath her t-shirt. She probably should have kept her jeans on as well, not to mention adding layers for extra protection, except that she knew all the clothing in the world wouldn't keep Alex MacDowell away from her. She had to rely on her own wayward sense of self-preservation.

She turned out the lights and curled up on the high bed, pulling the duvet around her. The room felt stuffy, with the musty smell of a closed-up house, and she opened one of the windows a crack to let in the cool spring air.

It was fresh and damp and oddly comforting. She bundled deeper into the duvet and willed herself to sleep before Alex could come along and tempt her.

HE'D LIED TO HER, of course, but lying to Carolyn Smith was second nature to him by now. He could reprogram the security system, but there were no guarantees that it would keep any determined MacDowell from entering. They knew this place too well.

Of course, given the amounts of money at stake, whoever was behind all this could always simply hire a professional to take care of them. But he didn't think they would. He could still see the outline of the person who stood and shot him on the beach at Lighthouse Beach, even though the face eluded his stubborn brain. But it had been a face he had known, of that much he was certain.

There were times when he'd wondered whether it was Sally herself who'd followed him down to the beach and tried to kill him. He'd been a trial and a terror, and once he knew she had no biological cause to love him, he had to accept the possibility that she was the one who'd tried to get rid of him.

He'd known the moment he returned that it hadn't been her. But somehow in the few weeks since he'd been back he was no closer to an answer.

The only thing he was closer to was Carolyn Smith.

She was curled up in a cocoon of covers on the high double bed, her back toward him, shutting him out. The moonlight streamed in the open window, spreading a silver glow throughout the room, and he wondered what she'd do if he climbed on the bed beside her.

He didn't. He'd learned to survive by his instincts, and his instincts told him their enemy was close at hand. He couldn't allow himself to be distracted by the very real temptation of the woman he loved.

It was a terrible mistake, falling in love with her, but then, it was nothing new. He'd wanted her for as long as he could remember, and even during his time in self-imposed exile he'd still dreamed of her.

He didn't bother taking off his clothes, he simply dropped down on the mattress and stretched out. The breeze from the open window was cool, a fact he welcomed, because he was hot. Outside he could hear the water lapping against the docks, a soothing, gentle sound, and he wondered if he dared let himself sleep.

And then he did.

Chapter Twenty-two

CAROLYN WASN'T sure what woke her. The room was very dark—only the faint silvery moonlight illuminated it, and she guessed it was somewhere around two or three in the morning. She lay very still on the high bed, listening, all her senses immediately alert. And then she realized that Alex was awake as well.

"Alex?" Her voice was little more than the breath of a whisper on the night air.

"Yeah?" he said after a moment, making no movement.

She rose on her elbows and looked down at him. He lay stretched out on the bare mattress, fully dressed, no covers, no pillows. If he'd slept at all it hadn't been much—even in the dim moonlight he looked haggard, lost. "Alex," she said again, not knowing what she was asking, not knowing how to ask.

"Don't."

"Don't what?"

He closed his eyes in despair. "Don't look at me with those big eyes of yours, don't curl up next to me and cry, don't tell me you're lost and hurting. For God's sake, Carolyn, leave me alone."

She gathered the covers and began to climb off the bed. "I'll just go in another room—"

He caught her bare ankle in his big, strong hand. "No, you won't. Lie down and go to sleep."

"I can't sleep."

"And I can't be your sleeping pill."

"What do you mean?"

"I mean this is hard enough for me, without having to dispense celibate comfort as well. I'm hurting. And I need you. I'm doing my damnedest to respect your wishes and keep my hands off you, but it would help if you wouldn't look at me out of those damnable eyes of yours and . . ."

She was suddenly quite calm. "I just wanted to ask you a question."

He sighed, obviously trying to control his temper. "What?"

196

"Does this bed really squeak?"

For a moment he sounded confused. "Yeah. See for yourself."

She moved, and the bed squeaked noisily. She moved again, settling onto the mattress beside him. "Do you really need me?" she whispered, putting her hands on his face. His skin was warm against her cool hands, and she could feel his sudden sharp intake of breath.

"I need you," he said roughly.

"Good," she whispered. And she leaned forward and kissed his mouth, with such gentle sweetness that he had to have guessed that she loved him.

But she knew men weren't the most observant creatures in the world, which had to be a mixed blessing.

He took her kiss as it was offered, sliding his hands up her back, cradling her. And then he kissed her back, a slow, languorous kiss, unlike any he'd ever given her before. He'd kissed her in a white-hot passion. He'd kissed her in fury and revenge and uncontrollable lust. He'd never kissed her with such sweet, simple pleasure.

She felt the desire curl in the pit of her stomach, spiraling up to her breasts. When he moved her onto her back she went willingly, closing her eyes as his mouth trailed hot, stinging little kisses across her cheekbones, her eyelids, the side of her mouth.

And then he sat up, and she felt bereft, her eyes flying open in the darkness. He was looking down at her, and she couldn't even begin to read his expression.

"I thought you said you needed me," she said.

"I do. I'm just not certain I want a martyr in my bed."

She laughed. "I wonder if Sally dropped you on your head when you were a baby," she said, half to herself. "Trust me, I really don't mind if you force me to have exquisite sex. I'm willing to make such a noble sacrifice."

"'Exquisite sex'?" he echoed, making no move to touch her.

Some of her amusement was fading. She'd been so sure she'd been safe enough, offering herself to him. That he wanted her, at least on a physical level, as much as she wanted him. Now she wasn't so certain.

"Are you about to offer me anything more?" she asked.

He didn't move, watching her for a long, thoughtful moment. And then he pulled his sweater over his head, flinging it across the room, and his chest was white-gold in the moonlight. "Yes," he said.

She wouldn't have thought him capable of such rare sweetness. She hadn't really thought he could make love to her, real love. She hadn't realized how very dangerous it could be, to let him love her.

He stripped off her clothes, slowly, pulling the t-shirt over her head with delicious deliberation, putting his lips against every inch of flesh he exposed. His skin was hot in the cool night air, gilded by the moonlight, and she felt strange, floating, like a pagan goddess with her hair spread around her naked body. His hands were deft, arousing, and then deliciously not-gentle, and she arched her back, crying out, only to have him cover her mouth with his, stifling her cry, drinking it in.

He pulled away from her, leaning back against the wall, watching her out of hooded eyes, and she knew what he wanted. He reached out his hand and she took it, she came to him, straddling him, clinging to his broad shoulders, trembling.

"Look at me, Carolyn," he whispered, a plea, not an order, and she forced herself to open her eyes, to stare into the deep depths of his Cossack eyes, as she slowly sank down on the fierce length of him, filling herself with his cock. She was hypnotized, silent, entranced, by the intensity of his face, by the invasion of his body, and when she'd finally taken all of him, deep inside, shudders began to wrack her body.

She gave in then, kissing his mouth, his face, with anxious, hungry kisses, all the while he held her body pressed against his, held completely still within her, until nothing but his very presence sent her over the edge, and she buried her face against his shoulder to muffle her cries as her body exploded and her soul incinerated, and he joined her, pulsing hotly, deep within her.

She collapsed against him, as weak and boneless as a rag doll, and his arms were around her, holding her, protecting her, loving her. She wanted to cry, she wanted to tell him, when suddenly she became aware of a sharp, acrid odor.

He must have sensed it at the same time. He lifted her off his body with a care that belied his strength. "Get your clothes on," he whispered. "Fast."

She was already scrambling for her discarded t-shirt. "What is it?"

"Gasoline." Such an ordinary word, and so horrifying in its ramifications. He was already dressed, towering over her, and she was struggling into her jeans when the explosion came, a fireball of light that dazzled and blinded her.

The flames seemed to surround them almost immediately, a wall of fire across the front windows of the house, and there was no escape. He kicked open the bedroom door, grabbing her hand and hauling her with him, directly into the billowing smoke of the hallway.

The fire engulfed the ancient building, coming up in sheets of white-hot flame on all sides, but Alex must have remembered that the back of the house was partly brick. There were no porch roofs on the back, and if there had been they would have been engulfed in flames, but he simply dragged her into her old bedroom, picked up a chair and sent it crashing through the window.

"Come on!" he shouted, starting through the jagged remnants of glass.

She tried to pull back, suddenly terrified, but he wasn't having any of it. He simply picked her up and shoved her out the window, then followed her a moment later.

He'd also remembered the boxwood that surrounded the back of the house, thick and solid enough to break her fall. For a moment she lay there, winded, aching, her lungs still filled with smoke as the inferno filled the sky, and then Alex crashed into the hedge beside her, almost landing on her.

A moment later he was up, dragging her with him. She could hear the fire sirens in the distance, but he seemed intent on ignoring them. He dragged her across the deserted back lawns of the summerhouses, over stone walls and across picket fences, pulling her into the shadows as the fire engines raced by.

"The car . . ." she managed to gasp.

"We'll find another one," he said ruthlessly. "Whoever torched the place will be waiting to make sure we didn't make it out alive. I'm not taking any more chances."

"How can we just find another car?" she protested. "It's the middle of the night—?"

"I'm an expert at stealing cars, remember? That's what started all this mess eighteen years ago. I'm out of practice, but I'm sure it's like riding a bicycle—once you learn you never really forget."

She stared at him in astonishment. He seemed almost lighthearted, and the flames shooting into the night air gave a satanic cast to his features. "Someone just tried to kill us," she said in a voice roughened by smoke. "The house is destroyed. What the hell do you have to be so cheerful about?"

"Because they're getting closer, and they're getting careless," he said. "In a matter of hours we'll know who's behind all this."

"In a matter of hours we could be dead," she said flatly.

"That too." He looked down at her. "Do you want me to find you a safe place to hide?"

"Is there such a place?"

"I don't know."

"I'm not leaving you," she said, not caring how it sounded

"I know you aren't," he said. "I wouldn't really let you." And he took her hand, heading off into the firelit night.

He stole a pickup truck with surprising ease, ripping out the ignition wires and starting it with an almost frightening efficiency even before Carolyn could climb into the front seat. It was a rusty old wreck, and if it ever possessed seat belts they'd been removed by an impatient owner, but the engine ran smoothly as Alex pulled out onto the highway heading toward the west end of the island.

Carolyn felt a lump under her butt, and she reached down and pulled out a crushed beer can. "Why couldn't you have stolen a Mercedes?" she inquired.

"They have too many antitheft devices. We were looking for transportation, not luxury," he said, concentrating on the road in front of him. Behind them the night sky was a brilliant canvas of orange and red and smoky blue as the historic MacDowell house went up in the flames of century-old timber, but the roads were devoid of traffic, and resolutely Carolyn turned her face forward. "Who was it?" she asked in a low voice.

"I still don't know."

"Where are we going?"

He didn't answer. He didn't need to. He was headed in the direction of Gay Head, and she knew without asking what he wanted to find.

"Take the first left," she said finally, as they were approaching the cliffs.

He slowed the car, turning to look at her in the moonlight. "What?"

"Take the first left. You want to see where the Robinsons lived, don't you? It's down that road."

His smile was slow and heartbreakingly sexy. "When did you start to know me so well?"

"Decades ago," she said.

The Robinson house was nothing like the architectural splendor of the MacDowell house in Edgartown. Menemsha and the southwest tip of the island were much more rural and far less upscale, at least in

Vineyard terms. The Robinsons had owned a small, rambling cottage off by itself on the backside of the Squibnocket Cliffs near Gay Head. A weathered-looking for-sale sign hung lopsided in the front yard, and the place looked lost and deserted.

He pulled the stolen truck into the driveway and climbed out. The eerie fire-glow had already started to fade in the distance—obviously the blaze hadn't spread to the other old houses surrounding the MacDowell place. The moon was low in the sky, getting ready to set, and there was just the faintest touch of pink on the eastern horizon. It must be near dawn, Carolyn thought dazedly, climbing out of the truck as well, her body stiff and aching.

"This place looks deserted." Alex had paused on the front steps, staring up at the cottage.

"I told you, the parents died and the only heirs were distant cousins. The house has been on the market for a while—it's priced too high, but no one cares enough to let it go."

He was as adept at breaking into houses as he was at stealing cars. She followed him into the dark, musty interior, flicking a light switch with no results. It was cold, a damp, bone-biting cold, and Carolyn sank down in one of the old mission oak chairs, shivering, while Alex prowled around with the aid of a small flashlight.

She thought he'd forgotten about her. He was staring at framed photographs on the wall, his back to her, and she wrapped her arms around her body, trying to control her shivers.

"I'll make a fire," he said, not even looking at her. Staring at an old photo of a young girl, her sweet young face oddly familiar. He was looking at his birth mother.

"I will," she said, moving toward the fieldstone fireplace, but he was ahead of her, settling her back in the chair.

He stripped the sweater from his body, seemingly impervious to the cold night air against his bare skin. "Put this on."

"Don't be ridiculous, you'll freeze," she protested, but he simply overruled her, pulling it over her head. It was warm, and it smelled like him, and it made her far too vulnerable.

In a matter of minutes he had a small fire going, warming the rustic living room, filling it with light.

He sat back on his heels once he'd coaxed the fire into a decent blaze, turning to look at her. "Can I ask you a question?"

"Can I stop you?"

His smile was slight. "There's always a chance we might not survive."

"A fairly good chance, if one can go by what's happened so far," she said.

"What was it you didn't tell me?"

"What do you mean?"

"Yesterday afternoon, you said there was something you felt about me that I didn't know. Or maybe that was lust."

"You already know perfectly well I lust after you," she said in a deliberately cool voice. She didn't want to be having this conversation, not now. Not with the smell of the burning house still clinging to her hair and clothes, not with him kneeling, shirtless in front of her. Not with the sky turning pink with dawn and a murderer out there, waiting for them.

"Then what was it?" He tilted back his head, watching her with utter stillness. "You aren't in love with me, are you?"

Odd, how her heart could stop beating, how her breath could stall in her body, and yet she could still appear perfectly calm. "That's idiotic."

He shrugged. "If I die I'd like to know I'll be mourned."

"Trust me, if you die I'll mourn you," she said dryly. "Though chances are if you don't make it, neither will I."

"Are you in love with me, Carolyn?"

"You're very annoying. You've pissed me off for as long as I can remember."

"That still doesn't answer my question. Are you in love with me?"

She made a disgusted sound. "Of course I am. Don't be so damned stupid. I always was, I expect I always will be, and I don't like it one damned bit. Happy?"

"Yes," he said, and reached up his hands to cup her face. He was lit by the firelight in the rustic old house, and she knew she was doomed.

She wasn't going down without a fight. Pulling away from him, she scrambled from the chair and headed for the front door. "I'm going to check something," she said nervously, flinging it open, ready to barge out.

The sight of the man standing there stopped her cold. It was growing lighter in the distance, but even in the predawn shadows and the firelight emanating from the room she never had any doubt as to who it was.

It was the first time she'd looked into Warren MacDowell's face since she'd found out he was her father. The effect was startling, and she stood in the doorway, frozen, terrified, waiting for something. He was her father, and she felt nothing more than she'd always felt. There was no sudden wash of filial love. No resentment, either. She was too busy facing the possibility of death.

She'd never seen him less than perfectly dressed. He was still wearing a jacket, but his tie was long gone, the shirt was wrinkled and stained, and he had soot streaks across his face. His silver hair was mussed, and the eerily calm expression on his face was the most frightening of all.

"I thought I might find you here," he said. "Where's Alex?"

She didn't make the mistake of looking behind her. Obviously, Warren couldn't see him, a small advantage they needed to take advantage of. "Somewhere," she said vaguely, horrified to hear her voice tremble.

"He's the real Alex, isn't he?" Warren said wearily. "He had me fooled, but then, he always was a conniving little trickster. I was a fool not to realize the truth, but then, I was so very sure he was dead."

"MacDowells are hard to kill."

"We both know he isn't really a MacDowell," Warren said gently. "And you are."

"Have you suddenly developed some paternal feelings for your long-lost daughter?" She kept her voice cool and cynical.

"You weren't long lost. Sally brought you home, much to my disapproval. I wasn't cut out to be a father. You were an accident, one that I would have much preferred to forget all about, but my sister liked to have her own way. She wanted you as a little playmate for Alex. I'm not sure she had in mind the kind of games you two must have been playing recently, however." Despite his rumpled appearance he was his usual waspish self.

"That doesn't explain why you'd want to kill us, Warren."

He looked utterly astonished. "Kill you? Why would I want to do that? I came to—" He stopped mid-sentence, an expression of absolute shock on his face. And then he collapsed at her feet in a soundless puddle, and she looked down to see the growing stain of red in the back of his perfectly tailored jacket.

She was too horrified to scream. She looked up, numb with shock, into the smug, pleased face of Cousin George. "You really are quite stupid, Carolyn," he said. "He didn't even have a gun. Why in the world would he want to kill you? The poor fool wanted to save your life."

"You," she said helplessly.

"Of course, me," he replied. "Now why don't the two of you come on along now, so we can finish this up? I need to get back to my dear mother's bedside before anyone realizes how long I've been gone. Come along, hmmm?" And he gestured sweetly with the big black gun in his hand.

Chapter Twenty-three

IT WAS A GLORIOUS sunrise. They walked up the winding path toward the cliffs, a bizarre funeral cortege. They'd left Warren's body behind in a growing pool of blood, and now they walked, climbing the hill that they'd climbed as children, with George chattering with inane cheerfulness as he drove them upward.

"How's your memory now, Alex?" he taunted. "Is the murky past all coming back to you?"

"Somewhat," he said, his hand tight around Carolyn's. "Seeing you standing there with a gun in your hand did wonders."

"I'm sure it did. I can't believe how you managed to fool Uncle Warren into believing you were an imposter. I knew it was you the moment I saw you, and I was the one who killed you before. Even my mother recognized you, though she was merely convinced you were the dead returned to torment her."

"Did they know you shot me eighteen years ago? Were they part of it?" Alex sounded distant, only slightly interested in what should have been of paramount importance.

"Yes and no. They knew after it was too late, and they had no choice but to cover up for me. After all, I'd done it for all of them, hadn't I? And Aunt Sally had always been ridiculously doting—it obviously wouldn't have mattered to her how big a stink it would have made if I'd been accused of murder, so they had to keep it a secret. Patsy and Warren would have made sure I wouldn't have been charged, of course, but it still would have been quite a mess."

"You want to refresh my memory?" Alex drawled. "Why kill me? Apart from the fact that I was a royal pain in the butt. As I remember, you weren't any too charming yourself back then."

"Oh, but that's where you're wrong. I was a perfect son. Devoted to his mother, always looking out for her best interests. I'm very observant, you know that. The night you were going to leave you caught me watching my mother and her latest boyfriend go at it. They were into kink, which made it particularly entertaining. You absolutely spoiled everything."

"What did I do?"

"Threatened to beat the hell out of me if I didn't stop watching. But of course, that's a habit that's hard to break." He grinned with impartial cheeriness. "You two were quite entertaining in the library a few days ago. I was hoping for a replay before I burned the Edgartown house, but you were so unobliging. Not that I believe for a moment you weren't going at it like rabbits. You just kept out of range of the windows."

Nausea rose in Carolyn's throat. "You watched us?"

"I watch everyone. It's my major pleasure in life, one I learned young. I don't usually have to resort to my own arrangements. I belong to a very discreet club in New York that organizes such things for connoisseurs like me."

"Perverts like you," Carolyn snapped.

"Now, now, dear cousin. There's no such thing as perversion among consenting adults. And you were very consenting indeed, I could tell. He does have a way with him, doesn't he?" George sighed gustily. "I wish we had more time. I don't know who I'd want to fuck more, you or him. But I doubt either of you would be terribly cooperative. Still, it would be so much fun to have the other one watch."

"Why are you in such a hurry?" Alex said in a silky voice, ignoring Carolyn's expression of sick horror. "I'm game if you are."

George laughed. "Very thoughtful of you, but you don't fool me for a minute. You just think if you have extra time you might be able to trick me. I'm afraid I've learned to sublimate my appetites to a greater good. You two need to be dead by sunrise. A lovely suicide dive off the cliffs."

"Why would we want to do that?"

"I'm not a psychologist; I can't explain the workings of your mind, dear boy," George said lightly. "Why would you want to sabotage dear Carolyn's car and then bring her away with you? And when your uncle came after you to try and stop you, you murdered him in cold blood. Who can explain that, any more than the fact that you burned the Edgartown house to the ground? I'll be at a loss, when they bring me the news at my mother's bedside. We'll all be distraught with grief." He smiled sweetly.

"Don't you think burning the house was a little drastic? I assume you're doing this for money, but whatever the insurance, the house was still worth more."

"Ah, but you know perfectly well you can't make an omelet without breaking a few eggs. I thought Uncle Warren understood that much." They had reached the top of the rise now, and the sun was coming up on the horizon, sending glorious arcs of light through the inky sky.

"George," Carolyn said softly. "I still don't understand why you would want to hurt us. Is the money that important? You have so much."

"One can never have too much, Carolyn. You always were pathetically naive. My lifestyle is extremely expensive, you know. But you're right, that's not the real reason."

"And what is the real reason?"

"Isn't it obvious? I'm sure Alex has figured it out. You're not real MacDowells. You're a bastard, he's a changeling. Neither of you belong in the family, neither of you deserve even a penny of the money my ancestors built up over generations. You're imposters, both of you. I've known it since I was a child—I told you I had a habit of watching and listening. I always knew I'd have to get rid of Alex sooner or later, and when he caught me enjoying my mother's little peccadilloes it seemed as good a time as any. I wasn't sure I'd have to do anything about you, but Warren was getting sentimental in his old age. He warned me not to touch you. Up until then I had no intention of doing anything, but such parental concern was far too dangerous." He halted. They were at the head of the steep cliffs. Below them were rocks, with the sea pouring in around them, and off to the left, bathed in the rosy glow of dawn, was the Gay Head Lighthouse. "Time to jump, children. You can hold hands while you do it."

"And what if we don't jump?" Alex said. "You'd have a hard time explaining bullet holes in our bodies, now wouldn't you?"

"Not particularly. You'll wash out to sea. By the time they find you there probably won't be enough to identify you, much less tell how you died. It's a chance I'm willing to take if you don't cooperate. The sea spat you out once. I doubt it will give you up again." It was windy on the headlands, and overhead seagulls screeched and whirled in the brightening day. Carolyn put up a hand to push the hair out of her face, and in the distance she thought she could hear the sound of a car.

George heard it too. "Someone's coming," he said pleasantly. "Who wants to go first?" The roar of an aging motor burst over the hillside, as headlights speared the twilight, illuminating them like a biblical tableau, coming faster than she ever imagined. George froze, like a deer caught in a poacher's light, as the old truck bore down on him at a fiendish speed. And with sudden shrieking despair, Carolyn knew who was driving.

"Get down!" Alex shouted, grabbing her around the waist and

throwing her to the rocky precipice, covering her body with his, covering her ears with his strong hands, pressing her face against his shoulder.

He couldn't block out the sound, or the truth. The stolen truck slammed into George's body as it went soaring over the cliff, tumbling over and over until it crashed onto the rocks below and burst into flames. And Carolyn could see his face, Warren's pale, determined face, as he plowed into George's body and took them both to their death below.

Slowly Alex untangled himself from her, climbing to his feet like an old man. He held out a hand for her, but she turned her head away, refusing to move. He walked to the edge of the cliff and looked down for long, countless minutes.

The sun had risen. Overhead the seagulls circled and cried, in the distance came the sound of a police siren. And inside Carolyn's heart, something bloomed and died.

Chapter Twenty-four

HE WAS GONE. Five days later he was gone, without a word to her. She knew the lies he'd spun for the police, and she'd gone along with them, numbly obedient. It didn't matter why he lied, it only mattered that he hadn't come near her, hadn't touched her, since the police had arrived on that rocky outcropping and taken them both away.

She moved through life in a daze. Sally was buried with pomp and circumstance, Warren was buried beside her. George was a different matter—his service was small and private, with only his two sisters in attendance. Patsy's latest drug overdose had shut off the oxygen to her brain long enough to cause damage, and she had retreated to a pleasant, hazy world of television soap operas and vodka and round-the-clock nursing care.

And Alex was gone. Alex, who told the police he was an imposter, that the real Alexander MacDowell had been killed by his cousin George eighteen years ago. It had been an elaborate yet simple tale, so believable that Carolyn began to doubt herself. Warren had sought him out, trying to expose his murderous nephew. And he'd left enough of a paper trail to prove that Samuel Kinkaid was just who he said he was. An expatriate drifter.

The months passed, spring into summer, summer into fall, and there was still no escape for Carolyn. Most of the MacDowells were gone now, but she was still tied to the house, the family. Patsy was settled into Sally's old rooms, and if she occasionally remembered that she had had a son the thought passed quickly, lost in a haze of fantasy and drugs.

For some stupid reason Carolyn kept expecting Alex to return. To suddenly show up in her room in the middle of the night, to turn up on the front doorstep as he had that wintry morning, setting everything on end. But he didn't. And as the first snow began to fly, Carolyn knew she couldn't wait any longer.

Of all the myriad lawyers the MacDowell family had employed, Carolyn trusted Gerald Townsend the most. He'd gently guided her through the complexities of the wills, respecting her need for distance, and she'd counted on him to make the right choices. They'd never discussed what had happened, merely talked in polite tones about funds and money markets and trusts.

But it was finally time for her to leave.

"I wondered when you'd get around to asking questions," the elderly man said gently when she walked into the library of the Vermont house. She'd offered to come to his office, but he'd insisted on coming to her. Clients as important as the MacDowells deserved special treatment, he'd insisted, and she hadn't bothered to argue.

"I don't have questions," she said. "I just want access to my trust fund so I can get out of here. Everything else is taken care of, isn't it? There's nothing else I need to do?"

"Nothing else you need to do," he said. "You're free. That's what you wanted to hear, isn't it? I told Sally she should have let you go years ago, but she was a possessive old woman, and she loved you dearly."

"I wouldn't have left her," she said.

"No, I expect you wouldn't." He sighed. "This entire business has been very distressing."

"Yes," she said dryly. "It has."

"I don't understand how that young man could turn his back on so much money," he said.

"He wasn't Alex." She said the lie by rote.

"Don't be absurd; we both know that he was. But he was absolutely adamant that he wouldn't take a penny of the MacDowell money, and now he can't change his mind. Not that he seemed likely to, or I would have built some sort of fail-safe into the agreements. It's out of his reach now, and he seems absurdly glad of it."

She jerked her head up. "You've been in touch with him?"

"Well, of course. I've needed his cooperation to make certain the legal aspects are taken care of. I also arranged for him to buy a little place on Martha's Vineyard, though given the circumstances I wouldn't have thought he'd ever want to come to the island again."

"The Robinson house," Carolyn said, a statement, not a question.

"Exactly. Though I can, perhaps, guess why."

"Where is he now?"

"Italy. He owns a place in a small village in Tuscany, I believe. At least, that's where he's been getting his mail."

"And how does he support himself?"

"I believe he started a small company when he was in his twenties that he sold for a tidy profit. He does what interests him. Not that his assets are anywhere near the MacDowells' in size, or yours for that matter, but people have different needs."

She stared at him in sudden surprise. "Mine? Sally was very generous with my trust fund, but it was a comfortable amount, just to supplement my income."

It was his turn to look surprised. "My dear child, haven't you been paying any attention to the legal work we've been doing these last six months?"

"No."

"With Alex MacDowell declared dead, Sally's estate, after minor bequests to you and the various servants, was evenly divided between her brother and her sister."

"I know that."

"And didn't you realize you were Warren's sole heir?"

She looked at him in shock. "I can't be."

"I assure you, you've signed papers acknowledging that fact. He made his will more than a decade ago. He was a good friend of mine, Carolyn, and despite his lapses he wasn't a man devoid of responsibility. His sizable estate, coupled with half of Sally's, comes to a very healthy sum of money." He hesitated. "I imagine young Mr. Kinkaid was well aware of that fact."

"He knew I was heir to all that?"

"He knew."

"And he left."

"Yes," said Townsend. "I'm certain he's quite happy in Tuscany. I gather Citté-del-Monte is a lovely little village, though it can be quite difficult to get to if you don't know the way. Fortunately, he was obliging enough to give me detailed instructions in case of emergency."

"How very fortunate," she said in a hushed voice.

"Perhaps I ought to pass those instructions along to you, just in case you might need them," the old man said, all sweet innocence. "I hadn't wanted to mention it before—you were in such shock after those terrible events in May, and I imagine Mr. Kinkaid needed some time as well. But I'm sure there's no harm in passing along the information at this late date. After all, what possible use could you put it to?" His kind smile was painfully paternal, and she found she had tears in her eyes as she smiled back at him.

"What possible use?" she echoed.

MR. TOWNSEND WAS right, Citté-del-Monte was almost impossible to find. Even with the lawyer's detailed instructions she managed to get lost three times on the winding country roads. By the time she drove her tiny little rented Fiat up the narrow road leading to the tumbledown villa, she was numb with exhaustion and fear.

She had no idea what she'd say to him. Maybe just good-bye. He'd left without that much; he'd left knowing she loved him. She deserved something, if only a polite farewell.

Even in the autumn it was a tangle of overgrown greenery. The stucco farmhouse was in the midst of repair—she could see the new roof, smell fresh lumber. In the distance she could hear the sound of hammering, and a laughing male voice.

She climbed out of the car, leaving her bags behind, walking on the uneven stones toward the house. And then she stopped, in sick, nameless horror, as a pretty, red-haired woman emerged from the front entry with a dark-haired baby on one ample hip.

"Can I help you?" she asked in a cheerful British voice.

Carolyn wanted to run. With all the lies, all the uncertainties, she'd never for one moment considered the possibility that he might be married. The woman stood there, welcoming, entirely at ease, and Carolyn wanted the ground to open up and swallow her.

"I . . . I must have made a wrong turn," she said in a faintly desperate voice. "I was looking . . . looking for my cousin. He's rented a villa around here."

The woman's pretty face creased in confusion. "I didn't realize there were any other Americans around here. Let me check with my husband and see if he knows. What's his name?"

"Don't bother!" Carolyn said, backing away from her. "I probably have the wrong village. Maybe even the wrong country. I'm sorry to bother you."

Too late she realized the hammering had stopped, and the male voices had grown nearer. She was almost at her car when Alex emerged from behind the house, shirtless, tanned, his hair too long, his face unshaven, his Cossack eyes bright with laughter. She couldn't move, couldn't tear her eyes from him.

He saw her, of course, immediately, and all the laughter fled from his face as he froze. The man beside him barreled into him, cursing and laughing beneath his breath.

"There you are," the woman with the baby called out. "This woman has gotten lost. She's looking for her cousin. Do you know of any other Americans around, Paolo?"

The second man shook his head. "No, *cara*. Just this mangy bastard here." He moved around Alex's frozen figure and planted a kiss on the woman's cheek. "Are we staying for dinner?"

The British woman looked from Alex's strange expression to Carolyn's, and a smile curled her lips. "I don't think so, darling. I think the young woman found what she was looking for, after all." She handed him the baby. "Come along, darling."

Carolyn didn't even see them leave. There must have been another way into the tangled property, because suddenly they were gone, and Alex had made no move toward her.

"What are you doing here?"

He sounded more reserved than unwelcoming, but she was past the point of being sensitive. "It started to snow in Vermont and I knew I couldn't stand another winter there. I thought she was your wife," she said abruptly.

That startled him. "Anna? She's married to Paolo. I've never been married. I told you that."

"You told me a lot of things."

A faint smile curved his lush mouth, the mouth that she remembered so well. "Yes, I did, didn't I?"

"Why didn't you take the money? Sally wanted you to have it."

"Sally got her way too much in this life. It was blood money, and I didn't need it."

"What about me?"

He shrugged carelessly, but she could see beyond his studied indifference to something that made her palms sweat and her stomach twist in delectable knots. "I don't know whether you need all that money or not. It's up to you."

"That's not what I'm talking about," she said. "You said you don't need the money. Do you need me?"

He looked absolutely trapped. "Do I have to answer that?"

"Considering I came thousands of miles to ask the question, yes."

She hadn't realized he was moving closer. A slow, dangerous pace, and she realized he wasn't the only one who was trapped—she was as well. Predator and prey, both of them.

He stopped in front of her, and his skin was smooth and silken in the bright Mediterranean sun, and she wanted to press her mouth against his throat. He cupped her neck, his big, strong hand, rough with calluses, gentle on her smooth skin. "I need you," he said. "I can even put up with all that goddamn MacDowell money if I have to."

He kissed her, a slow, deep, possessive kiss that was like the wellspring of life. When he pulled back there were tears on her cheeks and he smiled.

"Big of you," she muttered.

"Very big," he agreed. "I'm going to have to cancel my plane reservations. I was coming to get you next week."

"Great minds think alike," she said.

His hands were on her breasts, and all she wanted was to lie with him in the bright Tuscan sun. "I still haven't told you," he said.

"Told me what?"

"I'm in love with you. I have been since you were thirteen."

"Pervert." She smiled up at him and began unbuttoning her shirt. "Of course you are," she said. "Did it take you this long to figure it out?"

"No," he said. "I just had to give you enough time to make sure you knew what you're doing."

"At least we know you're not marrying me for my money."

He raised an eyebrow. "Who says I'm marrying you?"

"Are you?"

"As soon as I can find a priest," he said. He pulled her into his arms. "And guess what?" His mouth hovered over hers, tempting. "What?" she echoed dazedly.

"It hardly ever snows in Tuscany."

About the Author

Anne Stuart is currently celebrating forty years as a published novelist. She has won every major award in the romance field and appeared on the NYT Bestseller List, Publisher's Weekly, and USA Today. Anne Stuart currently lives in northern Vermont.

CPSIA information can be obtained at www.ICGtesting.com
Printed in the USA
LVOW13s1957210514

386772LV00008B/1189/P